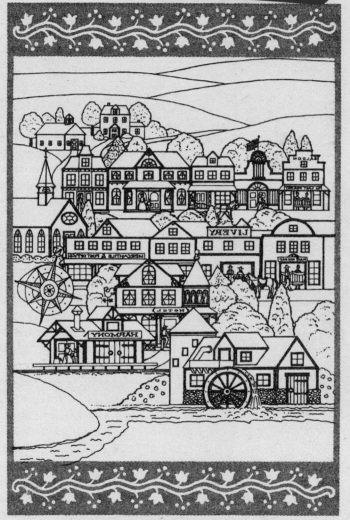

JAMES AND LILLIAN TAYLOR, *owners of the mercantile and post office* . . . With their six children, they're Harmony's wealthiest and most prolific family. Now their beautiful daughter Libby has come home again—and she's turned the entire town upside-down!

"LUSCIOUS" LOTTIE McGEE, *owner of "The First Resort"* . . . Lottie's girls sing and dance and even entertain upstairs . . . but Lottie herslf is the main attraction at her enticing saloon. And when it comes to taking care of her own cousin, this enticing madam is all maternal instinct.

CORD SPENCER, *owner of "The Last Resort"* . . . Things sometimes get out of hand at Spencer's rowdy tavern, but he's mostly a good-natured scoundrel who doesn't mean any harm. And when push comes to shove, he'd be the first to put his life on the line for a friend.

SHERIFF TRAVIS MILLER, *the lawman* . . . The townsfolk don't always like the way he bends the law a bit when the saloons need a little straightening up. But Travis Miller listens to only one thing when it comes to deciding on the law: his conscience.

ZEKE GALLAGHER, *the barber and the dentist* . . . When he doesn't have his nose in a dime Western, the white-whiskered, blue-eyed Zeke is probably making up stories of his own—*or* flirting with the ladies. But not all his tales are just talk—once he really *was* a notorious gunfighter . . .

A TOWN CALLED HARMONY

Delightful tales that capture the heart of a small
Kansas town—and a simple time when
love was a gift to cherish . . .

Available from Diamond Books

**A TOWN CALLED
HARMONY**

HOLDING
HANDS

Jo Anne Cassity

DIAMOND BOOKS, NEW YORK

This book is a Diamond original edition, and has never been
previously published.

HOLDING HANDS

A Diamond Book / published by arrangement with
the author

PRINTING HISTORY
Diamond edition / February 1995

ISBN: 0-7865-0075-1

Diamond Books are published by The Berkley Publishing Group,
200 Madison Avenue, New York, New York 10016.
DIAMOND and the "D" design are trademarks
belonging to Charter Communications, Inc.

PRINTED IN THE UNITED STATES OF AMERICA

10 9 8 7 6 5 4 3 2 1

For my wonderful nephews,
Jim and Donald;
and for all my beautiful nieces—
Tamara, Susan, Jennifer,
Kellie, Laurie,
Sara, and Emily.

HOLDING
HANDS

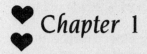 Chapter 1

Harmony, Kansas
December 1874

WHEN THE 9:30 Kansas Pacific pulled into the Harmony depot, Miss Elnora Perry grabbed her large valise and rose from her seat.

With the slamming of iron and a hiss of steam, the train came to a stop. Courteous as always, Miss Perry nodded her thanks to the conductor and wasted no time making her way down the aisle and descending the train's steps.

Although she was a tiny woman, she had no fear of traveling alone. Traveling was something she did quite often, given her many relatives and their many needs.

As usual, she wore a simple dress with a high, prim collar, and covering that simple dress was a warm, serviceable coat.

Her hair, however, was quite remarkable, often drawing stares of appreciation from men and women alike, to which Elnora seemed oblivious. It was a most lustrous chestnut brown and, as usual, was arranged in a fashionable nest upon her head.

The chill morning air nipped at her cheeks as she raised one eyebrow, scrutinizing her surroundings.

1

Almost every building within sight was a different color—the depot itself being a lovely shade of blue.

"Nora!"

Hearing her brother's voice, Elnora turned to see him coming around a bend, seated in a wagon. Six children and one on the way hadn't changed him much. Somehow she had expected him to look older, more mature, but his face bore the same eager, almost boyish expression that had always made her smile.

When the wagon rocked to a stop, he jumped down and ran to meet her.

At thirty-one, Gordon was one year younger than herself and the oldest of her five brothers. As children they'd been very close, often sharing secrets and creating all sorts of mischief together. The sight of him now, winded, his cheeks flushed, his clothes rumpled as though he had tugged them on at the very last minute, brought back a rush of sweet memories.

"Nora . . ." He stopped before her, his dark eyes bright with excitement. "I'm sorry I'm late. I had to wait for Maisie Hastings and Minnie Parker to come by so they could stay with the children. . . ." He gave her a quick look. "You look better than strawberries on cake in the middle of January." He swept her up into his arms and squeezed her hard, lifting her high off her feet.

"And you're still a terrible liar," she said, laughing. "Put me down, for heaven's sake!"

"Aw, Nora," he said, gently obeying her request. He towered over her and, shuffling his feet, pushed a lock of tousled hair off his forehead. "It's great to have you here. Thanks for comin'."

In that moment he reminded her of the gentle, genial boy he'd always been, and she felt another swift surge of affection for him. She smiled, and her intelligent honey-brown eyes sparkled with joy.

He bent and lifted her huge bag off the ground, then led the way to the wagon where it waited beside the pretty blue depot, beside Harmony's new pink hotel and restaurant. "I'll tell you all about Vivian and the children on the way out to the farm." He glanced over at her again. "Our latest addition is Mark Anthony. He's eighteen months old now."

Elnora arched one brow. "Mark Anthony? What an impressive name!"

Gordon shrugged. "Vivian's been doin' a lot of readin' lately. Says she got it from a book."

"I see . . ." Elnora paused a moment and eyed him with speculation. "Gordon, you've been a busy man—six children and another on the way. Have you and Vivian taken it upon yourselves to populate the earth all alone?"

Pretending to be insulted by her bold statement, he frowned. "Why, Nora, I'm surprised at you."

She lifted her chin a measure and gave a small huff. "I imagine you are. But I'm old enough to say whatever I please these days, and most of the time I do. But my real concern lies with Vivian. How is she?"

Gordon sobered, his steps slowing. "Doc Tanner said she has to stay in bed until the baby comes." His expression grew sheepish. "The house is a mess, I'm sorry to say. Maisie and Minnie organized a crew of women to take turns comin' out to see to meals and such, but havin' families and responsibilities of their own, there's only so much they can do." He took a deep breath, then added with a grin, "Vivian's sure lookin' forward to your visit. It's all she's talked about since you wrote and said you'd come."

Elnora smiled, her eyes becoming soft with understanding. A sudden blast of December wind caused her to pull her wrap tight around her throat. "You and I haven't spent a Christmas together since I can't remember when. And you know how much I've always loved Vivian."

Her answer cheered him. "Come on, then, let's go home." He hefted her bag into the wagon bed, then came around the side and helped her up into the seat.

"My, my," Elnora said as her eyes swept back to the bright blue depot, then came back to rest on the pink hotel once again. "I can't say as I've ever seen a town quite like this one."

Gordon took his place beside his sister and gave the reins a quick flick. "There isn't any town anywhere quite like Harmony, Nora. You'll see."

Elnora lifted one dark eyebrow. "I imagine I will at that."

As the Kansas Pacific blew its whistle to announce its arrival that morning, Russell Whitaker left Maisie Hastings and Minnie Parker's boardinghouse and headed down Main Street. Arthur, his dog, was at his side as usual.

As Russell passed by Harmony's barbershop, he saw Zeke Gallagher, the town's barber and dentist, opening his store for the day. Russell pulled out his timepiece.

9:40.

He grinned and snapped the lid shut. Zeke was late. He would have to bait him about that. He'd seen him head over to Cord Spencer's saloon, the Last Resort, after dinner last night.

Russell tucked his timepiece back into his vest pocket and rearranged his copy of Charles Dickens's *Great Expectations* under his arm.

He crossed the street to Whitaker's Bookstore, his

own place of business. It was a small, snug, orange building, planted squarely between Jane Evans's dress shop, You Sew And Sew, and the bright yellow mercantile and post office, owned and operated by James and Lillie Taylor.

Russell climbed the steps to his store and unlocked the door, then entered the darkened interior with Arthur following close behind.

The Kansas Pacific blew its whistle once more, and Russell went still a moment, listening. The sound of the train's arrival still stirred him at thirty-four years of age, filling him with a sense of adventure and sometimes reawakening the restless spirit that lay hidden deep within his heart.

He flipped the "Closed" sign around in the window so that it read "Open," then he set about repeating his daily task of lighting the oil lamps and chasing away the morning shadows. He inhaled the scents of his many leather-bound volumes and felt energized as he often did when he opened his store in the morning. Whistling, he lit the old stove that sat in the far corner of the store, then paused a few moments, holding his hands out to the welcome warmth.

He was glad he'd taken his morning meal over at the boardinghouse, as he often did, though Maisie and Minnie had bustled out that morning, leaving their guests to their food, saying they had to get out to the Perry farm.

When he was finally warm enough to venture back out into the cold, he donned his overcoat again and stepped out onto the porch to sweep away the thin layer of snow from his steps. With the Christmas season well under way, he expected his store to be busy.

With that thought in mind, he acknowledged that the little town of Harmony suited him well, much better than he ever would have imagined when he'd arrived six years ago aboard the Kansas Pacific on an early winter morn, much the same as this one. He hadn't planned on staying. He was only passing through on his way west, and if someone had told him back then that he would stay on, that he would be the owner and operator of his own bookstore, he never would have believed it.

But Harmony had grown on him.

And only rarely did he think of the past.

As Gordon steered the wagon down Main Street, he turned to his sister and asked, "So how's Pa these days?"

"He's much better." Elnora smiled. "He's getting around fine, though Mother clucks after him constantly."

Gordon chuckled and said, "Some things never change. I sure miss—"

A sudden loud shriek cut into the stillness of the morning, interrupting their conversation.

Quite suddenly from down the street a man charged through the doors of a bright purple building and out into the street. The building he ran from boasted a sign that read THE FIRST RESORT.

Elnora's mouth fell open.

He was half naked and coming their way!

Behind him, hot on his trail, chased a woman, brandishing a rolling pin and wearing nothing more than a filmy red wrap over her corset and bloomers. "You come back here, Clyde Finnegan!" she screamed. "You slimy, no good, son of a bitch! Nobody cheats Lottie McGee!"

Her voice, raised in fury, sent shivers rippling over Elnora's skin.

The man came chugging down the street, fast as his bare feet and knobby knees could carry him, hiking his trousers up over his bare backside. He ran a crooked line, zigging back and forth from one side of the street to the other, then directly into the path of Gordon's wagon.

"Whoa!" Gordon bellowed and pulled sharply on the horses' reins. He stopped the wagon, nearly unseating Elnora, whose eyes were straining their sockets as it was.

Another furious shriek, followed by another loud string of crude obscenities, caused the half-dressed man to steal a glance over his shoulder.

The moment cost him dearly.

Russell, who'd been watching the spectacle in silent amusement, waited until the man was abreast of his bookstore, then dipped low and effortlessly swung his broom out. He deftly caught the man across his ankles, sending him tumbling into a long skid over the frozen ground.

The shrieking woman was on him in a minute.

"Now, you pay up, Clyde, or I'll take this rolling pin to that worthless skull o' yours!"

"Aw, Lottie!" Clyde whined. "I can't pay ya'. If I go home broke, my wife is like to shoot me dead!"

"I'm like to beat you to death right here and now! Take your pick! Do ya wanna die now or later?"

"Pay the lady, Clyde," Russell said quietly. He walked over to where the disgruntled man lay on the ground. "Arthur, come," he ordered in a soft, even tone. The dog was at his side in a heartbeat.

"Aw, Russ..." the man wheedled, shaking his head from side to side.

"I mean it," Russell repeated. "Pay her, or I'll let her have a go at you." A slow grin tugged at the corners of his mouth, but his dark eyes were stone serious.

Clyde paused a moment, considering his predicament and Russell's unrelenting gaze. "Aw, shit!" he finally said and dug deep into his trousers. "Here!" He begrudgingly held the money out to the woman, who wasted no time in snatching it from his hands and counting it out, before depositing it in the deep hollow between her ample breasts.

"And don't you come back to my place, either!" she told him. "I ain't got time to waste on men who won't pay for services rendered from my girls!" With that said she turned to Russell and flashed him a flirty smile. "Thanks, Russ. You always were the finest gentleman this town ever saw."

Russell inclined his head slightly. "Anytime, Lottie." A gust of winter wind caught at his silvery blond hair and ruffled it so that it fell rakishly over one side of his forehead.

Glowering furiously, Clyde got off the ground and stalked off, muttering something unintelligible, but something Elnora was sure was quite obscene.

Bestowing one last positively wicked smile on her hero, and a brief polite nod to Elnora and Gordon, Lottie McGee turned on the heel of her fancy red slipper and, with her hips swinging, made her way back to the First Resort.

Still smiling, Russell looked up at the two seated in the wagon. "Hello, Gordon," he said as though nothing out of the ordinary had occurred.

"Russ," Gordon returned with a grin. "Arthur," he said to the dog. "Lively morning, isn't it?"

"Some are livelier than others," Russell agreed. His eyes left Gordon and found Elnora.

Her hand at her throat, she found herself clutching

the collar of her dress, as though to assure herself that she, at least, was dressed respectably.

"Elnora," Gordon said, noting Russell's shift of attention, "meet Russell Whitaker. He owns Whitaker's Bookstore. Russell, this is my sister, Elnora."

Russell's smile grew, revealing even white teeth. He took in the lady's pale face. "My pleasure, ma'am." He waited for her to return the greeting, wondering if she might teeter over the side of the wagon in a dead faint at any moment. Her wide honey-gold eyes seemed frozen open, and her pointy little chin—complete with one tiny impudent dimple—trembled with astonishment.

"Miss," Elnora choked out, feeling quite hot and bothered. "It's miss." Her mind was in a tither. A naked man, for heaven's sake! Thank God Almighty he'd gotten his trousers up by the time he'd reached their wagon!

"Ah, I see. My pleasure, Miss Perry."

"And mine, Mr. Whitaker," she managed while she studied him from the safety of her seat. He was tall and lean and dressed every bit the gentleman. He had a fine-featured face and square masculine jawline that was saved from sternness by his easy smile. But his eyes were the most unsettling. They were a deep dark brown and seemed to glitter with silent amusement.

"Please feel free to stop in and browse whenever you have time," he offered, gesturing behind him to his store.

"I'll do that," she said, thinking she'd rather be baked in mud than do any such thing. After all, the man knew "that woman" by her first name!

"Well, we'd best get home," Gordon said and gave the reins a flick. "I'll see ya, Russ."

Russell nodded, his eyes still on Elnora. Then, once

the wagon had moved on down Main Street, he chuckled quietly, patted Arthur, and turned back into the welcome warmth of his store.

The Perry house was a large, white, two-story structure that boasted a wide front porch, complete with a swing and two matching rocking chairs, which had been covered with large pieces of burlap to protect them during the winter months.

By the time Gordon and Elnora arrived at the house, she'd finally managed to compose herself.

Once inside, Gordon introduced her to Maisie and Minnie, who were obviously twin sisters. They were a matching set—all the way up their tall angular bodies to the iron-gray knots of hair on top of their heads.

"So," Maisie said, squinting and leaning in close to get a better look, "you're Gordon's sister?"

Minnie, whose eyesight was a mite better, studied Elnora from where she stood.

"Yes," Elnora answered, not in the least unnerved by their scrutiny. After all, what could be more unsettling than the scene she'd just witnessed?

Besides, she knew the two women were weighing her capabilities, and rather than be insulted by the fact, she was touched that they cared so much about her brother and his family that they wanted to be sure they left them in good hands.

"We're happy to have you with us," Minnie said at last, smiling. She nudged her sister with an elbow. "Aren't we, Sister?"

"Indeed we are," Maisie agreed, deciding Elnora would do quite nicely, despite her small stature. "Well, Sister, we'd best get back to our boarders."

"Indeed," said the other, equally satisfied with their replacement.

Gordon helped the ladies to their buggy, offering to see them home. They declined his offer, saying they might be old, but they weren't feeble yet.

When Gordon came back in, he turned to Elnora and with a sheepish grin said, "I should get to the chores. . . ."

She smiled and shrugged out of her coat. "Go on. I'll be fine. The children and I need some time alone anyway."

Once he'd left, Elnora gazed down at the several pairs of questioning eyes, not sure what to expect. She'd never taken care of so many children at once, but how hard could it be? Two or twenty, children were children.

With a heavy sigh, her gaze left the children and swept the room, taking stock of the confusion around her.

Though the town's ladies had done their best to keep the house in order, there was still much to be done.

Rather than be dissuaded, however, Elnora Perry felt a spurt of energy shoot through her veins.

She deposited her belongings in the bedroom that Sam, Gordon and Vivian's oldest boy, led her to, then she returned to the kitchen and sat down with all six of the Perry children. There was Sam, who was nine; Andy, who was seven; George, who was six; Sara, who was four; Emily, who was three; and of course, Mark Anthony, who was an extremely active eighteen months old.

Once she felt sufficiently able to tell one child from another, she plucked Emily's thumb from her mouth, replacing it with a peppermint and a kiss, then decided her next course of action was to see to Vivian's immediate comfort.

For the most part, there was not much that could rattle Elnora Perry's composure. She prided herself on being neat and tidy, precise and predictable. But, just the same, by late that afternoon, with her hair escaping its normally neat arrangement, and her apron spotted and wrinkled, she found herself questioning her own sanity.

With the noon meal barely over, Andy had clobbered George in the nose, and Sam, being his usual fair-minded self, was trying to pass judgment on them both by locking them out of the house.

To add to the confusion, Sara and Emily waited until Elnora was busy washing dishes, then decided to diaper the cat, and Mark Anthony, toddling along behind, gleefully donated his somewhat soggy diaper.

Amazingly enough, however, when evening finally came, Elnora had the Perry household under control. She'd polished and scrubbed her way through the house, and by suppertime she even had a pot of beef stew simmering on the stove and a pan of biscuits baking in the oven.

When Gordon came in from completing the day's chores, he took a deep sniff of the enticing aromas and decided he'd died and gone to heaven.

After Elnora settled him and the children at the table, she prepared a tray for Vivian and went up to visit her.

She entered the bedroom and carefully centered the tray over what little there was left of Vivian's lap. Then she sat down on the edge of the bed beside her.

Vivian savored a spoonful of rich broth and sighed with pleasure. "Oh, Elnora, this is wonderful. You don't know how much I needed you to come."

Elnora smiled. "I needed to come just as much."

"Everyone in town has been so good to us," Vivian

went on, "but it isn't like having your own family with you during times like these. . . . " She left off, her pretty blue eyes speaking volumes.

Elnora patted Vivian's plump hand. Vivian had always been a pretty woman. Now, with her usual plumpness exaggerated by her condition, Elnora still thought her lovely. She looked like a cuddly blond baby doll. "Hush, now. This will be good for me, too. Spending a Christmas with the children will be an occasion I'll never forget."

"Christmas in Harmony is a special time of year."

"I'll just bet it is." Elnora raised one eyebrow and thought of the spectacle she'd witnessed that morning, then feeling flustered all over again, she switched her thoughts to the colorful buildings they'd passed on their way through town. Gordon had told her that several years ago Lillie Taylor had organized a beautification committee to paint every building in town a different color. It was an odd though charming idea, Elnora silently conceded.

While Vivian ate a bite of her buttered biscuit, she studied Elnora silently. When at last she spoke, her voice was thoughtful and quiet. "You should have a family of your own, Nora. You're so good at all of this."

Elnora gave a small huff and dropped her gaze to the bed. She studied the patterned quilt intently, hoping to hide the secret yearning the other woman's words had elicited. "You know I don't have time for that," she said with a tight little laugh.

"That's because you're always taking care of everyone else," Vivian stated bluntly.

Silence fell between them for several long moments. When finally Elnora felt her composure had returned sufficiently, she raised her eyes to Vivian's.

"I'm quite happy, Viv. Really."

Vivian covered Elnora's hand where it lay on the quilt. "I hope so, Nora. I truly do."

"Besides, I'm too old to start thinking about marrying and bearing seven children."

Vivian snorted her disgust. "Thirty-two is hardly old."

"Old enough."

Vivian made a face and laid her head back against her plumped pillow. "Talk about old . . . this old mare ain't what she used to be."

Despite herself, Elnora grinned, and the two women shared an easy laugh. When Vivian sobered, she said once more, "I'm so glad you're here, Nora."

"Me, too," Elnora answered, her eyes warm and sincere. "I truly am."

The following Sunday Elnora and Gordon herded the children off to church, allowing Vivian a quiet morning to herself.

After services, Elnora met the Reverend Abe Johnson and his wife, Rachel. Next she met Zeke Gallagher, the town's barber and dentist, and who, she was told later, was a subject of Maisie and Minnie's constant competitions.

"Elnora!" Maisie called out from where she stood at the front of the church.

Elnora left her brother and joined the small group of women. "Good morning, ladies," she greeted. She would have addressed Maisie and Minnie personally, but she still wasn't quite sure which twin was which.

Maisie introduced Elnora to Lillie Taylor and to Lillie's recently wed daughter, Mary Hubbard.

Lillie nodded a greeting, and Mary said, "Welcome to Harmony, Elnora." Mary was an attractive young woman with a friendly smile and pretty brown eyes.

"Mary will have to tell you how she found her husband," Maisie said to Elnora. "It's quite a story." She changed the subject by turning to Lillie and asking, "Did you read yesterday's addition to our story in the *Sentinel*?"

"Why, yes, of course," Lillie said, as though it were absurd to think she hadn't.

Minnie leaned in close. "What do you think of the new lady of the court?"

Lillie smiled. "Maybe she'll be the one to win our knight's heart."

"Maybe," Maisie added before her sister could beat her to it.

"Then again, Sister," Minnie put in with an air of superiority, "we still don't know the identity of our knight, nor the identity of his creator—the author of the series."

"True," Lillie added, contemplating the thought, "and since we don't know who he is, there's not much chance of finding out anything before he writes it out for us."

"Humph! We'll see about that," Maisie retorted. "Mysteries are made to be solved." Then, noticing Elnora's puzzled expression, she hurried to say, "Forgive us, dear. We're referring to the serial that's featured weekly in the *Sentinel*. It's a wonderful addition to our paper. The story often adds new characters and takes them on exciting adventures."

"It's all very romantic," Minnie added with a twinkle in her eye.

"You need to read the stories, Elnora," Maisie decided for her. "I have all of the copies back to the very first one. And," she added conspiratorially, "we've begun to suspect that the author mirrors his characters after us, Harmony's townsfolk."

Mark Anthony, growing weary of the adult conversation, decided to let his impatience be known by making a fuss.

Gordon found Elnora and, with a sheepish grin, said, "I hate to interrupt, but this one's ready to go home."

Elnora smiled, agreeing.

They excused themselves with the proper amenities and gathered the children for the ride home. They were on their way out the church door when Gordon called out to the man in front of him. "Russ, hello!"

Hearing his name, Russell Whitaker turned.

Elnora recognized him immediately as the man she'd met the morning of her arrival, and despite herself she flushed anew.

"Russ," Gordon said, extending his hand, "how are you?"

Russell gave Gordon's hand a firm shake. "I'm well, thank you. I'm glad to see you. I wanted to let you know that the book you ordered for Vivian has come in."

"Good. I'll stop by and get it on Friday when I come into town for supplies."

"That'll be fine."

"And how's Arthur these days?" Gordon asked.

"He's fine. He's looking forward to a visit from your boys, I'm sure." His dark gaze left Gordon and fixed itself on Elnora.

It was at that moment that George chose to announce, "Pa, I gotta go!" He made a tortured face and squirmed in an effort to exaggerate his discomfort. "Now!"

Gordon grinned. "We'd best get home, Nora, 'fore these children make us sorry we dallied so long."

Elnora laughed at George's expression, glad for the diversion. Her laughter was light and sweet, warm and genuine.

It struck Russell that laughing was something Elnora Perry did very well.

She turned her attention back to Russell, her intelligent eyes alight with amusement, and because Elnora Perry was always a lady, she acknowledged his presence gracefully by taking her leave. "Goodbye, Mr. Whitaker."

"Goodbye, Miss Perry." He affected a small bow.

"I'll see you at the end of the week, Russ," Gordon called over his shoulder.

Russell nodded, his eyes still fixed on Elnora's retreating back. "I'll certainly look forward to it," he said quietly.

As the days passed, life settled into a hectic though pleasant routine.

Maisie and Minnie dropped by often, and when they did they left the past issues of the *Sentinel* for Elnora, just as they'd promised. Though she tried to tell herself she didn't have time to bother with such fanciful nonsense, in the evenings, when the children were safely tucked into their beds, she found herself reading the stories the folks of Harmony were so taken with.

To her surprise, it wasn't long before she, too, was looking forward to the next chapter of the story.

♥♥ Chapter 2

THE NEXT TWO weeks passed quickly for Elnora.

Winter took hold of Harmony much to the delight of the children, who waited so impatiently for Christmas, which was only days away.

It was on an especially frosty morning, while Elnora was preparing breakfast for the awakening household, that a loud knock sounded at the door. Surprised to have a visitor so early, she left the stove to see who it could be.

She opened the door to find a tall, muscular man filling the doorway. He wore a pair of dark trousers and a heavy overcoat, and on his head was a well-worn Stetson. His stance was sure and confident, and when his green eyes met hers, they hovered a second, then danced a reckless path over her entire form. When finally they came back to her face, he smiled and simply brushed past her, bags in hand, not bothering to wait for an invitation, forcing her to move sideways or be shoved onto her backside.

"I beg your pardon," Elnora said crisply, a sudden spurt of starch stiffening her spine. "May I help you, sir?"

He dropped his bags onto the floor with an announcing thud and turned, hooking his hands onto his hips. "I sure as hell hope so." He flashed her a

19

smile the size of Texas—a smile that would have turned a weaker woman's heart to mush.

But Elnora Perry was no weak woman.

"I'm Ransom Riley. Vivian's big brother." He affected a deep bow, his eyes never leaving hers while he swept his Stetson from his glossy dark hair. "And who, fair lady, might you be?"

A deep flush of color crept over Elnora's face. "I'm Elnora Perry," she answered with quiet dignity. "Gordon's sister. I'm afraid we've never met, but I've heard Vivian speak of you often."

Ransom shrugged and flashed her another confident grin. "If we'd met, I'd remember it." He paused a moment, his eyes raking her once again. "And so would you."

Astounded by his male arrogance, her eyebrows rose to new heights. She resisted the temptation to put him in his place and instead merely stared at him, hoping her silence was an insult in itself.

"I drop in on Gordon and Vivian every now and then, whenever I'm passing through these parts." His eyes left her and swept the kitchen, finally settling on the table, which was set with eight place settings. "It's been a while since I last came through. About three years. Looks like there've been a couple o' new additions."

Her back still straight as a fence post, Elnora said, "They would be Emily and Mark Anthony." She paused, then added, "There's another baby on the way, you know."

"No kiddin'?" He chuckled, his eyes widening in surprise. "Well, where the hell is that rascal Gordon?" He shrugged out of his overcoat and carelessly hung it on a peg beside the many others on the wall, then stalked to the stairway and boomed, "Gordon! Viv! Git up! Come on down!"

Within seconds the house was filled with the thumps of many feet rushing through the upstairs of the house and on down the staircase.

Sam and Andy made it to the bottom of the stairs first, both panting with excitement. Shyly they hung back a moment, uncertain of the big man they only barely remembered.

"Aw, come on over here, boys." Ransom stooped down onto his haunches. "You remember me, don't ya?"

Sam obeyed and approached the man. Andy followed close behind his brother. "Yes," Sam said in his most adult voice. "I think so." He held out his hand in greeting. "You're Uncle Ransom."

"That's right!" Ransom gave the boy's hand a hearty squeeze.

"And what about you?" he asked Andy, who blinked his confusion.

Gordon came down the stairs, pulling his suspenders up onto his shoulders. George followed, along with Sara and Emily.

Andy eyed his uncle for a moment, then remembering him, beamed a smile. "I remember you. Last time you were here you had a big bear rug with a head on it. It had teeth and claws."

"That's right." Ransom ruffled Andy's shock of blond hair so that it stood straight up on top of his head. The big man rose and strode across the floor to where Gordon stood watching. "Gordon!" He slapped his brother-in-law on the shoulder, nearly knocking him sideways. "Hell, it's good to see ya!"

Righting himself, Gordon forced a smile. "It's good to see you, too, Ransom. Vivian has been worried. It's been a long time since we last heard from you." His words reflected a quiet, though very clear reprimand.

"Aw, you know me. I ain't much for writin' ".

"Ransom!" Vivian called from upstairs. "Is that you?"

"Hell, yes, it's me!"

"Come up and see me!"

"She can't come down the stairs," Gordon explained. "She's had a hard time carrying this baby."

Ransom bounded up the stairs. "I'm on my way, Viv!"

"Well . . . " Elnora huffed her disdain, her nose lifting into the air an inch higher than normal. "He certainly knows how to make an arrival, doesn't he?"

She turned back to the stove to stir the boiling pot of thickening oatmeal, glad to have some semblance of sanity returning to the household. "This oatmeal is more than ready, I'm afraid." Pot in hand, she turned. "Come, children. Wash up, and we'll sit down to breakfast. I'll take your mother up something after a bit."

Once she'd fed the children and shooed the two oldest off to school, she settled the others down to play. Then she sent Gordon upstairs with breakfast for both Vivian and her brother, while she busied herself with tidying the house. When at last Gordon came down again, she studied him silently, her eyes full of questions he knew better than to ignore.

"He'll be staying with us for a while," Gordon said and poured himself another cup of coffee from the pot she kept warm on top of the stove.

"Vivian will enjoy that," Elnora remarked in a matter-of-fact tone.

"Yes," Gordon said, "she will at that. He won't stay long, though."

"I see," Elnora said, though she didn't see at all.

"He's a bounty hunter," Gordon explained.

Her head came up. To her knowledge, she'd never met a bounty hunter. Oh, she knew they existed, especially in this part of the country and farther out west where outlaws often made their presence known. But the thought that they would be housing one . . . For heaven's sake . . . "Well," she finally said. "I'm sure the children will enjoy his visit, also." With that said she resumed her chores, her mind conjuring up a bevy of sordid thoughts about Ransom and outlaws and other such unsavory subjects.

By evening she'd finally calmed herself. She'd promised the children they could pop and string corn so that the strands would be ready when Gordon brought in the Christmas tree on Christmas Eve.

Forgetting Ransom for a while, she admitted that she, too, was excited about Christmas. Though Vivian had said that the folks of Harmony decorated the large pine tree in front of the church for all to enjoy, Elnora wanted a tree of their very own in the house for the children. She'd been gathering gifts for weeks, knowing she would be spending the holiday with Gordon's family. At times she thought she was more excited about the holiday than the children could ever be.

The next several days passed in a whirl. Ransom's presence kept Elnora in a constant state of turmoil, though no one would have guessed it by her composed countenance.

She wondered why the man affected her in such a manner, then decided it must be that she wasn't used to having a man, his kind of a man, underfoot all the time. Or maybe, she decided, she'd simply been filling her mind with too much romantic nonsense about knights in shining armor and other such ridiculous imaginings.

She was especially disgusted with herself when one morning, two days before Christmas, while preparing breakfast, she realized how truly tired she was. She'd spent a restless night, tossing and turning, dreaming of the knight in the *Sentinel*'s story.

His name was Sir Ruggard, and no one in the court knew who he was or where he'd come from. He was a tall man whose face remained a mystery to all, hidden as it was beneath his silver helmet. Despite his mysterious past, he had become King Nefen's most favored knight, and it was rumored in the kingdom that he was taken with the new lady. In the latest chapter of the story, the author had finally given the new lady of the court a name: Lady Elvia.

Elnora heaved a great sigh that lifted her small breasts beneath the pleated bodice of her tidy white blouse. A familiar ache caught at her throat, awakening that great dragon of yearning that lay buried within her lonely maiden heart.

A sudden pop of bacon grease hit her arm and snapped her away from her colorful fantasy. Once again she chided herself for becoming so caught up in a make-believe world, while she reminded herself that some things were simply not meant to be, especially for a woman like herself.

Oh, in her younger days she'd often entertained romantic notions of marrying her one true love and having children of her own. Now, however, older and much wiser, she thought herself well beyond that hope.

Still, there was an emptiness within her that ached to be filled. She wondered how it would feel to have a husband love her—a husband she loved in return. She wondered what it would feel like to be held close in his arms at night. She wondered how it would feel to have her stomach swollen with his baby. . . .

She allowed herself a rare moment of self-pity and thought about what the folks back in Wichita said: "Poor little Elnora Perry. What a shame she'd never married. She's a spinster, you know. Just like her namesake, her great-aunt Elnora. It's a good thing she has so many brothers to look after. . . . "

Lifting her chin a notch, Elnora comforted herself with defending her vulnerability about the *Sentinel's* story, by reasoning that even the good folks of Harmony had begun to argue about who was who in the story.

Maisie and Minnie refused to believe they were the two elderly ladies in the story, who made it their business to know every detail about every subject of King Nefen's court.

Elnora smiled, shaking off the last remnants of her sadness. In fact, Travis Miller, the local sheriff, and Cord Spencer, the dashing owner of the Last Resort, had taken to arguing over which one of them was the brave Black Knight of the Valley. The Black Knight had spent his life searching for Sir Gawain, who was once the noblest knight in the kingdom, before he'd fallen from grace for transgressions he was accused of committing against the royal court.

Zeke Gallagher assured them both that neither was noble enough to fit the description of the great knight.

Elnora pushed the sputtering bacon around in the pan and chuckled out loud.

"You should laugh more often." A masculine voice cut into the silence, interrupting her reverie.

Startled, fork in hand, Elnora spun to find Ransom

behind her. "My, you're up early today, Mr. Riley." Her cheeks felt unusually hot, and the high collar of her blouse felt uncomfortably snug.

"I have some business in Ellsworth this morning. I thought I'd better git an early start." His gaze focused on the fork she clutched in her hand, and he affected a worried expression. "I hope ya don't plan on usin' that thing on anything but your breakfast." He took a seat at the table.

Unable to help herself, she relaxed a bit and laughed at his expression. "I'm afraid my aim is terrible. You're quite safe with me."

Ransom smiled. He liked Elnora Perry, though some would say she was a bit stuffy. Still, she was a woman and a pretty one, and he'd rarely met a woman of any kind he didn't like.

"You look real pretty this morning, Miss Perry," he finally said, hoping to coax another chuckle from her.

Befuddled, her smile faded into uncertainty, and she turned back to her task at the stove. She didn't know how to react to his compliment.

She'd been around men all of her life, having had a wonderful father and five younger brothers. But compliments from someone other than the men in her family were a rarity that left her feeling flustered and confused.

"I didn't mean to rattle you." Ransom rose to his feet behind her.

"You didn't, Mr. Riley." She kept her back to him and busied herself with taking the bacon from the skillet and laying the strips out onto a platter.

"I'd like it if you'd call me Ransom. 'Mr. Riley' makes me feel like I should be fat and baldin' and at least seventy years old."

"All right, Ransom it is," she conceded while secretly acknowledging he was anything but fat and balding.

"I'd like to call you Elnora." He waited, wondering what her reaction would be.

She paused a moment, thinking. "If you wish."

"I wish." He went to a cupboard in search of a cup. Finding one, he joined her at the stove, took the coffeepot, and poured himself a cup. "Gordon says you're a dandy cook."

"I can cook," she said briskly, feeling crowded and winded by his presence. "As to how wonderfully"— she shot him a quick glance from beneath her short thick lashes—"I'd say Gordon is a bit prejudiced about everything where I'm concerned."

Ransom was silent for a second. "Do you wanna know what I think?"

"What exactly do you think, Mr. Riley?" Elnora's voice was all business. She didn't bother to look at him while she tried to calm the restless beating of her heart.

"I think you take life much too seriously, if you don't mind me sayin' so."

Elnora huffed her disapproval and dismissed him by turning her attention to the oven. "Life is not a party, Mr. Ri—" Catching herself, she amended with, "Ransom. And if I don't get these biscuits out of the oven, they'll be black as coals, and then we'll leave no question as to what kind of cook I am."

Amused, Ransom chuckled and moved out of her way, while he kept his eyes firmly fixed on her backside.

Elnora shoved her head into the warm oven, wishing she could escape into its welcome darkness, while secretly she wondered what Ransom Riley would look like dressed in a silver suit of armor.

* * *

The day before Christmas Elnora took Maisie up on her offer to stay with the children and went in to town with Gordon.

Ransom had left for Ellsworth again, saying he had business to attend to and didn't intend to be back until nightfall.

Despite her reluctance to do so, Elnora planned to visit Whitaker's Bookstore. With Christmas almost upon them, she had nothing to give Ransom. Though she'd only known him a short time, it didn't seem right to have gifts for everyone else in the Perry household but nothing for Ransom under the tree.

And Elnora was always kind, if she was nothing else at all.

She had to admit that Ransom was interesting to have around. He took every moment as it came. He had countless tales to tell and at the drop of a hat took time to play with the children.

"Are you warm enough?" Gordon asked her, interrupting her thoughts. He climbed up onto the wagon seat beside her.

"Oh, yes, I'm fine." Elnora turned to him and smiled.

The air was crisp, the trees stark and barren. Their ghostly limbs lifted upward toward the bleak winter sky. With a lap robe tucked snugly around her legs, she relaxed and enjoyed the ride into town. After some time she finally broke the silence and surprised her brother by baldly asking, "Who exactly is Mr. Whitaker?"

Gordon shot her a look of confusion. "What do you mean?"

Elnora thought a minute. "Well . . . does he have a family? A wife?"

Gordon thought a moment. "Maisie and Minnie said he's never been married, but he does have a younger brother and sister somewhere up North."

Elnora laughed. "And how do Maisie and Minnie know all this?"

Gordon grinned good-naturedly. "Like it or not, those two women, along with Lillie Taylor and Rachel Johnson, make it their business to know everything about everybody in Harmony. Russell has put them out a bit, though. They've tried everything to get more information out of him, but he just smiles and ignores their prodding and goes about his business.

"All I know is he showed up six years ago, right after Viv and I did, and he stayed on. About two months later he opened his bookstore. He's not much for talking—especially about personal matters."

They fell silent, each thinking their own thoughts, and just before they reached town, light snow began to fall.

When they reached the bookstore, Gordon stopped the wagon, jumped down, and helped Elnora down to the frozen ground. "I have a few things to pick up over at the mercantile. You go ahead and browse. Russell will help you out. I'll be back in about half an hour."

"That'll be fine," Elnora assured him. She climbed the steps to the bookstore, then, stalling, she turned and called out, "Don't forget the candy sticks for the children's stockings."

"I won't!" He waved.

"And the apples!"

"Yes, Nora!" He hurried on, braving a strong gust of winter wind.

"And if you can find them, buy a set of ivory combs for Vivian's hair!"

He lifted his arm to indicate that he'd heard her.

Elnora turned, straightened her spine, and said to herself, *Oh, go on in, for heaven's sake!* Before she could change her mind, she did. A welcome warmth hit her immediately, and she quickly closed the door behind her, hoping to shut out the chilly air. A bell, fixed above the door, clanged merrily, announcing her.

The room was lit with the lustrous glow of the many lamps placed throughout. The burnished countertop gleamed beneath the light. Her gaze swept the room, taking in the many book-filled shelves that covered the walls from floor to ceiling. A tall ladder attached to a rail at the top could be moved from one end of the bookcase to the other to reach any book any customer might desire. "Oh, my . . . " she whispered, surprised and pleased to find such a vast selection of literature in a town as small as Harmony.

She was about to remove her dainty white gloves when the large dog she'd seen with Russell Whitaker the day of her arrival came from behind the counter and startled her.

He was a beautiful animal with tall pointed ears, large intelligent golden eyes, and silver-and-black markings.

"Don't be afraid," Russell said, coming out from his rooms in the back of the store. "Arthur is as harmless as they come." He was surprised but pleased to see her. From the way she'd looked at him the day she'd arrived in town, he figured his place was the last she'd frequent, other than Lottie McGee's. With one quick sweep of his gaze, he took in her conservative apparel and decided that Elnora Perry had more spunk than he'd originally thought.

She pressed a hand to her chest and laughed with

relief. "Well, he certainly gets the customer's attention, doesn't he?"

Russell patted his thigh, and the dog immediately found his place at his master's side. "We plan it that way, don't we, boy?" He scratched behind the dog's ears, his affection for the animal obvious.

"What kind of dog is he?" Elnora asked, her natural inquisitiveness taking over.

"He's part dog, part wolf."

"Where in the world did you find him?"

Russell allowed a small smile to tug at his mouth. His hand stilled on the dog's head. "He was with a circus that had set up outside of town. They were training him to be a fighter." At her look of confusion, he went on. "He was trained to fight other dogs so men could wager money on the winner."

Elnora's hand found her throat. "How horrible!"

"Yes," Russell agreed. "Arthur just didn't have the heart for it and was losing his first fight. I suppose he would have died had someone not heard his cries and interrupted the match."

Elnora's face mirrored her pity and revulsion, but her eyes lit with something akin to respect. "You interrupted the match?"

"Oh, nothing quite so gallant, I'm afraid. I merely offered to buy Arthur before the match could be finished. His owner was the one who stopped the match. I simply made sure the dog was worth more to him alive than dead."

Elnora was silent for a moment. "He must have cost you quite a sum."

"He did," Russell admitted without a glimmer of regret. He looked down at the dog. "He was worth every cent. So," he said, his head coming up, his gaze finding hers once more, "what can I help you with today, Miss Perry?"

Overwhelmed by the countless volumes to choose from, Elnora sighed. "I really don't know where to begin."

"If you give me an idea of what you're looking for, maybe I can help."

Her brow furrowed in confusion. "Well . . . I need a gift for a man."

"For Gordon or one of your brothers?" Russell asked, remembering that Gordon had said he was one of five Perry brothers.

"No. This man isn't related to me."

Ah, so the lady had a suitor already. Russell carefully masked his surprise, finding the idea vaguely disturbing. "Do you have any idea of the man's interests?"

Elnora shrugged and shook her head. "I'm afraid I don't know him very well. We've only just met. He's Vivian's brother, Ransom Riley. He'll be staying with us for a time. All I know about him is that he's a bounty hunter. What do *you* think would interest him?"

Russell's lips twitched with amusement. He thought a moment and when finally he spoke, he said, "Several years ago I read the book *Les Misérables*." He went to a bookshelf and withdrew a large leather-bound volume. "It's a story about one man's hunt for another for the space of most of their lives." He paused a minute. "The story is about love and hate. About redemption and revenge. I don't know if your gentleman would be interested in reading such a book, but his profession being what it is, he may well relate to the frustrations of the detective, Javert, as the

convict, Jean Valjean, eludes him time after time." He
held the book out to her.

Fascinated, she was suddenly very aware of Russell
Whitaker's maleness. He was dressed in black trousers and a white shirt that was left casually open at
the neck. His shirtsleeves were rolled up over his forearms, and his silvery-blond hair fell over one side of
his forehead, as though he'd been working on some
project before she'd interrupted him. She lowered her
gaze to his hands and took the book, remaining silent
for a long moment. There was much more to Russell
Whitaker than he allowed most people to see, she decided, intrigued. Much more than she had originally
thought. "Why, Mr. Whitaker ... " she said softly,
raising her eyes to his. She held his gaze and saw the
restless passion within. "You should write yourself.
You say things so eloquently." For a moment she almost forgot she'd been on a mission to find a gift for
Ransom and found herself completely captivated by
the man before her.

A wry grin touched his lips, and his eyes took on
a devilish glitter. "You think so?"

"Indeed, I do."

"Well, thank you, Miss Perry," he said and turned
away, pushing another book back into its place on the
shelf. "Who knows, maybe I will write someday."

Having no reason to delay further, Elnora paid for
her purchase. As she was about to leave, the bell
above the door clanged, and she turned to see two
men entering the store.

"Hello, gentlemen," Russell said.

"Hello, Russ," Frederick Winchester returned.

"Russell," Edward Winchester greeted with a nod.

Though Elnora had yet to meet the two, she'd heard
about them and recognized them by the description

Maisie and Minnie had given her. They were the owners of the Double B Farm.

Frederick, Edward's uncle, was often involved in Harmony's social events, and Edward, with his handsome face, polished manners, and memorable gray eyes had managed to win Suzanna Bailey's heart.

Seeing Elnora, Frederick smiled down on her. "You must be Miss Perry, Gordon's sister."

"And you must be Mr. Winchester," Elnora replied.

"Yes, I'm Frederick." He was tall and balding, and his eyes twinkled with merriment. "But Fred will do just fine."

"Nice to meet you, Miss Perry," the other man said with a charming smile.

"And you, Mr. Winchester," Elnora returned graciously.

"How did you know who we were?" Edward asked, though he was sure he knew the answer to his question.

"I think I'd know most of Harmony's citizens on sight, thanks to Maisie and Minnie's descriptions."

The two men chuckled, realizing the truth of her statement.

Just then Gordon stuck his head in the door. His hat was covered with a fresh dusting of snow. "Ready, Nora?"

"Yes," she answered and turned to go.

"Hello, Fred. Howdy, Ed!" Gordon hollered to the two men.

Elnora turned back to Russell. "Thank you, Mr. Whitaker."

"It was my pleasure," he said quietly. Surprisingly enough, his eyes held no trace of the restless passion she was sure she'd seen earlier within their dark depths. Again he smiled that slow easy smile. "Stop by again."

"I will," she found herself saying and went to the door. With her hand on the doorknob, she glanced over her shoulder one last time. "Merry Christmas, Mr. Whitaker."

"The same to you, Miss Perry," he returned.

Once the bell over the door had quieted, Frederick turned to Russell. "My, what a lovely woman. A bit stiff around the edges, but quite attractive just the same."

"Yes, she is at that," Russell agreed to both statements.

Ever the romantic, Frederick said more to himself than to anyone else, "I wonder why she has never married."

His nephew shrugged and said, "I suppose we all have reasons for living our lives the way we do." His eyes met Russell's. "Don't you agree, Russ?"

A shadow of a smile returned to Russell's mouth. "Indeed I do."

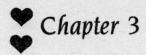 **Chapter 3**

CHRISTMAS DAY WAS delightful.

The Perry household awoke to a fresh layer of snow on the ground that morning. The tree branches drooped beneath the heavy weight of their bounty, and the air hung pregnant and ripe with anticipation of the festivities to come.

The children's excitement was contagious. Their simple, unaffected enjoyment of the holiday was a splendid gift in itself to Elnora.

The only awkward moment of the day was when Ransom unwrapped her package. For those few silent seconds she felt as inept and uncertain as a schoolgirl who'd given the teacher an apple complete with a big, fat worm.

Unsmiling, he held the large volume in his hands for several wordless moments, as though he wasn't quite sure what to do with it. The silence in the room seemed to thicken to grits, and Elnora found herself wishing she'd given him a plug of tobacco, a new pair of handcuffs—anything but a book!

Vivian, whom Gordon had carried downstairs for the day, noted the rush of color creeping into her sister-in-law's cheeks and exclaimed, "How thoughtful of you, Nora! Don't you agree, Ransom?"

Ransom's eyes found Elnora, and quite suddenly he

37

flashed her a bright smile that made her usually stable heart skip at least three good beats.

"Yes." His boyish smile was sincere. "Thanks, Nora."

His gaze continued to hold hers, and her blush deepened at the familiar use of her name. "You're welcome," she returned quietly.

His smile grew sheepish. "I'm not much for books—"

He was cut off by Sam's exuberant cry, "Thank you, Aunt Nora!" Reverently the boy ran his hand over the wooden stock of his new toy shotgun.

"Yeah, thank you!" Andy mimicked, adjusting his pistol belt above his practically nonexistent hips.

They threw themselves up against Elnora's chest, hugging her tightly, smacking wet kisses onto her smooth cheeks, and the awkward moment with Ransom was soon forgotten.

Russell Whitaker enjoyed Christmas Day, also. Maisie and Minnie's table was set generously with an abundance of breads, meats, stuffings, vegetables, and desserts. Their boarders joined them for the feast, as did Russell, who was one of their past boarders.

The day passed quickly with countless visitors, who stopped by to sample the sisters' famous recipes. There was little time for solitude or reflections of any nature for anyone amidst the celebrating.

Later that evening, however, with Arthur at his side, Russell found time for some reflection. As he walked down Main Street, his thoughts returned to the past, and to Clara.

There were times, though they were scarce, when he missed the hustle and bustle of city life.

Yet he knew that if he had the chance, he wouldn't

exchange the quiet life he now lived for any other.

Oh, he was lonely at times.

He supposed he could wander over to Lottie's and buy a night of physical enjoyment from one of her girls in an attempt to quell the loneliness. But he knew he would only feel emptier afterward.

What he craved could neither be bought nor satisfied in one night with a woman he hardly knew.

He'd never thought of himself as a family man. But lately he'd begun to wonder what he'd missed by making the choices he had. In his younger days his work had been everything to him. How could he have known that the work he loved so much would cost him so dearly?

He supposed he should have told Clara how much he cared for her when he'd had the chance. But being the young fool he was, he'd waited too long and lost the opportunity to express himself.

Her memory evoked feelings of loss and a twinge of homesickness. His sister Laura had written to say that Clara had given birth to her fourth child this past summer. Imagine that, he thought with amusement—Clara with four children. Clara, who'd never seemed to care for children at all. Laura had also written that Clara's much older, very rich husband's business was flourishing.

Well, that was just dandy.

A sad smile flitted across Russell's lips. If he were to be honest, he would have to admit he'd always known she wouldn't have chosen him anyway. She wanted stability and social acceptance among the ranks of Detroit's most prominent citizens. He could never have given her either had he remained in Detroit.

Maybe, he thought, things would have worked out

if he could have taken her with him.

He gave a small bitter laugh. *You know better than that*, an inner voice chided. Clara would never have appreciated Harmony's simplicity as he did.

And he would not have appreciated Clara for that.

Surprisingly enough, thoughts of Clara turned to thoughts of Elnora Perry. She obviously enjoyed Gordon and Vivian's children. Her easy laughter and smiling eyes had told him that much. But for some reason she held herself back, as though she was afraid of what would happen if she unleashed the woman who lived within. He sensed that beneath her proper Victorian blouse was a warm, passionate heart. He'd seen a telltale spark brighten her eyes the day she'd visited his store, the day he'd told her the story of *Les Misérables*.

For a moment Russell allowed himself to wonder what it would take to fan that spark into life. He smiled into the night. It was an intriguing thought, though he knew it was an impossible one for a man such as himself.

With the snow falling around him, he sighed heavily and looked down at his companion. "Come, Arthur. It's late, and we still have work to do." He turned back toward the bookstore and wondered what the bounty hunter, staying in Gordon Perry's house, had thought of Elnora Perry's Christmas gift.

Later that evening, after supper, Elnora grabbed her coat and went out for a breath of fresh air. The sky was dark, the moon well hidden from sight. The snow fell in a soft curtain around her. She leaned her shoulder up against a pillar of the porch and breathed in deep of the cool air.

Behind her the front door opened and closed. Expecting to see Gordon, she turned to see Ransom shrugging into his coat. She found herself both surprised and pleased.

"I thought I'd join you," he said with a smile. "I wanted to thank you for the book."

"You're quite welcome. I hope you enjoy it. Mr. Whitaker seemed to think you would."

"Mr. Whitaker?"

"Yes, he owns the bookstore in town."

"Ah . . . " Ransom nodded. He offered her his arm. "How 'bout a walk?" he asked, his eyes merry. "After all, we are living together. I'd say we know each other well enough."

Elnora snorted her disapproval at his words, even while her stomach quivered with something she didn't quite understand. "We may be staying beneath the same roof, Mr. Riley, but let me assure you—we aren't living together."

Rather than be dissuaded by her statement, Ransom was more amused than ever. He let loose with a loud hoot of laughter. "Beggin' your pardon, ma'am." He angled her a grin. "I thought we agreed you'd stop calling me Mr. Riley."

She thought about that. "Yes. I did, didn't I?"

"Yep. So how 'bout that walk?" He offered his arm again, cocking his elbow out at her.

She hesitated a moment, tipping her head to the side, considering the invitation. She finally decided there could be little harm in an innocent walk.

Knowing he was used to much more exciting activities than a mere walk on a winter's eve with a woman such as herself, however, she studied him with a suspicious look even as she took his arm. "A walk is a bit tame for a man like you, isn't it, Ransom?" She tried the name out and found it easier to say than she'd thought it would be.

He led her down the steps to the frozen earth below. "Hell, tame ain't so bad." He affected a serious expression. "It's boring that kills me."

Despite herself, she chuckled, and the tension she felt at being alone with a man on a dark winter night, with no chaperon other than her staunch Presbyterian propriety, lifted and was borne away on the chilly night wind.

They walked side by side toward the big white-washed barn that sat to the left of the house. Their footsteps crunched over the ground, cutting into the silence.

When at last they reached the fence that bordered the barnyard, their footsteps ceased. She dropped her hand from his arm, and he turned and folded his arms over the top rung of the fence, while he hooked one boot onto the bottom rung.

Elnora stared off into the dark field, feeling dwarfed by his size. Stealing a glance over at him, she realized, for perhaps the first time that she barely came to his shoulder. Though she was a small woman, she rarely thought of herself as such. Quite suddenly she felt vulnerable and feminine and sixteen again—very much the way she'd felt those many years ago when she'd allowed Henry Clemmens that one very brief, very wet, very innocent kiss.

It had been her first kiss—her first and her last.

She sighed, unaware that it was audible and that Ransom had heard it, too.

"Somethin' wrong?" he asked quietly, turning his head to stare down at the dark crown of her hair.

"No," she hurried to say. "Of course not." She wondered what topic of conversation would be of interest to a man like him, even as she wondered why she had allowed herself to be persuaded into taking a walk with him in the first place.

Although they'd lived in the same house together for the space of a full week, they'd never been alone long enough to exchange more than the most basic of pleasantries, except for the one morning he'd risen before the others.

Finally, because the silence felt oppressive, she bluntly asked, "Why would you want to spend your life hunting down other men?"

Surprised at her boldness, Ransom chuckled. Most women wouldn't have asked him about his work in such a blunt manner. "Money," he told her matter-of-factly. "The job pays well if you get your man."

"And if you don't?"

"I do."

"Every single time?"

"All but once." He turned to face her. His expression was hidden by the shadows, but she'd noted an abrupt change in his tone of voice, which was usually so lighthearted and confident. "There's only one I didn't get."

Elnora was impressed. "My . . . " was all she said.

A short silence fell between them.

"Do you ever think you'll find him?" she asked at length.

Ransom gave a short laugh. "Oh, yeah. Sooner or later." He fell silent again, then quite abruptly dismissed the subject by saying, "As I said, I wanted to thank you for the book—"

She waved off his thanks with an airy motion of her hand. "There's no need. You've already thanked me—"

"Nora . . . " The quiet, almost intimate way he said her name cut her off and made her go as still as the night around them. He took his boot from the railing and moved a step closer to where she stood with her small sensible shoes planted firmly to the cold earth. "I was hopin' you'd do me the honor of spendin' an evening with me. The townsfolk are holdin' a sleighin' party next Saturday night."

Thoroughly discombobulated, Elnora's mouth dropped open, and she palmed her chest wordlessly. Above them, the heavy clouds parted, and the moon shone down on them in a silvery haze of light. She looked up into Ransom's face. "Me?" she whispered in disbelief, her palm still at her breast.

As he took her other hand from her side, her heart did somersaults, and her knees weakened.

"Yes, you, Nora. I'd like to take you."

She continued to stare up into his face and was filled with a new sense of herself, while she wondered if he would dare attempt to kiss her.

He stared down into her face, thinking he'd like to do just that, wondering if he dare attempt the act with such a prim and proper lady.

Then quite suddenly she snatched her hand away and found the strangest words leaving her mouth. "Why, yes, I'd love to go with you." With that said, her face flaming, she pivoted on her heel and stalked back toward the safety of her brother's house.

Later, after everyone had retired, Gordon and Ransom sat in the cozy front room, smoking their pipes before the fireplace.

Ransom hooked his ankle onto his knee and leaned back into his chair. "That sister of yours needs to get out more," he said.

Gordon raised an eyebrow in much the same manner as Elnora often did. "What makes you say that?"

"She's a woman."

Gordon snorted, irritated by his brother-in-law's observation of his sister's gender.

Ransom gave him a long stare. "Didn't it ever occur to you that she might like to have a little fun once in a while?"

Gordon thought about that a minute and felt a sudden stab of shame. It had truly never occurred to him that Elnora would want anything more for herself than to care for her family. "I suppose I've never given it much thought," he admitted. "She's always seemed so content."

Ransom shrugged. "She probably is. Mostly. But a night out every now and then wouldn't hurt her any."

Gordon stared into the flames, thinking about that.

"I stopped over at the First Resort yesterday on my way back from Ellsworth."

"You'd best not let Vivian know that," Gordon warned. His eyes found Ransom's. "She may not say much about the way Lottie McGee and her girls make a living, but she wouldn't want to know you'd been visitin' Lottie's establishment."

Ransom didn't bother to explain what he'd been doing over at Lottie's. "When I was leaving I saw Jake Sutherland outside the livery."

Gordon nodded. "Jake owns the livery. He's a good man. One of the best."

"He said the townsfolk are meeting over at Hutton's Hotel and having a sleighin' party next Saturday night with a social afterward over at Alexander Evans's house. Jake said he and Abby Lee plan to go."

Gordon made a face. "I hardly think Vivian is up to a sleighin' party or a social of any sort, if that's what you're gettin' at."

Ransom frowned his disgust. "You're thicker than

the bark on an oak tree. Don't you think I know Vivian ain't up to socializin'?"

"I sure as hell would hope so."

"Well, I ain't talkin' 'bout Vivian."

Finally Gordon understood, and his eyes rounded. "You want to take Nora?"

"I think it'd do her good."

Gordon contemplated the thought. His usually amiable expression grew thoughtful and sober. When he finally spoke, his voice held a quiet warning. "We both know you have a habit of droppin' in for a visit whenever the need strikes you. Just the same, you make no bones about cuttin' out whenever things get a little too comfortable." He paused a moment, then went on. "I don't want to see my sister get hurt."

Ransom made no attempt to challenge his brother-in-law's words. Instead, he grinned and raised his palms. "I've already asked her, Gordon. And just so you know, I don't plan on hurtin' her."

"Just so we understand each other."

"We do," Ransom said. "Don't worry."

The evening of the sleighing party finally arrived, although Elnora had begun to fear it never would.

She dressed with special care, wearing a deep blue blouse with a high collar and long puffy sleeves, and a full skirt, pleated around the sides where they swept into a small bustle in the back. Her glossy hair was piled on top of her head in a style that accentuated her large eyes and smooth skin.

From her place on the bed, Vivian watched, clucking and fussing over every detail until Elnora felt like a chick being pecked alive by its mother.

"Oh, Elnora," Vivian gushed. "You look absolutely lovely."

Flustered, Elnora gave her hair one last look, still dissatisfied with what she saw reflected in the mirror. Her mouth was too wide, her chin too pointy. And that dimple! She groaned inwardly. Only the good Lord Himself knew what purpose it served. She straightened, hoping to gain an inch or two in stature, then decided it didn't help any. She was still too short. "Oh, well," she finally said, turning toward her sister-in-law, "I've spent far too much time fussing already."

But when she descended the staircase and Ransom's eyes spoke his appreciation, she was glad she'd taken the time to fuss.

He looked undeniably handsome, his hair damp and slicked back, his big chest puffed out and straining against the buttons of his best Sunday suit. His expression was eager, his smile bright.

She crossed the kitchen floor, her knees weak with a delicious sense of anticipation. As she allowed Ransom to help her on with her wrap, she tried to still her fast-tripping heart.

Before she and Ransom left, the children lined up in a tidy row in front of the door, awaiting their turn for a good-night kiss. Elnora made her way down the row, kissing each child, plucking Emily's thumb from her mouth, until at last she reached Sam, who, being the oldest, was last in line.

As she approached him, his dark eyes grew serious. He pressed himself up against her and hugged her neck tight. "You won't be late will you, Aunt Nora? I want you to read me more about Arthur and his knights." Since her arrival Sam had taken to Elnora like a bear cub to honey. He followed her footsteps throughout the house, carrying out her requests, as if he were her very own captain of the guard. Although he was fond enough of Uncle Ransom, he didn't like the thought of him courting Aunt Nora at all. Not even for an evening. Sam had already decided he was going to marry Elnora Perry himself when he grew up.

Her eyes tender with affection for the boy, Elnora smiled and placed a kiss to Sam's temple. "King Arthur and his knights will have to wait until tomorrow night, dear. I'm afraid your uncle and I won't be back until long after your bedtime."

Sam didn't bother to hide his disappointment. He angled his uncle a disgruntled glare that spoke volumes.

As they left the house, Ransom chuckled. "I think that boy's sweet on you, Nora."

"You think so?" she asked, surprised, not having considered the thought.

"Yep. I sure do."

Bemused, Elnora shrugged. "Imagine that," she said softly.

Ransom helped her up into the sleigh, then came around to the other side and leaped up beside her. With a flick of the reins, he turned to her and said, "I already have."

The night was cold and clear, the sky lit by a large pale moon and countless glittering stars.

When Russell Whitaker arrived at Hutton's Hotel, the gathering group was almost ready to depart for the evening ride.

Alexander Evans spotted him first and called out, "Russ! You're welcome to ride with Jane and me if you want! We have plenty of room!"

"Thanks!" Russell called back. "But I'm riding with Zeke."

Though Maisie and Minnie had each contended for Zeke Gallagher's company this evening, hinting pointedly for invitations, Zeke Gallagher was no fool. He'd decided to play it safe and had offered a seat to Russell instead. That way he wouldn't alienate either of the twins, and he'd still have his steady supply of baked goods from both women.

The twins, however, had decided to make him jealous and had accepted an invitation to ride with Frederick Winchester. When they'd climbed into Frederick's sleigh, they'd shot Zeke identical looks of satisfaction. It had taken Zeke ten full minutes to quiet his chuckles. Now seeing his partner arrive, he eagerly called out, "Russ, over here!"

Russell climbed into the sleigh, and a grin touched the corners of his mouth. "You're a sly old fox, Zeke. You know damn well those two women had intentions of wheedling an invitation out of you tonight."

Zeke chuckled, pleased with himself. He smoothed down his snowy-white whiskers. "An old bachelor like me has to look out for himself."

"And how do you plan to look out for yourself later when we all meet over at Alexander and Jane's for the social?"

"That's easy." Zeke's blue eyes twinkled mischievously. "It'll be well past my bedtime. I plan on gettin' home soon as I drop you off. Besides, I got a dime novel to get back to, and"—he angled Russell a devilish grin—"those two old gals ain't up to that kind of merriment any more than I am."

From her place beside Ransom, Elnora watched Russell Whitaker arrive. He glanced around at the others, took a seat in Zeke's sleigh, and immediately entered into a conversation with the older man. For some odd reason, Elnora felt strangely disappointed that he hadn't noticed her, though she didn't understand why. After all, she was with Ransom and she felt giddy with excitement at what the evening held in store for them.

"Everybody ready?" Alexander called out. Assured that everyone was, he flicked the reins, setting his horses and sleigh in motion. They headed around the mercantile and down Main Street, past the many shops and houses still decorated with their holiday greenery. When they reached the First Resort, they took a left and came up behind the mill. Then they crossed over the railroad tracks and headed out toward the Smoky Hill River.

Someone started singing "The Blue Tail Fly," and others joined in, not caring that it was hardly the season to be singing about flies. Everyone knew the words to the song which was all that mattered. Their voices filled the night air with gaiety and laughter. Some of the voices were lovely; others, however, were so horribly out of tune, they brought loud hoots of laughter.

But no one seemed to mind.

Least of all Elnora, who for the first time in years was having the time of her life.

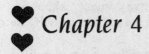 **Chapter 4**

ELNORA WAS WRONG. Russell had noticed her all right.

He'd also noticed her escort and experienced a very real prick of jealousy.

His reaction confused and irritated him.

As the group headed back into town over the bridge that spanned the river, he thought about Elnora and was glad the sleigh she rode in was behind him, rather than in front. He didn't want to have to stare at their backs as he wondered whether Miss Perry was becoming enamored of the dashing bounty hunter, or whether the bounty hunter would be the man who would light Miss Perry's fire.

He asked himself why it would even matter to him.

Elnora Perry was nothing more than a mere acquaintance.

But there was something about her—something sweet and vulnerable, soft and feminine—that she tried very hard to hide beneath that polished air of cool correctness.

As the group completed their travels and headed over to the Evans house, his thoughts left off.

Zeke dropped him at the door and made a hasty retreat before anyone had the chance to try to talk him into coming indoors for refreshments.

Russell entered the house, thinking he would have

been wiser to have followed Zeke's lead and gone home, too. But he felt a perverse curiosity about Elnora's escort, and, he had to admit to himself, he wanted to see Elnora again.

The Evanses' parlor filled rapidly, as couples filed in, their cheeks rosy from the cold. They chafed their hands together and called out greetings, while Jane flitted around, collecting their wraps and mittens.

Samantha Spencer, Alexander Evans's lovely daughter, dipped punch from a bowl for the ladies, while Alexander saw to the men's comfort by offering them glasses of his best brandy.

From where he stood by the window in the far corner of the room, Russell sipped his brandy and watched Elnora and her escort arrive.

She handed Jane her wrap, and Ransom handed her his coat. Then Elnora moved toward the parlor doors, leaving Ransom behind to speak with Alexander.

Maisie and Minnie stopped her in the doorway.

"Elnora," Maisie said, "how nice that you could come."

Elnora glanced back at Ransom, who was still talking with Alexander. "Vivian's brother brought me. He'll be staying at the house for a short time."

"Is that a fact?" Minnie asked. "I can't say as we've ever met him, have we, Sister?"

"No," Maisie answered thoughtfully. "Now that you mention it, though, I do remember Vivian talking about him. He's some kind of body hunter, isn't he?" She wrinkled her nose in distaste, her disapproval obvious.

Elnora hid her smile of amusement. "He's a bounty hunter."

"A bounty what!" Minnie squawked, not sure she'd heard correctly.

"Hunter," Elnora repeated patiently. "He's a bounty hunter."

"Land's sake!" Minnie said.

The twins swung around to get a better look at Elnora's gentleman, not at all pleased by this new turn of events. Their minds had been furiously clicking with plans to link her with another.

"Humph!" Maisie snorted her disapproval, turning back to Elnora. "Bounty hunters, outlaws, convicts—they're all the same to me. One is as unscrupulous as the other."

"Ransom is a very nice man," Elnora defended with a soft smile. "You'll have to meet him."

Minnie ignored Elnora's statement by saying, "A nice man is Russell Whitaker!" The older woman didn't bother to be discreet. "Don't you agree, Sister?"

"Indeed I do. He's a little shy and bookish, but he's a good solid individual, a true gentleman. A law-abiding citizen if ever there was one." Perpetually plagued by her poor eyesight, Maisie squinted at Elnora, trying to read her expression. "You've met him, haven't you, Elnora?"

"Why, yes, I have."

"Maisie! Minnie!" Lillie Taylor called from across the room. "Come over and settle this for us. Fred says we had our last pie eatin' contest in August, but I know it was September. . . ."

The twins huffed their disgust at the interruption of their matchmaking scheme and excused themselves.

Amused by their antics, Elnora entered the parlor, still smiling. She noticed Mary Hubbard standing near the table that held the punch bowl.

Mary's face brightened when she saw Elnora, and she waved a greeting. "Elnora, hello! Come join us. You haven't met Samantha yet, have you?"

Elnora crossed the room to join the two women.

"Samantha," Mary said, "meet Elnora Perry, Gordon's sister."

Samantha handed Elnora a cup of punch. "Welcome, Elnora." Samantha's smile was genuine and warm. "It's always nice to have another woman come to town."

The three chatted a while, and, remembering Maisie's remark about how Mary had found her husband, Elnora couldn't help but ask, "So tell me, Mary, how did you find Mr. Hubbard?"

Samantha laughed, and Mary blushed. "Well, believe it or not, I advertised for him."

Elnora's eyes widened. "You advertised for him?" She paused a moment. "How?"

Mary's eyes sparkled. "I placed a notice in several Kansas newspapers."

"Really?" Although Elnora was surprised, she was more amused than anything.

Samantha nodded. "She really did."

"And what did you get?" Elnora's curiosity was stoked.

"You mean for a husband?" Mary asked, laughing.

"Yes."

"Him." Mary pointed toward a tall, handsome man with light brown hair who stood across the room talking with several of the other men. She pressed forward and said, "Come by the mercantile sometime, and I'll tell you the whole story."

"I look forward to it," Elnora said. After a few moments she excused herself and went to look for Ransom. But as she crossed the floor, instead of finding Ransom, her gaze found Russell. Her steps halted.

For several silent seconds they took measure of

each other, then he lifted his glass in greeting. A slow easy smile tugged at his mouth, and he began to move across the floor toward her.

Elnora felt a sudden flush steal over her entire body, and her heart broke into an absurd canter. By the time he reached her, she'd begun to question her sanity in accepting Ransom's invitation. Normally she wouldn't have. But it seemed from the time she'd arrived in Harmony that nothing was normal any longer, including herself. Her common sense had all but abandoned her, and her once solid and stable life—the life that had always seemed so safe and so satisfying—now seemed sadly insufficient.

Russell stopped before her. He was taller than she'd realized, taller even than Ransom, and she had to raise her chin to meet his eyes.

"Good evening, Miss Perry." His deep, dark eyes held that all-too-familiar hint of amusement.

"Good evening, Mr. Whitaker," she managed, though she wasn't sure how.

His eyes swept her form in a discreet manner, never lingering anywhere for more than the briefest of moments. But when they returned to her face, his appreciation of what he'd seen was obvious in the sudden warmth of his gaze. "You look lovely tonight."

"Thank you," she replied, glancing away from his eyes, thinking Maisie and Minnie were truly mistaken if they thought this man was shy. From the very moment she'd met him, she'd thought him anything but shy. Oh, he was quiet all right, but shy? Humph!

"Your holidays were pleasant, I hope?"

"Yes, very."

"And your gentleman . . . was he pleased with the book?"

"He was," Ransom answered for her, taking his place at her side.

The two men studied each other for several silent seconds, and an instant tension sprang to life between them.

"Ah . . . " Russell said, a small secret smile taking hold of his mouth. "Good." He held out his hand in greeting. "I'm Russell Whitaker. It's nice to meet you, Mister—"

"Riley." Ransom's green eyes lingered quizzically on Russell's face while he shook his hand.

"Do you plan to stay in Harmony very long?"

"It depends."

A brief silence fell.

"Well, I certainly hope you enjoy your stay," Russell said, proving he was quite good at amenities, despite the animosity that hovered in the air. "Please feel free to drop in at the bookstore if there is anything I can do for you."

Ransom refused to smile. "I'll do that." He took Elnora's arm in a possessive manner that left no question as to who her escort was this evening.

Russell's face remained impassive.

Annoyed by his manhandling, Elnora prickled. She withdrew her arm from his grasp and was about to put him in his place when Samantha stepped into the center of the room and clapped her hands.

"All right, everybody!" Her eyes twinkled with mischief. "Please sit down. It's time for fun!"

Russell inclined his head to Elnora. "Miss Perry."

Elnora nodded politely, and Russell turned and crossed the room to sit down on a sofa beside Cord Spencer.

"Now," Samantha said, "we're going to play a game very similar to charades."

Everyone groaned.

Charlie Thompson, the bartender over at the Last Resort, whined, "Not another guessing game!"

"Hush, Charlie!" his wife Cora scolded and slapped his arm none too gently.

Everyone laughed, and Samantha smiled patiently. "The prizes will be worth it, Charlie." Her eyes rounded, and she hesitated just long enough to allow the room to fall silent. "You should know, however, that I'm making up the rules."

Her statement released another ripple of hearty chuckles. Everyone knew, especially Cord Spencer, Samantha's husband, that she always made up her own rules.

"Instead of guessing words or phrases this time, we'll be trying to guess objects. The women will take turns giving the clues, and the men will have to do the guessing."

"How come the men gotta do the guessing first?" Joseph Taylor wanted to know.

"Because I say so, that's why," Samantha answered amid another bout of laughter. She waited for the room to quiet once again. "The man who guesses the object correctly wins his prize. . . . " She paused, letting the suspense build, until at length she said, "His prize will be a kiss from the lady of his choice. . . . "

The room rippled with excitement. Some of the men hooted, while many of the younger women blushed and clapped their hands over their mouths.

Mortified, Elnora's mouth fell open. Her rigid sense of Victorian propriety rose to life.

Beside her Ransom whooped and slapped his knee.

Across the room, Russell Whitaker chuckled quietly and turned to Cord Spencer. "Leave it to your Samantha to come up with this one."

Cord nodded, his appreciation of "his" Samantha evident in his shining eyes.

"I'll begin," Samantha said, pursing her lips thoughtfully. "I'm thinking of an item of clothing. I'm always worn by women—at least I should be. . . . "

That brought another round of laughter.

"I always follow and never lead . . . as my hindsight is much better than my foresight. . . . " She looked directly into her husband's eyes, and he quietly said, "You're a bustle."

"Oh, Cord!" she exclaimed, stomping her foot. "You weren't supposed to guess the answer that quickly!"

Everyone clapped, and Samantha pouted, but most of the townsfolk knew that things had worked out exactly as she had planned. Cord rose from the sofa, offered his hand, then tugged his lady off into the hall to claim his prize privately, while titters and catcalls followed in his wake.

Watching the two leave the room, Elnora sat stiff-shouldered and stone still. She felt flushed and uncomfortable, drawn and repelled at once. She wondered if all unmarried women felt as she did. She immediately decided that they must—kissing was such an intimate act, just one step beneath that one unmentionable act that occurred between a man and his wife on their wedding night.

She glanced around the room, and her gaze collided with Russell's.

His dark eyes held hers, and she felt an insidious stirring in the lower part of her stomach. Bewildered, her eyes danced away, and she studied the varied pattern of the wallpaper to the left of his head.

When Samantha returned a few moments later, she was flushed and grinning like a cat who'd gotten her mouse. She turned to Faith Hutton and said, "Go ahead, Faith. It's your turn."

Faith rose from her seat beside her husband, Kincaid, and took her place in the center of the room. "All right," she began, "I am tall, dark, and handsome. My offspring are timekeepers. My hands often get in the way of my face—"

She looked at her husband, who was indeed tall, dark, and handsome, and widened her eyes, waiting for him to shout the answer. But when he continued to stare up at her blankly, she finally huffed, "Oh, I can't make this much easier. . . . "

A low murmur could be heard in the room while the men put their heads together.

"Welllll . . . " Palms up, Faith looked truly disgusted.

"You're a grandfather clock," came the quiet answer from a deep male voice.

All heads turned toward Russell Whitaker.

"That's right!" Faith said, clapping. "Choose your lady, Russell."

Russell rose from the sofa. Elnora clutched her hands in her lap, her gaze fixed downward. She sensed him moving toward her, and she forgot to breathe, waiting, waiting, her heart beating in her throat, choking her along with the much-too-tight collar of her staid blouse.

He stopped before her, his shoes within her view. "Miss Perry," he said, his deep voice soft.

A hush fell around them.

Her gaze lifted to his. Her honey-brown eyes grew large and round in her face. He held his hand out to her and gestured with a tilt of his head toward the hall. "Shall we?"

Ransom coughed his surprise.

Elnora blanched.

Russell waited.

Maisie and Minnie looked on, smiling their approval.

When finally Elnora found her voice, it was nothing more than a mere whisper. "Oh, Mr. Whitaker, I . . . I . . . couldn't . . . I . . ." Her face flaming, she glanced over at Ransom, who looked as befuddled as she felt.

"You have to honor the request, Elnora," Faith called out. "It's the rule."

"Yes, Elnora, you must!" Samantha urged.

"Atta boy, Russ!" someone hollered.

Everyone laughed. Everyone except Elnora, Ransom, and Russell.

Realizing she had no choice but to comply, Elnora rose slowly. Once again Russell gestured toward the hall and stepped back, waiting for her to lead the way. She heaved a great sigh, refusing to meet his gaze, then like Joan of Arc being dragged to her death, she walked stiffly out of the room, thinking, *Shy, my bustle!*

Once out of earshot, she turned on him immediately. "How dare you, Mr. Whitaker!" she said, planting her hands firmly on her hips. "I thought you were supposed to be a gentleman!"

He studied her for the space of several seconds, then grinned and said, "Imagine that." He seemed truly amused by the thought. "I never would have guessed you thought so from the way you looked at me the first day we met."

"I didn't exactly say I thought so," she amended in a harsh whisper, remembering very well the day they'd met and the events thereof, "but there are others in this town who do think so."

He paused, then said, "I'm sorry to disappoint you,

but I did guess the answer to the riddle." He leaned a shoulder up against the wall, his dark eyes glittering with enjoyment.

"But, but ..." she sputtered, knowing she was being a poor sport by not observing the game rules. She lowered her gaze and wrung her hands. "This is not my game. These are not my rules...."

When he didn't answer, she went on in a wild flutter of words. "Maisie and Minnie said you were shy and ... and ... bookish ... and ... and ... after the day I came to your store, I thought ..." She lifted her eyes to his once again, and with a start realized she found him far more attractive than she wanted him to be, dressed in his gentleman's clothing, his beautiful silvery hair falling forward, his smiling eyes staring down on her. She noted, for perhaps the first time, that his mouth was a most handsome one, and an odd sensation skittered through her veins.

He crossed his arms over his broad chest and waited. "You thought what?" His voice was low and persuasive.

"I don't know," she said, flabbergasted. "I don't know what I thought." She felt petty and childish, knowing she was trying to forestall the moment when he would claim his kiss.

He studied her silently, allowing her a few moments to gather her composure. When he finally spoke, his words puzzled her. "Things are not always what they seem, Miss Perry. People often see only what they want to see."

"But, Mr. Whitaker ..." It was a soft plea.

Quite suddenly he began to suspect what the problem was. Maybe ... Elnora Perry had never been kissed before. And maybe, by choosing her as he had, he'd embarrassed her terribly by forcing her to face that fact. A sudden empathy for her rose within, and he felt the need to champion her. "Don't worry, Elnora," he said quietly, "I won't force you to pay up."

The sound of him speaking her first name for the very first time seemed so intensely intimate, her lips parted in surprise. She remained silent for several long moments and, staring up at him, read the compassion in his eyes.

And it hurt.

She'd seen that look before—from her parents, her brothers, her neighbors and friends. . . . Poor Elnora Perry, who'd never been properly kissed; poor Elnora, who had no one of her own; poor Elnora, who'd grown up to be just like her great-aunt, who'd gone to her grave a lonely old maid . . .

Quite suddenly a fierce pride lit within her breast, and she drew herself up to her full height. "I beg your pardon, Mr. Whitaker," she said tartly, trying to keep her voice low. "Let me assure you. I always pay my debts!" To prove it, she leaned forward and squeezed her eyes shut tight, tipping her chin up toward him.

He stared down at her pretty puckered mouth, finding her sacrifice undeniably appealing. He forgot the gallant words he'd spoken a moment ago and, very gently, cupped her shoulders, pulling her toward him. She went stiff as a tree trunk, so he waited a moment, then urged her toward him once again. "Come here, fair lady," he whispered.

She took one reluctant step, refusing to open her eyes, a lump of foreboding lodging in her throat.

Then she felt his warm breath upon her face.

She remained stiff and unyielding, even when his lips brushed across hers—lightly, oh, ever so lightly . . .

It happened so quickly, so painlessly, that she

wasn't sure it had happened at all. She opened her eyes and gazed up into his face. In a voice she didn't recognize as her own, she said, "Oh, my . . ." Then, as though of their own accord, her eyes drifted shut in expectation of more. . . .

She forgot the others who waited in the parlor, she forgot she was a respectable woman who would not think of engaging in such a private act with a man she barely knew; she forgot she was thirty-two and as untouched as the virginal snow that had fallen on Christmas morning. . . .

Though she was willing, the kiss went no further.

With a heavy sigh of resignation, Russell eased her away from his chest, knowing the game had gone far enough. Elnora Perry might be a full-grown woman, but she was an innocent all the same. There was something within him that rebelled against taking advantage of that fact, despite the tempting picture she presented.

Her eyelids parted, and she stared up at him, her eyes full of questions. There was more to kissing, she was sure . . . and whatever it was, she hungered for it. . . .

A half-smile caught at his mouth. His hand came up, and his thumb brushed across her full lower lip. "Thank you very much, Miss Perry."

Reason returned like a sudden flash of lightning, and her face flamed. "You're quite welcome, Mr. Whitaker," she said stiffly, gathering her composure.

He gestured toward the parlor and, her back straight, her chin parallel to the floor, she spun and led the way into the parlor without ever saying another word.

* * *

When finally Elnora and Ransom left the Evanses' house, Elnora felt she could finally breathe again. The cool night air brought relief; the darkness brought a welcome respite.

Ransom was uncharacteristically silent the entire ride home. He was sulking. It irritated him that Whitaker had chosen Elnora for his prize. It surprised him, too.

Oh, it wasn't that Elnora wasn't attractive. In fact, Elnora was more than attractive, she was downright beautiful. . . .

But she was so small, and she dressed in such a simple manner, a body had to get close enough to notice.

And Whitaker had noticed, all right. Ransom was sure of it.

Just the same, Whitaker hadn't seemed the type to be so bold as to choose anyone for a prize, least of all Nora, whom he hardly knew.

He stole a covert glance in her direction, seeing her in a new light—a light he was sure Gordon would not approve of.

When finally he stopped the sleigh in front of the Perry house, he turned to her and said, "Well?"

Elnora gave him a puzzled stare. "Well, what?" she returned innocently, but her voice sounded higher than normal, even to her own ears.

"Did he kiss you?" he asked, his expression sulky.

Exasperated, Elnora stared at him in silence, but the moon above revealed her blush and gave him his answer.

"He did!" Ransom exclaimed, his eyes widening. Whitaker had beat him to it! A spurt of jealousy jolted a wicked path through him, and he slapped his knee so hard he hurt himself. "Well, I'll be damned!"

"Ransom, please!" Elnora said, appalled at his vulgarity. "What is wrong with you?" When he didn't answer, she lifted herself out of the seat, ready to get down on her own. "I think I've had just about enough of this nonsense for one night," she huffed, disgusted.

But a hand on her shoulder stayed her. She turned to find Ransom's eyes on her face.

"I was hoping to have the pleasure." His face reflected an almost boyish disappointment.

"Oh, for heaven's sake! Come on around, then," she snapped, sitting back down, thinking he meant he wanted the pleasure of helping her out of the sleigh.

"That's not what I meant." He leaned in closer. "I meant I was hopin' to have the pleasure of kissin' you myself tonight."

Astounded, her eyes rounded with surprise. If ever there was a time in her life when her nervous system had been taxed as it had this evening, she surely didn't remember it. Suddenly her heart pounded, and her palms felt damp despite the cold, moistureless air around them.

When she didn't answer, he flashed her one of his most charming smiles. "How 'bout it?" He paused. "You let him. . . . " When still she didn't answer, he slumped back into his seat and affected another sulky face.

Her amazement faded somewhat, and she laughed at his expression. "Oh, all right. But just one."

Immediately Ransom seemed to puff up in his seat. "One's all I'll need," he stated arrogantly, his wide smile returning. He swept her up against his chest and planted his mouth squarely on hers, stealing the breath right out of her lungs.

His mouth was insistent, his kiss warm and wet. His tongue rode the seam of her lips, forcing them apart, willing her compliance, which she gave in lieu of curiosity about what Russell had denied her earlier. As Ransom's tongue swept her mouth, she found herself thinking: *So this is it. Well . . . I didn't miss so very much after all.*

The beginning of a kiss, she concluded, was much better than the end.

To her surprise, from out of the past came the memory of the one and only kiss she'd shared with Henry Clemmens the summer she was sixteen.

When at last Ransom lifted his head and stared down into her eyes, she found herself vastly relieved that the kiss had ended.

His eyes glittered, and he strove to catch his breath. He waited a moment, then his hand sought the back of her neck, and his head dipped toward hers once more.

But Elnora halted him, gently placing her palms against his chest. "We'd better go in, don't you think?"

Disappointment wiped Ransom's face clean of passion. He took a giant breath. "Yeah. I suppose we'd better 'fore Gordon comes out with his shotgun." With that said, he released her and jumped down to the ground, then came around to her and offered his hand. "I had a good time, Nora." All teasing aside, his eyes spoke his sincerity.

Elnora smiled down into his handsome face and honestly said, "So did I. It was an evening I'll never forget. Thank you, Ransom."

That night as Elnora lay in bed on her back, a thick quilt clutched tight to her breasts, her mind churned over the events of the evening, thinking about Ransom, thinking about Russell . . . wondering if she'd lost her mind . . . deciding she surely had. . . .

She'd spent most of her life wondering what it would be like to be kissed by a man, and in one night she'd found out what it was like to be kissed by two. . . . Imagine that.

She sighed into the night, her eyes sinking shut in exhaustion.

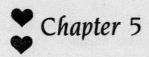 Chapter 5

MAISIE AND MINNIE arrived at the Perry farm early Monday afternoon.

When Elnora answered the door, they bustled in, bringing with them the most recent edition of the *Sentinel*.

"Elnora, we couldn't wait to tell you about the story!" Maisie exclaimed, her eyes snapping with excitement.

"Imagine that," Elnora said, amused. She offered the ladies a seat at the kitchen table, then set about brewing a fresh pot of tea. Her back to the sisters, she smiled. She felt certain it wasn't the story they wanted to discuss nearly so much as it was the events of last Saturday night.

They were going to be greatly disappointed, however.

She wasn't about to discuss anything with anyone, especially when she felt so confused about everything herself.

She wasn't sure about herself anymore.

The Elnora Perry she knew would never kiss a man she'd just met.

But she had. Not only had she kissed one, she'd kissed two! She groaned inwardly, feeling a rush of remorse at having given in to Ransom's plea for a kiss.

He had been especially attentive since the sleighing party. Though she appreciated his attention, to her surprise the fast-tripping excitement that had filled her when he'd first come to stay with the family had dulled somewhat, but she didn't know why. She'd hoped it was because her common sense was finally returning, but she discarded that idea when she found her mind befuddled with thoughts of Russell Whitaker and his kiss. Her smiled faded, and her eyes narrowed. His decidedly stingy kiss!

Now that she'd been kissed by Ransom, she knew Russell had shorted her. Well, see if she ever sacrificed herself again for such a scanty little peck!

"There's to be a jousting match!" Minnie said from behind, breaking into her thoughts. "Between the Black Knight and Sir Ruggard."

Elnora turned to face the women, glad for a diversion from thoughts of Russell Whitaker. "A tournament?"

The women nodded.

"But why? They're both knights of Sir Nefan's court."

"Yes, but the games are not to the death, but for fun and entertainment, for competition. The two knights are competin' for Lady Elvia's favor."

"Ah," Elnora whispered, intrigued.

"You know, Elnora," Maisie said matter-of-factly, "we've been discussin' it among ourselves, and we've decided that Lady Elvia is you."

"Me!" Elnora pressed her hand to her chest. Wide-eyed, she looked from one twin to the other. "Whatever gives you that idea?"

"We've already figured out that the subjects of King

Nefan's court are too much like our townsfolk for it to be a coincidence. No sooner did you come to town, than Lady Elvia appeared in the story."

"That's right," Minnie agreed heartily, "and she looks like you, too. Right down to that tiny dimple you got pressed into that pretty chin of yours."

Embarrassed, Elnora blushed and gently scoffed, "I think you're both imagining things."

"It's not just us," Maisie said. "Lillie Taylor and Rachel Johnson think so, too."

Still, Elnora huffed her disbelief and dismissed the idea by returning to the subject of the tournament. "Who do you think will win the joust?"

"The Black Knight—"

"Sir Ruggard—"

The sisters exchanged baffled looks.

"I didn't know you favored the Black Knight," Maisie all but accused, her expression turning sour.

Minnie lifted her nose into the air. "I can favor whoever I please, Sister. Besides, I know he'll win."

"Fiddle dee!" Maisie snapped, offended. "Sir Ruggard will knock that big black can of metal right off his horse!"

"Humph!" said one.

"Humph!" said the other.

Elnora laughed and joined them at the table with the pot of tea. "Now, ladies, there's no need to squabble over the matter." She sat down between the two and poured them each a cup. "I'm sure the truest, most deserving knight will win."

Agitated with each other, the two sisters sipped their tea in silence, almost forgetting they'd come on another much more important mission: To interrogate Elnora, of course.

Remembering their goal, Maisie brought up the

subject. "So, Elnora, did you enjoy the sleighing party Saturday night?"

Smiling, her eyes crinkling at the corners, Elnora took a cookie from the platter on the table. "Indeed, I did."

"And," Minnie jumped in, uniting with her sister in their purpose of attaining information, "did you enjoy the social afterward?"

"Why, yes," Elnora answered, offering nothing more.

"And Vivian's brother, the body hunter . . ." Maisie hesitated, glancing around the room as though she expected Ransom to appear out of the woodwork at any given moment.

"The bounty hunter," Minnie amended with a glower, having decided Ransom wasn't quite so bad after all. He'd sampled her pumpkin pie Saturday night and declared it the best he'd ever tasted.

"Ah, yes, well, whatever." Maisie waved her sister's correction aside. "Did he enjoy himself?"

"Very much so." Elnora's smile was secretive.

"I wonder if Russell did," Minnie commented, her eyes innocently wide.

"I wouldn't know." Elnora's face was as impassive as a deck of cards placed facedown.

"Oh, Elnora," Maisie snapped, flabbergasted. "Did he kiss you or not?"

A spurt of orneriness lit in Elnora's eyes. "Why, yes, as a matter of fact, he did." Then, seeing the satisfied smiles on both their faces, she couldn't help but add, "They both did."

"When do you think the baby will come, Aunt Nora?" Sara asked as she, Emily, and Mark Anthony sat at Elnora's feet four days later.

Both girls looked like their mother—fair and blond with enormous blue eyes. Mark Anthony looked more like Gordon. His eyes and hair were dark, his face almost always wearing a smile. He had a pleasant disposition and an enormous appetite, and day by day Elnora was becoming so attached to him and the rest of his siblings that she sometimes wondered how she would ever be able to leave them.

But leave them she would once the baby came and Vivian was up and about.

James Taylor had brought her out a letter yesterday from her cousin Sally. Sally had written to say she was getting married in June, and she was hoping Elnora could come and help her design and sew her wedding dress.

"Aunt Nora?" Sara prompted, wanting an answer to her question.

Elnora took another stitch in the sock she was darning and smiled down on the four-year-old. "If your mother's calculations are correct, your new brother or sister should arrive sometime before Easter."

"How will it get here?" Sara questioned, her wide eyes innocent.

Elnora's stitches halted. Her cheeks warmed. "Well, my goodness. What a question!" She thought a minute, then said, "Your mother will deliver him or her, of course."

"But how?"

Elnora's mind clicked furiously. How does one explain such things to a child? "Well . . . when the baby is ready, he or she will let us know."

Sara thoughtfully considered her aunt's words. "But how?" she asked once again.

Elnora laid her sewing in her lap and took a deep breath. "Darling, it's all very complicated. . . . " She left off a moment, then remembered the children's cat had delivered a litter of kittens prior to her own arrival. "Do you remember when Prissy had her kittens?"

"Yes," Sara said, wrinkling her brow thoughtfully.

"It will happen in much the same manner for your mother."

"Oh!" Sara's expression brightened, as though the entire matter was now quite clear. "I hope it's a sister."

"And why is that, dear?" Elnora was relieved to return to a less delicate topic of conversation. She retrieved the sock once again, and her stitching took up a steady rhythm.

"Well," the child said, "we have lots of brothers." She held up her hand, splaying out a pudgy thumb and four equally pudgy fingers. She counted the brothers off, one by one. "We have Sam and Andy and George and Mark Anthony . . . "

George! Elnora's head snapped up, and her eyes rounded. Her stitches halted. She hadn't seen George since breakfast, and it was almost noon. She tried to keep the panic out of her voice as she asked, "Have either of you seen George this morning?"

Sara shook her head silently, while Emily stared dumbly up at Elnora, thumb corked to mouth.

Elnora reached down and plucked out Emily's thumb, causing an audible *pop*. "Emmy, have you seen George?"

Never one for many words, Emily nodded her head up and down silently.

"You have?"

The little girl blinked and nodded again.

"Well," Elnora said in a voice that rose an octave, "tell Aunt Nora, darling."

"He left. Right after Sam and Andy left for school."

Fear shot a wicked path through Elnora's veins, and she vaulted from her chair, dropping her sewing to the floor. She stooped down beside the little girl and took her by the shoulders. "Are you quite sure, Emmy?"

Emily nodded again.

"Oh, sweet Jesus," Elnora whispered, never having uttered a blasphemous word in her entire life. She imagined the worst. George, more than any of the other children, worried her the most. Despite his easy charm, he tried her patience time and again. He was fearless and adventurous, bullheaded and willful. Elnora was sure he would grow up to be exactly like his uncle Ransom if he lived long enough.

She flew around the house, gathering her coat, mittens, and Mark Anthony, then shooed the two girls on up to Vivian's room, all the while berating herself for being so irresponsible.

"Viv, I've lost George!" she exclaimed, bursting into Vivian's bedroom and unceremoniously dumping Mark Anthony on the bed beside his mother. "I'm so terribly sorry. I don't know what's gotten into me lately. I've been so addle-brained. How could I lose a child of all things! How could I not have noticed that he was gone?" The words left her in a panicked rush.

Not nearly as frantic as her sister-in-law, Vivian sat up in bed and adjusted her pillows behind her back. "Oh, Nora," she said calmly, "don't work yourself into a fit of vapors. Knowing George, he's fine. I lose him at least twice a month. He has a habit of taking off on his own every now and then."

But Elnora wasn't comforted. She'd never lost anything before—never in all her orderly life, least of all a human being. Her solid constitution completely deserted her in the face of her fear. "He's only six years old!" she cried as gruesome visions of him lying frozen in a snowdrift jelled in her mind.

"He's a very self-sufficient six-year-old," Vivian said.

But the words meant nothing to Elnora. She spun on her heel and left the room, racing down the stairs, her skirts almost tripping her. "I'll be back as soon as I can," she hollered.

Dragging her coat on, she ran for the barn in search of Gordon and Ransom. "Gordon! Ransom!" When she couldn't find them, she hitched a horse to the buggy and lit out on her own, fearing to waste any more time.

By the time she reached town, she was in a mindless tizzy.

She stopped at the schoolhouse first, wondering if Faith had seen him and allowed him to stay through the morning classes rather than send him home alone. But Faith said she hadn't seen him, and Sam and Andy said they hadn't noticed him following them into town.

Wild with worry, Elnora hopped back into her buggy and set her horse on a reckless path down Main Street, almost running down anyone who dared venture into her way.

She jerked the buggy to a stop before the boardinghouse, jumped down, and took the stairs two at a time, in a most unladylike manner. She knocked twice, then waited impatiently for one of the twins to come to the door.

It was Maisie who finally did. "Elnora!" she said, surprised to see her. "What brings you into town?"

"George slipped out on me this morning, and I can't find him. Have you seen him?"

"Well, no . . ." Maisie turned to Minnie, who'd joined her at the door. "Have you seen George this morning, Sister?"

"Can't say that I have."

"Well," Elnora said, swallowing back her tears, "thank you just the same." She whirled and raced back down the stairs. She swung back up into the buggy, hitching her skirts high, not caring that she revealed a significant length of shapely leg.

She was about to set off again when Russell Whitaker stopped her by stepping in front of the buggy. He took her horse's bridle in hand, holding the horse steady.

"Elnora . . . what is it?" he asked, genuinely concerned. He was surprised at her appearance. Her eyes were crazed, her hair a riotous disarray of chestnut waves that had escaped its usual neat nest and hung in a tumble clear down to her waist. For a moment he hadn't been sure it was her when he'd seen her come careening down the street, bouncing and bumping to a stop in front of the boardinghouse.

She dropped back into the seat of the buggy, her brow tight, her eyes suddenly bright with unshed tears.

"It's George. I've lost him."

"I beg your pardon?" Russell looked confused.

"Well, I didn't exactly lose him." She wrung her hands, her distress so evident that Russell felt a swift rush of sympathy for her. "He left the house this morning without my knowing it." Her throat got tight, and her eyes found his. "I don't know where he went and I'm so afraid something might have happened to him."

Without asking for permission, Russell swung up into the buggy beside her. "Well, then, we'll just have to find him. George can be quite a rascal. If I remember correctly, he did much the same thing a month or so ago." He paused, then said, "I think I know where he is."

Immensely relieved, Elnora never stopped to think of propriety, or about the kiss they'd shared less than a week ago, or about the fact that the kiss was a stingy one, indeed. She allowed him to take the reins from her hands and was simply glad he was there and willing to help her.

Russell gave the reins a quick flick and turned the buggy around. "Come, Arthur," he said quietly, and the dog followed behind.

"He should have told me," Elnora said. "He shouldn't have left without getting my permission."

"Yes, well, sometimes men have a way of up and taking off that way," Russell said in an attempt to comfort her.

They headed back down Main for a short while, then quite abruptly he jerked the buggy to a stop directly in front of a bright purple building whose sign read: THE FIRST RESORT. She immediately recognized it as the building Clyde Finnegan had run from on the morning of her arrival.

Confused, Elnora turned to Russell, her gaze questioning.

He slid her a glance that told her nothing and ran a hand through his sun-lit hair. "You want to find George, don't you?"

Appalled, her eyes widened. "You can't be serious!" she cried, caring little that her usual soft voice carried clear over to Zeke's barbershop and caused him to nick a customer's chin.

"Yes, well," Russell said and shot her an apologetic grin, "I'm afraid I am."

A few moments passed, while some semblance of sanity returned. "Well," she finally said, her back rigid, "you just wait until I get my hands on that young man!" She jutted her chin forward and, without waiting for Russell to offer his help, hopped down to the ground into the center of a slushy puddle of mud and melting snow.

She gave her splattered, rumpled skirts a sharp shake. "George Perry!" she hollered. "You come out here right this minute!" Then she stomped off toward the door, chest heaving, arms pumping.

Behind her, Russell watched, his eyebrows lifting in surprise. He remembered her pale face and her wide-eyed shock the day Lottie had chased Clyde into the street, and the last thing he'd expected her to do now was take off for Lottie's establishment like a crazed woman chasing down an errant husband.

But the soft-spoken, ladylike Elnora Perry was on a mission far more important than that of chasing down a faithless husband. She was about to snatch a child from the ruinous claws of corruption.

Holding back his grin, Russell decided he wouldn't want to be George Perry for anything in the world right now.

He hopped to the ground and sauntered off behind her, while from his place on the side of the road, Arthur plopped down on his rump to wait.

When she reached the door, she took one long agonizing breath, then attacked the door with both hands, making such a racket that Russell feared she'd bring Lottie to the door with a gun in hand.

Hearing the commotion next door, Jake Sutherland, wearing his leather apron, hammer in hand, came out the livery doors and stared at the two. "Everything all right, Russ?" he called out, his expression perplexed.

Russ raised a hand to stay the man's concerns. "Just fine, Jake. I'm helping the lady run an errand of sorts, that's all."

Elnora ceased her pounding and glared over her shoulder at him. "An errand!" she yelled. "Are you out of your mind, Mr. Whitaker? There's a young, innocent boy inside this, this, house of . . . of . . . " She jabbed a finger at the door, her mind searching for a term that fully explained her opinion of Lottie's establishment.

Deciding no such term existed, she spun back to the door and was about to begin her attack once more when the door swung open, and she found herself face to face with Luscious Lottie McGee, the town madam.

Elnora planted her feet squarely and stood eye to eye with "that woman" for the space of ten full seconds. Lottie was dressed almost respectably today in a wine-colored dress, with a nipped-in waistline and low bodice. While she stared at her, Elnora realized that Lottie was older than she had originally thought her to be. The paint she wore on her once pretty face was unable to hide the heavy toll the years and her profession had taken.

When at last she spoke, Elnora's voice was steady and firm. "I've come for George."

Lottie's shrewd gaze swept Elnora from top to bottom. She took in the younger woman's worried eyes, her untidy hair, her disheveled clothing, her muddied shoes.

With genteel grace, Lottie held the door open and stepped aside. "Please, Miss Perry," she said respectfully. "Do come in."

Elnora hesitated only a moment, her desire to find George overriding any sense of propriety. She crossed over the threshold, half expecting thunder to boom and lightning to flash.

Behind her Russell followed, immensely enjoying himself.

Lottie led the way through the parlor, past a series of nude portraits displaying woman in various poses, on down the hall, to the kitchen in the rear of the house. When they reached the kitchen door, Lottie went sideways and said to Elnora, "He's having his cookies."

Elnora's gaze locked with Lottie's. "His cookies?" she questioned stupidly, her brow furrowed.

Lottie smiled. "Yes. Whatever did you think he came here for?"

A slow flush stole over Elnora's face, and she peeked her head inside the kitchen to see George sitting at the table with several woman, who were all covered considerably better than Lottie had been the first time Elnora had seen her.

Lottie went on to explain, "He stops by every now and then to see us. He's quite a charmer and a favorite with the girls."

As Elnora's eyes came back to Lottie's, an ugly sense of shame rose within. Cookies. He came for cookies. Her eyes sank shut in abject humiliation. She suddenly realized that women, all women, despite their walks of life, could share some common ground. Especially something as pure and precious as a love for children.

"I'm sorry," Elnora said, her sincerity evident in her soft tone. "I'm not exactly sure what I thought, but I'm ashamed of it nevertheless."

Lottie's eyes softened. "There's no need to apologize. Come, let's get George for you."

They stepped into the kitchen, and George's eyes found Elnora immediately. "Uh-oh," he whispered, ducking his head. He face paled, and he glanced around frantically, as though searching for a route of escape. But all escape routes were barred, so he gave a great sigh and turned his gaze back up to hers, knowing his days were numbered.

She marched across the floor to where he sat, cow-eyed, staring up at her. Planting her feet wide, she glowered down at him, hands on hips, mouth puckered with fury. Then, quite suddenly, she dropped down on her knees and dragged him off his chair and into her arms. She clutched him to her breast and whispered hoarsely, "George Perry, I ought to put a switch to your backside, but I'm so damned happy to see you, I simply haven't the heart for it."

From the door, Russell watched her and felt an odd stirring within his chest. Whatever it was Elnora Perry kept so securely locked within her was fast coming to the surface, whether she wanted it to or not.

Lottie stepped forward, her expression suddenly vulnerable and uncertain. She clasped her hands before her and quietly asked, "Would you care for tea, Miss Perry?"

Elnora gazed up into the other woman's heavily painted face and suddenly found herself remembering the words that Russell had spoken to her the night of the party. *"Things are not always as they seem, Miss Perry. People often see only what they want to see."* Elnora smiled. "Why, yes, that would be lovely."

That evening gossip hit the homes of Harmony like the worst blizzard in history.

"Elnora Perry, having tea with Lottie McGee! Whatever is the world coming to!" Lillie Taylor exclaimed to her husband in horror.

"Our Elnora?" squawked the elderly twins when they heard the news. "Well, for land's sake!" Their hands pressed to their chests, they raced for the smelling salts.

Zeke Gallagher chuckled, and the Reverend Abe Johnson smiled.

Vivian popped up in bed, her eyes aglow with curiosity. "What does it look like in there?" she wanted to know immediately.

"The hell she did!" Ransom bellowed to Gordon, not believing it for a minute. Befuddled, he looked across the table at Elnora. "Did you?"

"Why, yes," she answered calmly. "I did."

"Are you losing your mind, Nora?" Gordon asked, angry with her for the first time in his life.

Elnora's chin rose defensively. "I had tea, Gordon, that's all. And Russell Whitaker was with me."

"In a whorehouse!" Gordon's face took on an unhealthy shade of purple. "You had tea in a whorehouse!"

Elnora stood and, her movements unhurried, began clearing the table of the supper dishes. "Oh, Gordon, steady yourself before you pop a vessel." She pinned him with a determined gaze and very clearly stated, "I've spent most of my adult life taking care of people . . . mainly the men in my family. If I decide I want to have tea with Lottie McGee, then what should it matter to you or to anyone else? The only difference between her and me is that she takes care of men in her way, and I do in mine."

Astounded, Gordon's mouth fell open. When finally he could speak, he said, "Elnora, it—it's not the same thing. There's no comparison. Those women do things you haven't . . . you haven't even—"

"That's right, Gordon, they do. And don't think anyone is more aware of that fact than I am."

His expression furious, Ransom banged his fist on the table and interrupted with, "What got into that fool Whitaker, taking you into a place like that?"

Annoyed, Elnora shot him an irritated glance. "Lower your voice, Ransom. You'll wake the children." When his expression turned sheepish, her eyes softened somewhat. "He was helping me, that's all."

Gordon growled, his temper still escalating, "That young George has some explaining to do!"

But Elnora was having none of that. "George and I have already talked the matter through, and I scolded him quite soundly for taking off without telling me where he was going. I gave him my word no more would be said about the matter. Besides," she added, her tone firm, "he was only having cookies."

"But . . . but . . . you, in that place—" Gordon sputtered, trying to imagine his sister sitting at a table socializing with a troop of loose women. The image was totally absurd.

"I was only having tea, for heaven's sake," she reminded him calmly, then leaned down and pressed a kiss to his cheek. "Good night, Brother. Good night, Ransom." Then she slipped off to bed, leaving them both to gape after her in bald astonishment.

Sleep came reluctantly to Russell that night.

He found himself thinking of Elnora long into the morning hours. He linked his hands behind his head, rested his head in his palms, and stared up at the dark, shadow-splotched ceiling. When he'd left her that day, she'd looked up at him with those big honey-brown eyes of hers—as though he were her champion in helping her find George.

As he thought about that, he thought about kissing her again—really kissing her this time.

His thoughts raced on, beyond the innocent act of kissing, and his desire rekindled.

He groaned, flopped onto his side, and reached down to pat Arthur's head.

"You're a champion all right, Whitaker," he said to himself, "a real knight in shining armor."

Arthur's head popped up. Whining his sympathy, he nudged his master with his wet, spongy nose.

With a sound that was half sigh, half curse, Russell turned onto his stomach, pressing his aching flesh into the warmth of his bed while he smothered his face into his pillow.

Whitaker, you fool! If she knew about you, she sure as hell wouldn't see you as a knight in shining armor. . . .

But those words did little to quell the raging fire in his body or the restless yearning in his heart.

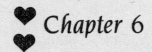 *Chapter 6*

THE WEEKS PASSED, and January slid into February. Winter hovered, and time seemed to stand still. The snow melted, then returned with force once again, bringing with it an especially frigid blast of arctic air, chasing most Harmony citizens indoors for days on end.

The Perry children grew restless. Vivian grew larger. And Ransom stayed on.

For the most part, Elnora was contentedly busy.

Ransom was underfoot constantly, teasing and flirting shamelessly, making her laugh as she'd never done before. Whenever they were alone together, he'd beg for another kiss, but she'd simply dismiss his nonsense and go about her chores.

Yet, oddly enough, she began to wonder what it would be like if she were to give in to his kisses and he were to stay in Harmony.

Although his presence no longer sent her heart tumbling into a mindless flutter, a quiet, much more tolerable affection for him had blossomed. She'd begun to wonder if maybe this calm affection wasn't better somehow than that first wild rush of excitement she'd experienced when they met.

She thought about her feelings for him often as the days passed, but at night, when the house was still and quiet, she allowed herself the pleasure of returning to the story. . . .

The subjects of King Nefan's court were planning a feast and decorating the great castle in preparation for the tournament. There were to be trumpeters and magicians, and everyone in the kingdom, even the serfs, would be allowed to participate in some way.

Meanwhile, Lady Elvia was making preparations of her own. She'd come to King Nefan on a quest. All of her life she'd heard about her family's heirloom, the blue diamond. It was the most beautiful stone in the land, coveted by many. Years ago, it had been taken from her ancestors' castle by enemies of King Nefan's court.

The women of the castle had believed the men to be friends and had foolishly allowed the intruders to enter that fateful day. Their men had perished defending them and their lands, and the Penwick clan had lost the blue diamond to the enemy.

Because of the women's bad judgment, the oldest maiden of the family had placed a curse upon all females who bore the name of Penwick. All the daughters of the lineage were destined to a lifetime of maidenhood—to live their lives through, without ever knowing the love of a man. . . .

But Lady Elvia was not content to accept the pronouncement. She sought out Balin, King Nefan's magician.

Balin told her the only way to break the curse was to find the blue diamond and restore it to Penwick Castle. In doing so, she would free herself and those women who came after her from the power of the curse.

So she'd set off for King Nefan's court, hoping he

would honor her request and allow her the services of his best knight.

And honor her request he did.

The knight who would win the joust was to be her champion and would accompany her on her quest. . . .

Often Elnora fell asleep with the *Sentinel* still in hand. Her dreams were clouded with mysteries and chivalrous knights.

Oddly enough, her dreams were often riddled with images of Russell Whitaker.

There seemed to be little purpose to his part in her dream, except that his face was always hidden from her, as was Sir Ruggard's.

But she knew it was him. She knew it by his silvery sun-struck hair and by his kiss. . . .

When dawn finally lit her room and she woke, his image remained imprinted in her mind. Throughout the day she felt flustered and hungry for something she had yet to taste, something she suspected was finally, for the first time in her life, within her reach.

In the meantime, Ransom grew more attentive.

Despite her confusion about her dreams and about Russell, she found herself looking forward to Ransom's company. His carefree smile lent a certain warmth to the chilly days, and his shameless bragging gave her endless amusement. He was like having all five of her brothers rolled up into one.

When the weather finally broke, Harmony's locals gathered together to plan another winter social. This one was to be a Valentine's Day dance to be held over at Hutton's Hotel.

As soon as he heard about the event, Ransom asked Elnora to accompany him. He wasn't taking any chances that Whitaker would beat him to it.

At first, though flattered, Elnora refused him, saying she was much too busy to attend. The truth was, she hadn't been to a dance in years, and she didn't have anything special enough to wear to such an event. Nor was she at all sure she remembered the steps to the waltzes she'd learned so many years ago.

But Vivian claimed she had a dress for Elnora to wear, and with a few minor adjustments it would do quite nicely. She insisted that Elnora go.

So she accepted Ransom's invitation and went to the dance wearing Vivian's best rose-silk dress. It was a lovely dress, but the lower-than-usual bodice was a source of consternation for Elnora.

Still, she laughed and danced and found she managed the steps to the dances quite easily.

Almost everyone in Harmony attended.

Everyone but Russell Whitaker.

Elnora watched for him throughout the entire evening. She told herself she only wanted to thank him again for his help in finding George. But deep within she knew it was more than that. He never did come, and she was left feeling oddly disappointed.

Later that night before they went inside, Ransom and Elnora stood on the porch and silently gazed up at a silver slice of moon.

After some time Ransom looked down at her and without warning drew her close. With his green eyes teasing, he asked her once again, "How 'bout it?"

Amused by his persistence, she smiled. "How about what?"

He wiggled his eyebrows wickedly, and she laughed out loud.

When finally she quieted she gazed up into his broad, dear face, and she felt a swift surge of affection for him. Very quietly she said, "I don't see why not. We are living together."

He chuckled and looked so pleased she almost felt guilty for having held him off so long.

He didn't give her a chance to change her mind. He swept her up against his big chest and kissed her soundly.

The kiss was a replica of the one they'd shared those many weeks ago in the sleigh. He worked her mouth over feverishly, his tongue delving deep, and when at last his head lifted, she came up gasping for air. "Oh, my . . ." she whispered, blinking.

Though the kiss was thorough and not at all unpleasant, it did little to ease the hunger that burned within her heart. Instead of feeling sated, she felt she'd missed something.

Later that night, alone in her room, she sat staring out the window, counting the many stars that glittered like diamonds against the velvet night sky. She decided she was far too much of a romantic. She would never have admitted it months ago, but time had shown her the truth. A woman her age should feel thankful to be kissed at all—let alone be sought out and kissed by someone as manly and attractive as Ransom Riley.

She should be engulfed by passion, she thought, scolding herself. She should be wilting with need . . .

Yet all she felt was sleepy. So, yawning, she climbed into her lonely bed and clutched the quilts to her breasts, and took a trip into the past . . . to the days of kings and magicians, to a time of knights and their ladies. . . .

The next Wednesday morning, Gordon went out to do the morning chores, and Ransom stayed behind.

He found Elnora alone in the kitchen, folding laundry, stacking the items on the table in neat piles to take upstairs.

"Nora," he said, crossing the floor to stand before her.

His voice was so quietly serious, her head came up immediately. She turned to him, her brow wrinkling with concern. "What is it, Ransom?"

The expression on his face was sober, lacking its usual carefree smile. "I feel I should tell you . . . I'll be leaving Harmony soon."

Sadness gripped her, and she realized she'd grown quite attached to him in the past six weeks. "When?"

"Friday morning."

Still holding Mark Anthony's diaper in her hands, she lowered her arms to her stomach. "Why?" she couldn't help but ask. She'd always been artless and direct, and she saw no reason to be anything else at this late stage of her life.

"A job. There's a man with a price on his head. I'm gonna find him and bring him in." He read the disappointment in her face and added, "It's what I do, Nora. I have to go."

She nodded, understanding. "Is this the one you've been searching for all these years?" she asked, remembering the conversation they'd had so many weeks ago.

He gave a short, dry laugh. "No. I wish it were. Maybe then I could settle down to a normal life." The words left his mouth before he realized he'd even thought them. In the past, settling down had always been an unpleasant thought. He'd always viewed marriage as the ultimate end of his freedom—as a prison as binding as the ones to which he returned his captives. Now, finally, at thirty-five years of age, as he stared down into Elnora's pretty face, the thought of settling down was not so frightening.

He reached for her, taking her shoulders gently in his big hands. "I'll miss you, Nora." His voice was soft, his gaze steady.

"I'll miss you, too, Ransom," Elnora returned honestly. "Will you come back?"

"You can count on it."

"When?"

"As soon as I catch him. I promise. I'll try to get back by spring."

"Do you think you will?"

"I'll do my best."

He lowered his head and kissed her—this time with far more tenderness than ever before. Her heart softened, and she tried to define what she truly felt for this big, handsome man.

When he lifted his head, he gazed down at her and wished he didn't have to leave her. He thought about Whitaker and the way he'd looked at her the night of the sleighing party. He'd kissed her, too, damn him! The thought still sent him into a sulk.

Although Whitaker had kept his distance, Ransom realized the man was competition, even if Elnora didn't.

Ransom found himself wishing Vivian's baby had already come and that he could take Elnora with him. "Wait for me, Nora," he said on a whim.

His face was so solemn, so earnest, it touched her deeply. Bemused, she dropped her gaze.

For the very first time ever, she acknowledged that she had indeed become like her great-aunt Elnora, passively allowing the years to slip away—burying her loneliness deep in her quest to care for others. She'd avoided taking responsibility for her own life, her own happiness, her own needs and desires, by putting everyone else's needs and desires ahead of her own.

She lifted her eyes to stare into the face of the man before her, and she realized that he might be her last chance to claim happiness, that another opportunity might never come her way. She wanted so desperately to know love. . . .

With those thoughts in mind, she smiled and very quietly said, "All right, Ransom. I'll wait for you."

March arrived gently, bringing warmer temperatures and sunny skies. The snow began to melt, and Elnora bundled the children into their coats and allowed them outdoors to play.

One day, noticing that she was unusually quiet, Gordon said to her, "Why don't you take the buggy into town today and get the supplies we need over at the mercantile? I'll stay here with Vivian and the children. A little visit with Lillie and Mary will do you good."

"Oh, Gordon," she whispered appreciatively, her eyes lighting, "I'd love to. Are you sure you wouldn't mind?"

"Of course not."

Elnora was only too happy to accept his offer. She'd thought of Ransom constantly since he'd left, but despite her promise, she was still so unsure of what it was she felt for him. She cared for him, that much she knew. But did she love him? Her emotions were so unsettled, so hard to define, that she felt burdened by the confusion. Her nightly dreams about Russell didn't help matters.

The trip into town would be a welcome emotional reprieve.

But when she reached town she found her gaze drawn to Russell's bookstore, which sat directly beside the mercantile. Remembering her dreams, she blushed hotly and averted her gaze. She shook off the memory and hurried into the mercantile, hoping no one would notice the color in her cheeks.

She was fortunate. Mary and her mother were busy helping a woman choose a length of material from several bolts they had spread out on the counter. Elnora recognized the woman, having seen her at church, but she had yet to meet her.

"Elnora!" Mary said, looking up. "How are you?"

"I'm well, thank you." Elnora smiled at the three.

Lillie introduced Elnora to Rachel Johnson.

"I've heard a lot about you," Rachel said. "It's nice to finally meet you."

"Likewise," Elnora returned, amused, remembering what Gordon had told her about Lillie and Rachel knowing everything about everyone in Harmony.

James Taylor, Lillie's husband and Mary's father, came through a door at the back of the store, carrying a huge sack of flour over his shoulder. "Hello, ladies," he said, then deposited the heavy sack on top of several others near the wall. He smiled at the group, then disappeared into the back of the store once again.

"How is dear Vivian?" Rachel asked Elnora.

"She's anxiously awaiting her time, but she's doing fine," Elnora said.

Rachel paid Mary for the material. "Well, give her my best, won't you? And let me know if you need anything."

"Thank you. I will."

On her way out the door, Rachel turned to Mary. "When's Matthew coming home?"

"Next week," Mary answered a bit wistfully. "And

that's not nearly soon enough. I miss him terribly." Her eyes twinkled with a wicked merriment. "I hope he's well rested when he gets here."

"Indeed . . ." Rachel huffed and raised her brows, shocked by the young woman's eagerness for her husband's attentions.

When Rachel left, Mary came out from behind the counter, openly chuckling over Rachel's expression. "What can I help you with today, Elnora?"

Elnora read off the items on her list, and Mary and her mother bustled around the store, gathering the supplies and sharing small talk and news about the townsfolk.

When they'd finished with the task, Elnora said to Mary, "Before I go, you promised to tell me the entire story behind your marriage to Matthew."

"Yes, I did, didn't I?" Mary said and laughed, while Lillie rolled her eyes to the ceiling and took herself off to the back of the store to see what her husband was up to.

"Well, come and sit down, and I'll tell you all about it." Mary led the way to a couple of chairs that sat near a window.

Once they were seated, she began.

She told Elnora about how she had placed advertisements in various newspapers for a mail-order husband. She told about how Matthew had answered the advertisement, surprising her by being far more handsome and far more wonderful than she had ever dared hope he'd be. She admitted that it hadn't taken her long to realize that he was the one for her. She talked about their sometimes turbulent courtship— about how she'd had to court him to win him back after she'd made him angry when she'd provided him with a list containing her requirements for a husband.

"You did that?" Elnora asked, shocked and amused at once.

"Yes, I did," Mary said. She laughed often while telling the story, but her eyes held a constant tender warmth that spoke of her happiness and her love for her husband.

Elnora couldn't help but wonder if her own eyes would hold the same tenderness, the same warmth, the same happiness if she were married to Ransom.

They visited for well over an hour, with Lillie and James scuttling around them from time to time.

It wasn't until the afternoon began to fade that Elnora reluctantly rose to leave. She realized she'd found a friend in Mary. "I can't tell you how much I enjoyed this. I love the children and Vivian, too, but it's good to get out and visit with others once in a while."

"I understand," Mary said. "I'd love it if you'd come by more often." She paused a moment, tipped her head to the side, and with a thoughtful look on her pretty face asked, "That handsome man who escorted you to the sleighing party and Valentine's Day dance . . . he's Vivian's brother, isn't he?"

"Yes," Elnora said.

Mary's eyes took on an inquisitive, mischievous glint. "How nice to be courted by two gentlemen."

"Two?" Elnora looked genuinely confused.

Mary smiled indulgently. "Come now, Elnora. Everyone saw Russell Whitaker choose you for his lady the night of the social."

"Oh, that." Elnora blushed, embarrassed. "That was only a game," she huffed.

Mary raised one dark eyebrow. "Was it?"

Elnora's gaze held Mary's. "Why . . . yes . . . of

course," she finally managed, her heart fluttering with a new wave of confusion.

"Well, we'll see," Mary said lightly and helped Elnora gather her supplies.

"Stop by again, Elnora," Lillie called out from a back room, letting the two women know that she'd heard every word they'd spoken.

Elnora and Mary exchanged amused glances, then laughed out loud.

"Goodbye, Lillie!" Elnora called out. Her arms full, she told Mary she'd see her soon and went out to her buggy, her mind busily working over every single one of Mary's words about being courted by two gentlemen.

After she deposited the supplies on the seat, she climbed up into the buggy, then stole a covert glance at Whitaker's Bookstore.

Ransom was one thing, but Russell Whitaker courting her . . .

What an absurd notion!

Ransom had been gone two weeks when Maisie and Minnie dropped in for another visit.

"Hello, Vivian!" the twins called up on their way past the staircase.

"Hello, ladies," Vivian called down from her bed.

The twins took their customary places at the Perrys' kitchen table while Elnora prepared the tea.

When Elnora sat down to join them for a cup, Maisie turned to her and snapped, "The tournament was an even match! Did you ever hear of such a ridiculous thing?" Thoroughly disgusted, she took a sip of her tea, then lowered her cup to the table. "All that fuss, and neither knight won! Why, I'll tell you, if I knew who the author of this whole thing was, I'd give him a good piece of my mind!"

"It makes the story more fun this way," Minnie said with a gleam in her eye. "Now Lady Elvia must choose which knight will accompany her on her quest."

"She'll choose the Black Knight!" Maisie leaned forward, going nose to nose with her sister.

Minnie refused to back down. "She'll choose Sir Ruggard!"

Normally Elnora would have been amused by their antics, but not today. With a heavy sigh she gazed out the window at the blue sky and barren fields.

With Ransom gone, the house seemed unbearably silent, even with six children clamoring about. She missed him far more than she ever imagined she would. Could it be she truly loved him? she wondered. Was this what love really felt like—this uncertainty, this confusion, this loneliness? She had thought it would feel much different. She remembered what Mary had said—that it hadn't taken her long to know that Matthew was the one for her. Did it happen that way for everyone? Surely it didn't. Everyone was different.

That thought did not comfort her, however. She felt more confused than ever.

"Who do you think she'll choose?" Maisie asked, turning to Elnora.

"Yes, Elnora," Minnie said, "who do you think?"

The two women pressed forward expectantly, waiting for Elnora's answer, but when she remained unresponsive and silent, continuing to stare out the window, they realized she had not heard them.

"Elnora!" Maisie exclaimed, insulted by her lack of attention.

Her thoughts interrupted, Elnora came back from

her reverie and smiled apologetically. "I'm sorry, ladies. I haven't been myself the past few days."

"Is something wrong?" Minnie asked, genuinely concerned.

Elnora shook her head and filled their teacups again. "No, not really."

A suspicious glint appeared in Maisie's narrowing eyes. "Where is your body hunter these days?"

"Bounty hunter!" Minnie amended. "He's a bounty hunter, for heaven's sake!"

Maisie waved her off airily. "Humph! Body hunter, bounty hunter . . . " She pinned Elnora with her sharp gaze. "So, where is he?"

"He's gone. . . . He left last week."

Both women snapped to attention.

"Indeed," Maisie drawled, her eyebrows rising.

"You don't say!" Minnie exclaimed, her eyes widening.

Maisie tried to affect an impassive expression. "Will he be returning to Harmony?"

"Yes," Elnora said a little wistfully. "He says he will."

"When might that be?" Minnie prodded.

"It's hard to say, but he hopes to return by spring."

The two women exchanged a very quick, very secretive glance.

"Well," Maisie said briskly, rising from her chair, "the tea was wonderful, but we really must go."

"Busy, busy, busy." Minnie bustled right behind her sister. "Thank you for the tea, Elnora."

They grabbed their coats and barely gave themselves time to shrug into them before marching out the door.

Once they were seated in the buggy, they turned to each other.

"This is perfect!" Maisie didn't bother to hide her glee. "With him out of the way, it will make our task so much easier. But it doesn't give us much time." She pursed her lips thoughtfully. "It's the first week of March already." Her mind clicked over the details of their plan.

"Elnora will never go for it," Minnie stated flatly. "Even if she did, Russell won't."

"They'll go for it," Maisie said confidently.

"And if they don't?"

"Then we'll bring out the big canon, Sister!"

Minnie looked puzzled. "What exactly is the big canon?"

Maisie turned a sugary smile on her sister. "Why, guilt, of course."

"Ah . . ." Minnie nodded, understanding now. She brightened instantly. "An ingenious strategy! Still, we have so little time. . . ."

"Then we'd best hurry!" Maisie flicked the horse's reins, and the buggy shot forward, nearly unseating the two old women. "Onward!" she hollered, punching her fist into the air. Off they raced for Harmony.

Two days later they were at Elnora's door again. This time they brought along Sissy Taylor.

"Elnora," Maisie said, "we've come to humbly beg your assistance about a very important matter."

"Come in, ladies," Elnora invited with her usual quiet grace. She held the door open wide. "Hello, Sissy," she said to the sixteen-year-old.

"We've brought Sissy along to stay with the children."

Elnora looked from one to the other. "But why?"

"Because we want you to come into town with us," Maisie said.

"But why?" Elnora asked again.

"We're on a mission, Elnora," Minnie explained.

Puzzled, Elnora shook her head. "I'm sorry, ladies, but I truly don't understand."

"We intend to find out the identity of the author of the story if it kills us, and we've elected two people to help us on our quest."

Baffled, Elnora's brows rose, but after several silent seconds her brows leveled, and her eyes narrowed with suspicion. She heaved a great sigh, crossed her arms over her chest, and shook her head. "I have my own responsibilities here. I have more to do than I can possibly keep up with. And," she added firmly, "Vivian's time is not far off. I'm sorry, but—"

"Now, Elnora," Maisie interrupted, affecting her most distressed tone, "before you say no, hear us out."

"Yes, Elnora," Minnie begged, "pleeeease listen."

Out of respect for the two older women, Elnora went silent, but her pointy little chin was fixed with determination.

Minnie nudged Maisie, and taking her cue, Maisie launched into her rehearsed speech. "Sister and I will take turns seeing to the children so that you'll have the time to do this for us. And Sissy"—Maisie turned to the younger girl—"loves the children and said she would not mind taking turns with us. Lillie said she would help out, too. If Vivian's time should come, well, someone would find you immediately, of course." Maisie elbowed her sister, and they leaned into each other, wearing the two most piteous expressions Elnora had ever seen. "We're not getting any younger, Elnora, and we want to know who's writing the story before the good Lord takes us home. And who knows, at our age it could happen just like that." She snapped her fingers for emphasis. "Please, Elnora, find him for us."

Incredulous, Elnora stared at them for several long moments, then despite herself she laughed heartily. She knew she was being manipulated by two of the craftiest schemers in Kansas, and yet they were so obvious about how they did it and so very dear to her that she simply didn't have the heart to be angry with them.

Realizing they were close to victory, Maisie warmed to her subject. "You know we truly do love you, Elnora. And Gordon and Vivian, well, there just isn't *anything* we wouldn't do for them and the children. If there was anyone else we could send on this search, we'd ask her. Besides, aren't you just the tiniest bit curious about who the author is yourself?"

Elnora looked from one to the other, trying her best to look disgusted. "Oh, you two . . . "

The twins folded their hands before them in a plaintive gesture and blinked their eyelids rapidly, managing to generate a suspicious dampness onto their sparse gray eyelashes.

"Oh, all right," Elnora said in defeat. "I'll do it."

"Oh, Elnora!" they chorused, and hugged her diminutive form between them, almost squashing her.

"You are a true saint, Elnora!" Maisie exclaimed.

"You won't regret this," Minnie assured her.

Maisie grabbed Elnora's coat and pointed Sissy toward the children, who watched the exchange, wide-eyed and curious.

"It's going to be so much fun," Maisie insisted. "Hurry, now. Put your coat on, and we'll take you to meet your partner."

* * *

As they rode into town, the "partner" part of the agreement worried Elnora. Try as she might, she couldn't persuade either twin to tell her the person's identity.

The fact alone was enough to make Elnora reconsider the wisdom of her decision to help them. By the time they'd reached town, she truly wished she hadn't been so hasty in giving in to their scheme.

When they stopped the buggy in front of Whitaker's Bookstore, it was all she could do not to jump down and run back home.

"Absolutely not!" she stated firmly, her voice stiff with conviction. She crossed her arms over her chest and refused to budge from her seat. She hadn't seen Russell Whitaker since the day they had hunted down George. Though she appreciated his help well enough, she'd decided that since she'd given her promise to Ransom, it was better for her to keep a distinct distance between herself and Russell. There was something about the man that made her heart go crazy, like a broken compass, spinning wildly in all directions. Thoughts of him brought confusion and sleepless nights. Now that her feelings for Ransom had grown, well, there simply was no point in spending time with Russell and tempting fate.

"Elnora, you aren't being fair," Maisie insisted, puckering her mouth like a sewed-up buttonhole.

"You should have told me it was him." Elnora skewered the twins with an angry look.

Minnie sighed heavily. "What difference does it make? Don't you see? Russell is the perfect choice! He knows everyone in town. He knows what everyone reads. He knows everyone's tastes in literature. If anyone would know how to find the author, Russell would. Elnora—"

Just then the door of the bookstore opened, and Russell stepped out onto the porch. His eyes found Elnora immediately, and he inclined his head in greeting.

She nodded briskly, blushing profusely, wishing she could melt into the buggy seat.

He was dressed much the same as he had been the first time Elnora had visited his store. He wore black trousers and a white shirt with the collar open and the sleeves rolled up over his forearms. Elnora noticed that his arms were nicely muscled and covered with a fine dusting of blond hair.

"Ladies," he said, leaning against the doorframe and pushing his hands down into his trouser pockets. A slow smile tugged at his mouth. "Won't you come in?"

Maisie looked at the stubborn set of Elnora's chin, and her eyes took on a mischievous glitter. "Well, actually we'd love to, Russell, but Elnora—"

Mortified, Elnora snapped her head around to glare at Maisie. She shot out of her seat and hopped down from the buggy, inwardly quoting some very vulgar words. Her back straight, she marched up the steps, brushing past Russell and on into the bookstore. Behind her came the two sisters, smiling their most satisfied smiles.

Once Russell had closed the door behind them, he crossed the room and took his place behind the polished counter.

As always, Arthur greeted the visitors, then he returned to a small oval rug before the stove to resume his midday nap.

Placing his palms on the counter before him, Russell leaned over toward the twins. "So what can I do for you?" Though his gaze was fixed on the two elderly ladies, he was quite aware of Elnora's presence in his store. The clean, fresh scent of her had tickled his nostrils as she'd passed him. And the memory of that scent had lingered, even after she'd wandered off into a corner to study the contents of one of his book-shelves. She looked lovely today—a little mussed, her hair not quite so perfect—as though she hadn't taken the time to primp before setting out. He decided he liked her this way. Hell, he admitted silently, he'd like her any way.

Wearing their most doleful expressions, the twins turned to him, and Minnie, using the same words her sister had used on Elnora, launched her attack. "Rus-sell, we've come to humbly beg your assistance about a very important matter."

From her place in the corner of the room, Elnora closed her eyes and groaned, drawing attention from Arthur. She had never been so humiliated in her life. Not only were they throwing her at Russell Whita-ker's feet, but he apparently had no knowledge of this whole ridiculous scheme.

"You see, Russell, if we could do this ourselves, we would. But we're gettin' on, and we just don't get around like we once did. . . . "

Russell listened to the practiced speech and had to fight to hold back his smile. Gettin' on! Ha! He'd be willing to bet the old girls could wrestle a bull to the ground if they had a mind to.

"We put our heads together, though, and we all decided that you and Elnora would be the two best choices to attempt this search—"

Finally Elnora could stand no more. "Ladies, please." She turned and walked to the burnished counter, her head held high, her cheeks a bit brighter than usual. Her eyes found Russell's, and very quietly she said, "Mr. Whitaker cannot possibly take time away from his store to bother with such nonsense."

"But, Elnora . . ." The twins began to sputter their dismay, while Russell studied Elnora for a long moment. In her eyes he saw vulnerability and a quiet intelligence and strength and something else . . . something he was not quite sure about.

Whitaker, he thought, *somebody ought to shoot you and be done with it.* He knew he was about to do something very foolish. Something very foolish, indeed.

He stepped out from behind the counter and slowly walked over to where Elnora stood. "Fair lady," he said, his voice low, "it would be my pleasure to accompany you on this quest."

♥ Chapter 7

BY TACIT AGREEMENT, Russell came for Elnora the following Tuesday afternoon. He waited for her just inside the door while she went to get her coat.

She'd only managed to get one arm into a sleeve when Maisie and Minnie all but shoved her out onto the porch. Amused, Russell helped her get the rest of her coat on, and as they crossed the yard to his buggy, they were both quite sure that the sisters watched bug-eyed from behind Vivian Perry's frilly white kitchen curtains.

He helped her up into the buggy, then walked around to the other side and swung up onto the seat beside her.

Almost immediately, she tossed him a cool glance and said, "You didn't have to agree to do this, you know." The words were spoken softly, but there was a spunky edge to her tone that commanded his full attention.

His gaze met hers, and a smile tugged at one corner of his mouth. "I know."

She turned her head away sharply and stared straight ahead. "There's no need to feel sorry for me, Mr. Whitaker."

"What?" he barked, incredulous.

She colored and sat up a little taller in her seat. "You heard me correctly."

Amazed at her assumption of his motives, he gave a soft chuckle. "That's hardly the reason I agreed to this," he told her truthfully.

"Then why did you?" Her pert little nose lifted into the air the tiniest notch.

He considered her question a moment, then said, "Because I wanted to."

Slowly she turned to look at him. Her eyes met his, then narrowed with speculation. "But why?"

Russell's smile grew wide and warm, and the skin around his eyes crinkled. "Quite honestly, Miss Perry, it's because you fascinate me."

Flabbergasted, Elnora's mouth dropped open a fraction. She wasn't sure how she felt about that. It was hard for her to imagine anyone being fascinated by someone as predictable as herself—least of all someone as dashing as Russell Whitaker.

There was a long silent pause.

"So what do you say we humor the old girls?" he asked at last.

Elnora snapped her mouth shut and pretended to consider his question even though she'd already made up her mind. She'd told herself she owed Maisie and Minnie for looking after Gordon and Vivian. She told herself she was fond of them and wanted to please them. She told herself many things. But the truth was she wanted to see Russell Whitaker again. She wanted to know what it was about him that drew her, puzzled her, intrigued her. Despite the danger it presented, she wanted to know why, even after she'd promised Ransom she'd wait for him, it was Russell who continued to haunt her dreams.

"Well?" he asked, wondering if she would turn him

down, thinking it would be best if she did—hoping she wouldn't.

She gave a heavy sigh of resignation. "I think we should find our author."

Russell smiled and took the reins in hand. Despite a sharp prickle of guilt, he felt happier than he had in years. "Where do you think our quest should begin?"

"To tell you the truth, Mr. Whitaker," Elnora said, "I've been giving the matter some thought and I've come up with a few ideas. . . ."

"Wait," he said, holding up a hand. "I know one thing for sure. Since we're going to be spending some time together, I'd appreciate it if you'd call me Russ or Russell, whichever you'd prefer, and I would like to call you Elnora."

She gave him an assessing look, then decided his request was within reason. "If you wish."

"I do. After all, we know each other well enough to dispense with formalities."

Elnora thought about that a few seconds. She supposed a kiss, even a stingy one, did make them more than just passing acquaintances. Remembering his paltry little peck, she allowed him an equally sparse smile. "You're right, of course. Russell, it is." That settled, she decided to get down to business. "As I said, I've been giving the matter some thought and I think we should visit Frederick and Edward out at the Double B. Whoever is writing the story is an educated, well-read man. Obviously he's quite familiar with the Arthurian legends. Given that fact, the first persons who come to my mind are the Winchesters." She cocked her head to the side. "They are from England, aren't they?"

Russell nodded, impressed with her deductions.

"As a matter of fact, they are." He flicked the reins and set the buggy in motion. "You know, Elnora," he said and gave her that slow smile that sent her heart into a tumble, "you'd be one hell of an investigative reporter."

She huffed her disbelief, while inwardly she felt warmed by his approval.

They rode along in silence for a long stretch of time, each wondering what the quest would bring them. She sat, her heart thudding, while his presence brought back the memory of her dreams with force. He sat, seemingly relaxed, but hardly so, ever aware of his budding attraction to the woman who rode so silently at his side.

The weather was unusually mild for March. The roads, though quite wet and sloppy, were passable. The sun was warm and bright—so bright it hurt their eyes, so warm Elnora felt uncomfortably hot beneath the heavy weight of her winter coat.

He stole a look over at her, studying her profile much longer than was prudent, noting her short dark lashes, her perky little nose, the stubborn chin that jutted forward slightly, the high prim collar of her sparkling white blouse, and her breasts, small and firm, pressing ever so slightly against the material of her coat.

She turned to catch him staring, and he glanced away, fighting back an avalanche of heated curiosity about what lay beneath that coat, that blouse . . .

Elnora peeked sideways at him, noting how the sun glinted off his blond hair, casting it gold and silver, and she was struck anew by a nagging sense of familiarity, as though she had lived this very moment before, as though . . .

Unsettled, she snapped her gaze back to the road.

A robin hopped across their path, and she was reminded that spring was not far off and that Ransom would soon return. That thought brought a turbulent rush of emotions—happiness, confusion, uncertainty, relief.

She gazed off into the distance at the fields, which were splotched with patches of brown and muted green where the snow had begun to melt. They passed a busy stream that gurgled with life anew, now that the spring thaw had begun. The trees that lined the road were still bare of leaves, but their awakening buds gave them a furry, almost fuzzy appearance.

Thadeus Green, driving his wagon, met them on the road just before they reached the Double B. Without stopping, he called out a "Hey, folks!" which Russell heartily returned.

When they reached the ranch, Russell stopped the buggy before the front doors of the house and hopped down to the ground. He came around to Elnora and reached up and took her by the waist, effortlessly lifting her to the ground before him.

He kept his hands at her waist for only the briefest, most appropriate of moments, but in those few moments Elnora felt the strength of his hands through her coat, while Russell felt the enticing firmness of her tiny waist.

"Russ! Elnora!" Frederick Winchester called, coming out his front door. "What brings you two out this way?"

"We've come on a mission," Russell called back.

"Then, come in. Come in!" Frederick exclaimed, eager for the company. He led them into his house, took their coats, then showed them into the parlor. "Sit down," he urged, and when they did, he asked, "Can

I get you something? Some tea perhaps?"

"Thank you," Elnora said graciously, "but not for me."

Russell declined the offer also and waited for Fred to take a seat himself.

"What can I do for you, then?" Fred asked, his curiosity sparked.

Russell and Elnora exchanged glances. Turning back to Fred, Elnora said, "Maisie and Minnie have elected us to search out the author of the *Sentinel*'s serial."

"You mean the author who writes the stories about Sir Ruggard and Lady Elvia?"

"Yes." Elnora nodded and fixed her gaze on him. "We haven't any real clues as to who the author is. But I know whoever he is, he's well acquainted with the legend of King Arthur and his noble knights. It seems to me that a person so knowledgeable about old England just might have come from that country." She raised an eyebrow and paused a long meaningful moment, then pointedly asked, "Are you the author, Mr. Winchester?"

"Me!" Frederick's eyes widened in surprise. He sputtered for a moment, then gave a hearty chuckle, his face turning as red as a ripe strawberry. When he quieted, he leveled his gaze on her and said, "My dear lady, let me assure you I am not the man you seek, although I truly wish I were. I'm afraid, though I am an avid reader, my interests do not lie in the creation of stories. I simply haven't the knack for it."

From his place beside Elnora, Russell listened to the two in silent amusement. His gaze left Frederick and found Elnora once again. She was so determined, yet so poised, and he felt his admiration for her grow.

Elnora studied Frederick for a few moments, considering his words. "Could it be Edward, do you think?"

"Hardly," Frederick blustered, without even giving the idea much thought. "He's too busy keeping up with Suzanna and with the chores around the ranch. I'm afraid he wouldn't have the time to write stories, even if he had a mind to." Reading the disappointment on her face, he kindly interjected, "I'm truly sorry, Miss Perry, but I'm afraid you won't find your author here."

Elnora gave a small sigh of defeat. She glanced over at Russell, then back at Frederick. "Do you have any idea at all who the writer could be?"

Frowning, Frederick thought a minute. "Well, Zeke Gallagher always has his nose in one of those dime novels. Everyone knows he's quite a reader, but as to his writing abilities . . . I honestly could not comment on the matter." He left off a brief moment, then hurried to say, "It certainly wouldn't hurt to talk to him, though. Being the town barber, he has access to a slew of gossip. Maybe he knows something we don't." Suddenly his face brightened. "My word! Why didn't I think of it before! You should talk with Samantha Spencer, too, of course. She's the one who prints the story. If anyone has a clue about the author's identity, I would say it would be her or Billy Taylor, the young man who gathers all the latest town gossip for the *Sentinel*."

Russell and Elnora exchanged sentient glances. "Thank you, Mr. Winchester," Elnora said to Frederick. "You've been most helpful." Smiling, she rose from her seat and turned to Russell. "I suppose we should be on our way. Heaven only knows what the children have done to Maisie and Minnie. They could be roasting them at a stake this very minute."

Russell chuckled and stood, extending his hand to Frederick. "Thanks, Fred. Give Ed and Suzanna our best, won't you?"

"You can be sure I will." Frederick showed them to the door and helped them on with their coats. As he saw them out, he added, "And do let me know when you solve this mystery. It will be interesting to finally meet our author."

On the ride home, Elnora turned to Russell. "What do you think? Is he telling the truth?"

Russell grinned. "Oh, yes. Fred isn't the kind of man to lie to a lady."

Elnora sighed, suddenly at a loss for direction. "Where do we go from here? To Samantha or to Zeke?"

Where indeed, Russell thought, but what he said was much more direct. "To Samantha Spencer's office, I suppose."

They lapsed into silence once again, and the sun, a great orange ball, sank low in the horizon. The air turned chilly, and they felt the coolness on their faces while they sat beside each other, separated by a prudent amount of space—each very aware of something awakening and growing between them. . . .

She thought of Ransom and her promise.

He thought of the past and the price of growing close to anyone.

But they both knew that what they felt, though it was indefinable and insidious at this point, was as compelling and inevitable as the coming of spring.

When Maisie and Minnie came by the following week, they were both furious.

"He did it again! I can't believe it!" Thoroughly disgusted, Maisie marched into the kitchen and dropped her tall, thin body into a chair before the table.

Minnie followed behind, her expression an exact replica of her sister's. She plopped into a seat of her own.

Baffled, Elnora looked from one to the other. "Who did what?"

Maisie wrinkled her nose in disdain. "That dad-blamed author, that's who! He had King Nefan send the Black Knight off on another search for Sir Gawain. It appears Sir Gawain may be innocent of the deeds he was accused of committing, and if he is, the king wants him exonerated."

"So . . ." Elnora prodded, still confused.

"So," Minnie jumped in, "the King appointed Sir Ruggard to escort Lady Elvia on her quest. We're an-gry because in sending the Black Knight off, he freed Lady Elvia from having to make a choice between the two."

"Ah . . ." Elnora smiled. "I see. And you wanted her to have to choose."

"Of course!" Both women said at once, as though Elnora were a ninny.

Maisie screwed up her face in an expression of pure misery. "You really must discover the identity of our author, Elnora. I can barely stand the suspense of wondering who he is any longer. Besides, he and I are going to have a long talk about this story of his—"

"Have you any clues yet?" Minnie cut in, looking over at Elnora.

"Not a one." Elnora took a seat at the table between the twins. "We visited the Double B last week, but the visit yielded us very little. Frederick claims he hasn't the vaguest notion who the author is. He suggested we talk to Samantha Spencer and Billy Taylor. So we're off to the *Harmony Sentinel* today. If our visit doesn't offer us any new leads, we'll talk with Zeke Gallagher.''

Maisie's eyes narrowed. ''That old fool ain't gonna be any help to you! He hasn't a romantic bone in his whole ancient, decaying body!''

''Ohooo,'' Minnie crooned, ''so he's an old fool today. Ha! You didn't think so last week when you baked him those oatmeal cookies.''

Maisie blushed clear up to her iron-gray roots. ''You're one to talk, Minnie Parker. You baked him an apple pie just two days ago and used that innocent boy, Harry Taylor, to sneak it over to the barbershop so I wouldn't know!''

The two sisters glared venom at each other until finally Elnora laughed and said, ''Ladies, you're forgetting the reason for this conversation. We're trying to discover the identity of our author, remember?''

The two women sniffed and lifted their noses.

Finally Maisie said, ''Well, I certainly hope Samantha can help you.'' She sent another malevolent glance over at her sister. ''Still I'm sure, had she the choice, Lady Elvia would have chosen the Black Knight!''

''Nooo, she wouldn't have,'' Minnie argued, shaking her head from side to side. ''She would have chosen Sir Ruggard.''

''Humph!'' said one.

''Humph!'' huffed the other.

They went nose to nose, preparing for another heated battle over the matter.

Elnora was spared from witnessing more of their rivalry by Russell's knock on the door. She rose from her chair to let him in, her heart tumbling into an excited spin.

She opened the door to find him standing in a golden slice of March sunshine. He looked undeniably handsome, his dark brown eyes twinkling with good humor. "Elnora," he said quietly, his gaze sweeping over her appreciatively, taking stock of the enticing fit of her pretty blue dress.

"Come in, Russell." Elnora held the door open wide.

"Hello, ladies," he said to the frowning twins as he stepped into the house.

But the two women were so caught up in their argument they ignored his greeting.

"She'll have to choose between them eventually," Maisie told her sister waspishly.

Elnora walked over to take her coat from a peg on the wall.

"Who will have to choose whom?" Russell asked conversationally.

"Lady Elvia," Elnora explained, shrugging into her coat. "She'll have to choose between Sir Ruggard or the Black Knight."

"Ah," he said, turning to help Elnora on with her coat. "I see." He eased her coat up onto her shoulders, fighting the urge to let his hands linger a moment.

"Maisie and Minnie are in opposition over whom she'll choose." Elnora glanced at him over her shoulder. "They're angry that the author of the story keeps teasing us by never forcing Lady Elvia to make her choice."

Russell looked from Maisie to Minnie. A hint of a smile tugged at his mouth. "Maybe he doesn't know yet which one she'll choose."

Their expressions stubbornly fixed, the two women thought about that. Then quite suddenly Maisie's expression brightened. "Of course!" she exclaimed. "I'm sure you're right about that, Russell."

"It does make sense," Minnie agreed, her mouth

still puckered thoughtfully.

"Well, maybe we'll find out something today," Elnora said cheerfully. "We'd best be on our way, though, while Mark Anthony is still taking his nap." She halted her steps on her way out the door. "Please don't forget to keep an eye on George," she reminded the ladies. "You know how he is."

"Don't worry, dear," Maisie said. "We certainly shall."

They found Samantha at her desk, bent over a typewriter, her brow knit in deep concentration.

Even though she'd married Cord Spencer last year, she continued to work at the newspaper, helping her father and fourteen-year-old Billy Taylor to churn out a weekly edition of the *Harmony Sentinel*.

Samantha had often singed the ears of the townsfolk with her impassioned prose and her straightforward presentation of a story, but they still looked forward to each edition, wondering what new reform she'd decided was necessary, or what new bit of town gossip Billy Taylor had unearthed.

"Hello, Samantha," Russell said, standing in the open doorway of her office.

Samantha looked up from her desk. Almost instantly her face lit with pleasure. "Russell, Elnora! Come in, please." She rose from her chair and came around the desk to usher them in. As always, she was dressed in the latest fashion, her long blond hair swept up onto her head, her blue eyes flashing with liveliness.

She offered them a seat, then asked, "What brings you out today?"

Russell's gaze was very direct. "We're on a quest to find someone. We thought if anyone in town would know where to find this person, you would."

Always intrigued by a good mystery, Samantha chuckled with pleasure. "Well, I'll certainly help you if I can. Who are you looking for?"

Elnora leaned forward in her chair. "The author who writes the weekly series for your newspaper."

Samantha frowned thoughtfully. "You mean the author of the story about King Nefan's court?"

"Yes," Elnora said, while Russell got comfortable and leaned back in his chair, hooking one foot onto his knee.

Her mind clicking, Samantha went silent a moment, her gaze shifting from Russell to Elnora, then back to Russell once again. "I see." She took a deep breath, then said, "Well, that's a good one. To be honest with you, we don't know who he is. He comes at night, leaving the next chapter of his story under the front door. Billy has tried to wait up for him and catch him in the act, but he ends up falling asleep almost every time. And when he doesn't fall asleep, our mystery writer is so quiet and sly, he's here and gone before Billy can see him."

"Well," Elnora said, disconcerted, "it seems we're chasing a ghost."

"He's no ghost," Russell put in quietly, his gaze fixed upon his boot.

"It seems to me," Samantha said, leaning her bustle against the desk and crossing her arms over her chest, "that whoever he is, he relishes his anonymity. There has to be a reason for that."

Amused, Russell raised one eyebrow, his gaze lifting to Samantha. His dark eyes twinkled with some hidden merriment. "Maybe." Then he turned to Elnora. "Don't be discouraged. We still have more leads to check out."

"Yes," Samantha said. "There's Zeke. Everyone knows how he loves to read. And you should talk to Jake Sutherland." She bent forward and added conspiratorially, "He recites poetry to his horses while he shoes them, though I'm sure he'd shoe me if he knew I'd told you. And don't forget to speak to Harry Taylor. He's the biggest romantic this town ever saw, even though he is still a boy." She was silent a moment, and her expression grew thoughtful. "It seems to me that whoever is writing the series has a very romantic heart." Samantha fixed her gaze purposely on Elnora, "I think the author is sweet on you, Elnora."

Abashed, Elnora sniffed and blushed vividly. "You're as bad as Maisie and Minnie."

"What do you think, Russell?" Samantha asked.

A small smile tugged at Russell's lips. "I agree with you wholeheartedly."

Samantha nodded. "There!" She clapped her hands together. "So you have it, Elnora. Find the author of the series and you've found the man whose heart you've won."

As they rode back to the Perry farm that afternoon, Elnora was unusually silent. Around them she saw and heard the evidence of spring—a gentle whisper of wind, the call of a mourning dove, the gurgling of water running through a creek bed, and a playful scrambling of chipmunks, cutting across their path.

After a while Elnora cast her companion a sidelong glance. "Who do you think it is, Russ?" Her voice was soft with entreaty. "Really." She'd never before used the shortened version of his name, but the sound of it now felt right upon her lips.

Taken aback, he turned his head to look at her. His

dark eyes grew earnest, and he allowed her the slightest smile. "Samantha's right, Elnora. Whoever he is, he has lost his heart to you."

"But I'm not Lady Elvia," she said quietly.

"Aren't you? Look closely. The similarities are no coincidence." His voice was so deep, so mellow, it stirred something within her, and a latent fire that she hadn't known existed sputtered into life, leaving her flustered and confused.

She dropped her gaze to study her tiny, sensible shoes where they peeked out from beneath her modest skirt. "I would not want to be her. I would not want to choose."

Her words brought a sudden prick of pain, and he swallowed thickly. "Is it because you think she loves both knights?"

"No," she answered, bereaved. "It's worse than that. I don't think she knows what love is at all. She can't make a choice until she knows. And how could she know?" She lifted her gaze to his for a brief moment. "She's never had the chance to know much of anything for sure. . . ." Her gaze skittered away.

Gently Russell tugged on the horses' reins, stopping the buggy in the middle of a bridge that forded a small stream. He sat in pensive silence, staring at his hands, weighing the consequences of what he was about to do, knowing all too well that he was courting disaster. Then, deciding disaster was a worthy price to pay, he turned to her and very gently lifted her chin, turning her face to his. "What is it you want to know, Nora?"

Her eyes lifted to his, and from out of her dreams came the memory of a gallant knight and a hint of something she had yet to acknowledge. Her pulse fluttered, and her heart kept time to an unknown melody, and she forgot about her promise to Ransom, she forgot about propriety, and she forgot to object as Russell's hands found her shoulders and urged her toward him.

She went willingly this time, like morning dew to a flower's petals, and when his lips grazed hers, a small sigh escaped her. She remembered the very first time, the only time he'd kissed her. Somehow she knew this time would be different.

And it was.

This time his mouth settled over hers, bringing a shock that went straight to the core of her heart. His mouth opened, and his tongue touched her bottom lip ever so softly, ever so gently, gliding across the seam of her mouth in a way that sent arrows dancing through her limbs. She gave a soft gasp of surprise, and his tongue came searching, awakening a yearning within her that she'd never imagined was possible.

Without even thinking, she kissed him back—following his lead, eager to learn what he would teach her.

When finally Russell lifted his head, her eyes remained closed. Her lashes cast dark shadows on her pale skin, and he felt a river of tenderness rush over him. His thumbs stroked her shoulders through the thick material of her coat, while passion flared, and he wondered what her skin would feel like.

She lifted her arms and hugged his neck, pressing close, laying her head on his shoulder. His eyes slid shut, and he stifled a groan, enfolding her close. Her soft hair brushed his jaw, and her breasts pressed against his throbbing heart. "Nora," he whispered, letting his feelings take him on a ride beyond reason.

The sound of her name woke her from her dream-like state. She lifted her head from his shoulder and stared up at him with open fascination, feeling her cheeks grow hot.

His common sense grew strong again, and he found the strength to set her back from him.

She cleared her throat and blinked twice as though to clear her mind. "Russ . . ." She swallowed, a sudden sadness overtaking her. "I should tell you . . . I promised Vivian's brother, Ransom, that I'd wait for him to return."

The muscles in Russell's cheeks twitched slightly. It was the only indication that her words unsettled him. He managed something of a smile and only said, "I see," while he thought to himself that the lady had made a decision after all. Disappointment grew rife, and he turned his attention to the road. Taking the reins in hand, he set the buggy in motion.

♥ Chapter 8

IN A SEEDY little hotel room in St. Louis, Missouri, Ransom lay trying to read the book Elnora had given him for Christmas, but it was a difficult endeavor for him. He'd never been much of a student, and as a result, he was a poor reader.

He'd muddled his way through school by charming his teachers, which he learned at a very early age was considerably easier than mastering his letters or numbers.

"What're ya readin', sugar?" crooned a silky voice at his side.

Ransom held the book propped open on his bare stomach with one hand, while his other hand slid down over the smooth curve of a shapely female hip. "You wouldn't be interested, Lacey, honey."

The woman snuggled up against his warm, hard length. She rubbed her cheek seductively against his shoulder. "You tryin' to tell me I ain't smart enough to read a big book like that one?" She turned her pretty face up to him and fluttered her eyelashes in an exaggerated manner that made her look as brainless as a pigeon.

He glanced down at her, then threw back his head and laughed. "Hell, I ain't hardly smart enough to read a book like this one! But I promised a gal I know I'd give it a try."

The woman pouted and fluffed her long red hair off her shoulder. "Readin' always did seem like a horrible waste of time to me," she said in a smooth easy drawl. Slowly she ran her bare foot up the long length of his naked leg.

"Whoa, girl," he said, catching her foot before it reached his hip. "I'm tryin' to get some learnin' done, and you're takin' a terrible toll on my concentration."

Lacey chuckled low and husky. "Now, what would a good-lookin' man like you need learnin' for? Honey, you're just fine the way you are."

"Ya never know," he said almost defensively. "I might be turnin' over a new leaf." He shot her a quick glance to gauge her reaction. "I might even get married." In stating the words, he felt a sudden swell of pride.

She gave a short disbelieving huff, and her hand went searching over the hard planes of his lower stomach. "Yeah, you'll get married, honey," she whispered as his body hardened, instantly reacting to her touch, "when bulls grow teats."

"Aw, Lacey," he groaned, and the book toppled off his hip and onto the bed. "Now look what you went and done." He looked down at his awakening body, then rolled over on his side and went length to length with one of St. Louis's finest young working women. He gave her a broad sexy grin. "Well . . . this bull ain't got teats, but I got somethin' else you're gonna like a helluva lot better."

"Oh, darlin'," Lacey said, snuggling close, "I can hardly wait. . . ."

* * *

Later that night after Lacey had left him, Ransom relaxed in his bed, tired and sated. For a moment he grew melancholy. He missed Elnora. He wondered if Whitaker had attempted to call on her, then comforted himself, thinking Elnora had promised to wait for him, and Elnora Perry would never break her word. Besides, what would she want with a man like Whitaker when she could have someone like himself?

He sighed deeply. It was a shame, though, he couldn't have taken her with him. But Vivian needed her more than he did.

It had been a long time since he'd been to St. Louis and visited Lacey Long. He smiled into the darkness and settled more comfortably into the middle of the bed. She sure as hell knew how to show a man a good time. And if there was one thing he never could turn down, it was a good time.

He'd always had a weakness for women.

Still, he'd have to learn how to temper that weakness, he reminded himself. If Elnora would have him, he'd soon be married, and times like these would be few and far between.

He couldn't imagine Elnora putting up with him sneaking off to the local whorehouse whenever the urge took him.

With his thoughts on her pretty face, he finally slipped off to sleep. Several hours later he awoke with a start. From somewhere in the deep, dark recesses of his mind, a thought nagged at him, but he couldn't quite call it forth, couldn't quite put it into words. It was a small, subtle inkling that left him feeling as though he'd missed something somewhere along the line.

Now fully awake and growing frustrated, he rose and lit the lamp in his room, then sat down in a chair by the window to read more of *Les Misérables*. Mastering the words written in the book was difficult, but he struggled on, becoming caught up in the fascinating story of Jean Valjean and the detective, Javert.

Suddenly his head came up, and he knew what it was that was bothering him. It had been eating at him since he'd first begun to read the story.

Why had Elnora chosen this particular book?

She'd given him the book before he'd told her about the man he'd been hunting for years. Yet it was as though she'd known all along about his search and had picked this story out especially for him.

But how could she have known?

The question brought him no peace, so he promised himself that once he caught up with Claude Johnson, the man he'd been tracking since he'd left Harmony, he'd return and ask Elnora himself.

Yessir, he thought. That's what he'd do.

The decision made, he relaxed some and returned to his reading.

Still, it wasn't until the pale light of dawn slipped across his chest that he finally dropped the book onto his lap and fell asleep once again.

But even in his sleep his mind was troubled by the odd coincidence.

The next two weeks passed quickly.

Russell and Elnora continued their quest in earnest.

They visited Zeke Gallagher and Jake Sutherland. That same day they chased down the youngest romantic in town, Harry Taylor.

A few days later they talked to the Reverend Johnson and his wife, Rachel, and even spent an hour interrogating Charlie Thompson, the bartender over at the Last Resort, who always knew the latest gossip about almost everyone in town.

They questioned them all, but their inquiries yielded them very little of the information they sought.

As for Russell and Elnora, the atmosphere was different between them now. Since the day he'd kissed her, they were ever aware of the burgeoning of their emotions. Yet they both worked hard to suppress the evidence of any such thing.

They kept a careful distance, always polite with each other, sometimes even lighthearted with their banter, but always, always, by some unspoken agreement, they held themselves and their feelings carefully in check.

The temptation to do otherwise was heady, however, so Elnora reminded herself daily of her promise to Ransom, and Russell reminded himself that their quest would eventually end, and so would his time with Elnora.

The thought played havoc with his heart, and he admitted for the first time to himself that he, like the author of the series, had fallen in love with Elnora Perry.

The fact that he loved her was his redemption, though, giving him the strength to do the honorable thing and respect her choice.

She'd made the better choice, he told himself often, though something within him rebelled at the thought and made him want to fight all the harder for her. When he thought of her with Riley—when he thought of the man touching her, it made him feel ill.

It was a bitter irony to him that after all these years he'd finally met a woman with whom he wanted to spend the rest of his life.

And it didn't matter.

He felt sure that if she knew the truth she would see him much differently, and he knew he couldn't bear to witness the disappointment in her eyes.

April brought rainy days and steely skies.

The children grew bored and restless once again.

Elnora's nerves stretched thin as she fought her attraction to Russell. She believed it was dishonorable to allow her heart to betray her in such a manner when she felt she owed her loyalty to Ransom.

Her feelings for Russell must have stemmed from her loneliness for Ransom.

But at night in her dreams it was Russell who came to her, it was Russell who kissed her. She often awoke feeling heavy-hearted and hollow, her breasts aching, her body aroused and yearning for that secret something that she had never known.

It was on one such morning she rose and hurried to the washstand to splash cold water onto her face. She sighed and gazed into the mirror, wondering about the woman who stared back at her, feeling confusion overwhelm her. "What is wrong with you, Nora?" she asked herself out loud. "Where is all your common sense? Where is your predictability, your sense of propriety? What in heaven's name is happening to you?"

A piercing howl from the family cat interrupted any further introspection.

She grabbed her robe and rushed down the stairs to find George completing the cat's haircut. The result left Prissy looking disgruntled and half naked and, Elnora was quite sure, suffering with a serious nervous condition.

She chided George more harshly than normal and sent him off to wash up while she prepared breakfast for the household. She called up the stairs to wake Sam and Andy. They balked at getting up for school, and she had to threaten them with the exposure of their latest pranks to get them motivated. In the meantime, Mark Anthony, tired of waiting for her attention, decided to change his own diaper. In doing so, he made a mess Elnora would remember till the end of her days.

When she finally managed to get the two oldest boys off to school, she chased Gordon out the door with George and then prepared Vivian's breakfast. She took Mark Anthony up to Vivian's room and sat him down on a rug to play with a pile of wooden blocks, then she went back downstairs to get the breakfast tray and Sara and Emily.

Glad for the respite, Elnora sat down on the edge of Vivian's bed to visit for a short while. "Well," she said and gave a great sigh, "I don't know how you do this day in and day out, Viv."

Vivian laid the *Sentinel* down and smiled. "You're getting a lifetime of experience in these few months, aren't you?"

Elnora chuckled softly. "I have to admit this is one visit I'll never forget. I used to think taking care of several children could be no more difficult than taking care of one or two." She widened her eyes and gave a short self-deprecating laugh. "It's not that it's so difficult, it's just that I only have two hands and two eyes, and there are six of them, all with the same number of parts as me. . . ." She laughed again. "Well, you know what I mean." She took the napkin from the tray and shook it out, placing it over Vivian's swollen belly. "Come now, eat."

Vivian leaned her head back against her pillow. Her face was unusually pale. Her pretty blue eyes showed signs of fatigue. "I'm afraid I'm not very hungry this morning, Nora."

"Well," Elnora said with forced cheerfulness, "that's all right. We'll visit for a while, and maybe you'll change your mind."

Vivian picked up the *Sentinel* and handed it to Elnora. "She's falling in love with Sir Ruggard, you know."

Elnora took the paper from her hand and lowered her gaze. "I know," she said quietly.

"She's made her choice," Vivian said, "even though she doesn't know who he really is or what he even looks like."

Elnora's expression grew soft and wistful. "She knows his heart. That's all that matters."

"I suppose you're right. But does he love her?"

The question gave Elnora pause. Her eyes lifted to Vivian's. "I believe he does."

"But their quest has brought them nothing. They have yet to find the blue diamond."

"They've found each other, and he'll find the diamond for her. I know he will."

They fell silent for a moment and listened to the children giggle as they played together. They listened to the clock down the hall, sounding out the hour. From outside came the sound of heavy rain pelting the house.

"Elnora?" Vivian said softly.

"Yes . . ."

"You know I love my brother."

Elnora smiled. "I know you do."

"He's big and handsome and fun—"

"He's all those things and more," Elnora admitted.

Vivian's expression was almost solemn. "But I love you, too."

Confused, Elnora's brow wrinkled. "What is it, Viv?"

"Look deep inside your heart, Nora. Make sure of what you feel for him, for any man. A woman has a right to be in love with her husband."

"Did you know for sure how you felt about Gordon at first?" Elnora asked quietly.

Vivian thought a moment, and her expression became tender with remembrance. "Oh, yes, I knew. He caught my eye the very first time I saw him, the very first time I heard his voice. And when he kissed me that first time, ah, well, he had my heart from that day forth. . . ." Suddenly she left off, her eyelids sinking shut, her face contorting with pain. A soft moan escaped her, and she turned her head into her pillow to muffle the sound.

Alarm clawed at Elnora's insides. Slowly she rose from the bed, her eyes widening with understanding. "Viv, it's time, isn't it?"

When the pain ebbed, Vivian opened her eyes and nodded. "The pains started coming sometime before dawn."

"Good heavens, why didn't you tell me?" Elnora whispered fiercely, not wanting to frighten the children. "I would have sent Gordon into town for Doc Tanner."

Vivian smiled wanly. "It should be a while yet, Nora. None of my children were in a hurry to enter this world. But if this one is, we'll manage just fine. You'll see."

"Oh, my . . ." Elnora pushed an errant lock of hair back from her face. She looked around the room frantically, as though searching the walls for strength. Finally her eyes came back to Vivian. "This is going to be quite a day."

And it was.

Vivian's labor continued slowly.

The next contraction was harder and sent her crouching up into a sitting position, causing her to fight for her breath for all of a minute.

When the contraction eased, Elnora pressed her back down onto the pillows, quietly crooning soft words of encouragement.

She gathered the children and, despite their disgruntled protests, put all three down for a nap.

Then she returned, took Vivian's hand, and sat down on the edge of the bed. Elnora had spent most of her life taking care of people, but helping a child into the world was the one thing she'd never done, and she was scared to death. "I know we've talked about this at least a dozen times. But now that the time has come, my mind is in a muddle. I'll need you to tell me once again what you need me to do."

Patiently Vivian repeated a long list of instructions. Elnora rose and followed them down to the minutest detail—gathering the scissors, a pile of clean cloths, and laying a newly laundered white sheet beneath Vivian's arching back.

Then, certain she would be all right for a few moments without her, she went downstairs to put several pots of water on to boil.

Once that was done, she shrugged into her coat and, her heart pumping wildly, raced out into the rain to look for Gordon.

Despite the rain and muddied roads, Russell climbed into his buggy and set off for the Perry farm. He'd recently received a shipment of books, and in it was a copy of the Charles Dickens novel, *A Tale of Two Cities*. He thought Elnora might enjoy it.

Actually it was as good an excuse as any to see her.

He knew it would be better if he stayed away, but he couldn't.

With only a few more of the townsfolk to question, their adventure would soon come to an end. Acknowledging that fact, time pressed in on him, making him less cautious than he would normally be.

When he arrived at the farm, he saw her making a dash from the house to the barn, so he steered the horse toward the barn and stopped the rig before the broad doors.

He leaped down to the ground, and with his head bowed against the pelting torrent, he raced for the doors. He entered the barn, banging the doors shut behind him, and came face to face with Elnora. Her eyes were wide and frightened, her face drawn with worry.

"Nora," he said, taking her by the arms, "what is it?"

She stared up into his handsome face for the sparsest of moments, and as though it were the most natural thing in the world for her to do, she went up against his broad chest, wrapping her arms tightly around his waist.

Instinctively he held her close, his eyelids slipping shut, his heart thudding, as she laid her cheek against the rough material of his coat and whispered, "Oh, Russ, I'm so glad you're here. It's Vivian. The baby's coming."

"Where's Gordon?" he asked, his voice suddenly hoarse, his jaw brushing against her soft, mussed hair.

"I don't know. But I need to get to Doc Tanner."

Gently Russell set her back from him. "I'll go for the doctor. You go on back to Vivian."

Her eyes lifted, and she searched his face. She felt

a deep stirring within her breast. "What if you don't get back in time?"

He took her hands and squeezed gently. "Just do what Vivian tells you. It'll be all right."

Her eyes mirrored her uncertainty. "I've never helped with a birthing. . . ."

Russell's eyes took on a mischievous glitter, and a wry smile pulled at his mouth. "Elnora Perry, there isn't anything in this world you couldn't do if you put your mind to it."

"You think so?" she asked softly, gazing up at him, feeling his strength flow into her.

"I know so," he said without hesitation.

A warm, wonderful feeling swept her, and as if by some mysterious magic, her heart opened at last and revealed its secret.

Quite suddenly the confusion lifted, and she knew . . .

She was in love with Russell Whitaker.

It had been he she loved all along—this handsome, decent man who humored elderly ladies and loved books, who'd given her her first grown-up kiss and rescued dogs, who calmed her and helped her find a lost child—this man, who treated everyone he knew with respect and kindness.

She was amazed it had taken her so long to figure out the truth.

She opened her mouth to speak, her heart billowing with the need to voice her newfound discovery, but he took her arm, reminding her that there was a much more pressing matter to attend to. "We'd better get you back to Vivian."

The truth lifted the heaviness from Elnora's heart, so she was content to remain silent in the face of Viv-

ian's need. Together they dashed from the barn back
to the house.

Once he saw her through the door, he ran back out
into the rain. "I'll find Gordon, too, if I can," he hollered, and then he was gone.

Gordon and George came back before Russell did.
Gordon sent the boy off to his room, then helped
Elnora gather the rest of the items Vivian had re-
quested. Sam and Andy came home from school, and
Elnora fed them, then shooed them off to their bed-
rooms, too.

The children seemed to understand their coopera-
tion was needed and for once brooked no arguments.

Gordon hurried around the house, fussily perform-
ing the tasks with which he was so familiar, and while
he did, he promised himself he would never put his
wife through this again. Not only had this pregnancy
been difficult, but the labor seemed harder than any
she'd suffered before.

Evening came, and Russell did not return with Doc
Tanner. Fearing Vivian could wait no longer, Elnora
prepared her for delivery. She followed Vivian's instructions carefully, washing her thighs, her swollen
genitals, and her bulging stomach with gentle but
quaking hands. "Oh, Viv . . ." she whispered, aggrieved, blinking back tears. "You must hurt terribly."

"It h-hurts, Nora," she managed. "I won't try to tell
you it doesn't. B-but it's worth it in the end. You'll
see."

Elnora's vision blurred. Would she? Oh, would she
ever see? Did she really want to?

"Oh, sweet Jesus," Vivian moaned, and she began
to pant as another contraction began. Elnora grabbed

her hands, hanging on tight, her eyes riveted on Vivian's constricting belly.

A rasping cry tore from her throat, and Elnora felt the bones in her hands grind together as Vivian squeezed tightly. She lifted her hips from the bed, her face contorted with agony.

In time she relaxed back onto the bed once again, and Elnora took a cool damp towel and wiped the beads of sweat from her brow. She pushed back the wet, darkened strands of blond hair and felt another rush of sympathy for the other woman.

The respite lasted only a few brief moments. Another hard pain took her, her thighs tightened, and she strained against the pain, a sob escaping through her clenched teeth.

Time ticked by, and Vivian's labor became more intense.

"Come on, Viv," Elnora whispered, taking her hands once again. "It can't be much longer." She glanced down at Vivian's distended genitals, and what she saw brought a swift rush of relief and amazement at once. "It's coming! I see the baby's head!"

Elnora peeled Vivian's hands from her own and placed them around the narrow columns of the brass headboard. She moved down to the bottom of the bed, ready to welcome her newest nephew or niece. Oddly enough, her hands steadied, and her stomach calmed. The doctor would not make it in time, she knew. But she was there, and she would do everything she could to see this new life safely into the world.

She reached forward, waiting, while once again Vivian arched, a terrible scream tearing from her throat as the baby's head slipped through, face downward.

"Oh, Viv . . ." Elnora whispered, cradling the tiny dark head in her hands, feeling her throat swell shut, feeling her eyes sting with fresh tears, knowing she was witnessing the most wondrous of miracles.

Then without warning Vivian groaned and bore down hard, and out eased a shoulder, then the other, and suddenly a tiny new life slipped out into Elnora's waiting hands. "Oh, it's a girl," she whispered, tears streaming down her cheeks. Elnora made an odd sound, half laugh and half sob. "Look, Viv. You have another beautiful daughter!"

Vivian fell back, panting. "Lord have mercy . . ." she whispered, exhausted, catching her breath. "Turn her onto her side, Nora," she instructed quietly, her voice thready. "Clean out her mouth with your finger."

Elnora did as instructed, and within seconds the baby gave a soft gasp, and a tiny mewing sound escaped her puckered little mouth.

Just then the bedroom door opened, and Elnora turned to see Doc Tanner come through carrying his black bag.

"Well, what do we have here?" he asked. Calm and composed as always, he peered down at the child Elnora held so carefully, then set his bag down and went over to the washstand to scrub his hands. "Seems to me Whitaker made a wasted trip chasing me all the way to Ellsworth to bring me back for the birth of this baby. You ladies did just fine without me."

Elnora felt her heart swell. *Oh, Russ,* she thought, *you went all the way to Ellsworth. . . .* She held the baby cradled in her hands, while the doctor came over and tied off the umbilical cord.

Then the baby was on her own, hiccuping and

squalling, flailing her arms wildly like a tiny princess warrior.

Elnora gave the child to the doctor and went over to wash herself. Drying her hands, she approached Vivian's bedside. "She's the most beautiful thing I've ever seen, Vivian." She bent over her weary sister-in-law and pressed a gentle kiss to her forehead. "Thank you for sharing her with me."

Vivian smiled weakly and closed her eyes. "Thank you, Nora. For being here."

Elnora left her with the doctor and stepped out into the hall, closing the door softly behind. All six children were lined up outside the door, six pairs of eyes blinking up at her, their expressions worried.

Sam stepped forward. "Is Mama gonna be all right?"

Elnora knelt before him and took his hand in her own. "Oh, yes, Samuel. She's going to be just fine."

"We heard her crying," Andy all but accused, his dark eyes shiny with plump tears he refused to shed.

"Yes, I know you did, darling. It's like that sometimes when women have their babies." She reached out and brushed a lock of hair from his eyes.

"When can we see her?" George asked, his bottom lip quivering.

"Soon. Just as soon as the doctor finishes taking care of her. I'm sure he'll let you all go in for a little while."

"What'd we get?" Sara wanted to know.

Elnora smiled and pulled the little girl into her arms, hugging her close. "You have a baby sister. Just like you wanted."

Emily and Mark Anthony looked on, blinking. Elnora plucked Emily's thumb from her mouth and asked, "What do you think of that, Emmy?" Silent as always, the little girl's grin was answer enough.

Doc Tanner opened the bedroom door. He, too, was met with the force of the children's young questioning eyes. "Come on in. Your mother has someone she wants you to meet." He held the door open wide, and solemnly the Perry children filed in to meet their new sister.

Happier than she could ever remember being, Elnora descended the steps and paused at the bottom of the staircase. Gordon sat at the table, his head in his hands, his shoulders slumped forward in exhaustion. Across from him sat Russell, looking every bit as weary as the new father. Her heart swelled anew with love for him, confirming the truth of her feelings for him. Sensing her presence, he looked up from studying his folded hands, and their eyes met and held.

"It's a girl," she said softly, and his eyes told her that he shared her joy.

Gordon's head came up, and he vaulted from his chair. "A girl!" he exclaimed, excitement lighting his face as though the child were his firstborn.

Elnora nodded, her smile stretching wide, making the skin around her eyes crinkle attractively at the corners. She walked over to the table. "Yes, you have another beautiful daughter, Gordon."

He let out a wild whoop and hugged her, lifting her high off her feet, spinning her around in a circle, while she threw back her head and laughed with enjoyment of the moment. He set her down and ran for the stairs, taking them by twos.

Russell rose from his chair. He smiled down at her, noting her mussed hair, her pale face, her spotted and wrinkled clothing, but her eyes . . . ah, her beautiful honey-brown eyes were shining with a light that made his heart grow weak. She'd never looked love-lier.

She gazed up into his wonderfully familiar face, and she realized that what had started as a most disastrous day had ended up being the most beautiful, magical day of her life.

They studied each other—thinking, assessing, hearts thrumming, time ticking. Because this day was special, and because she was fast learning that life was not always so predictable and neither was she, she went up on tiptoes and pressed a light kiss to his mouth. "Thank you, Sir Knight," she said softly, "for coming to my rescue once again."

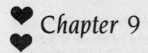 *Chapter 9*

ELNORA FOUND HERSELF busier than ever now that the baby had come.

Vivian was allowed out of bed for short intervals, but she tired easily, and Baby Alice was quite a handful at times. Consequently, Russell's and Elnora's quest was temporarily delayed.

Elnora often thought about what Vivian had said the day Baby Alice was born—about Ransom, about making sure of what she felt for him or anyone else.

She was sure now. What she felt for Russell was strong and sweet and true.

But there were so many things about him that puzzled her, so many things she sensed he could not or would not share with her.

Those things gave her pause, along with her promise to Ransom. . . .

Inside the office of the Kansas City jail, Ransom waited for Sheriff Mobely to finish counting out his reward money.

Sheriff Mobely glanced up from his task and smiled. "Fine job ya did o' catchin' that fella," he said, his voice echoing his respect. He picked up the money and held it out to Ransom, who took it with a nod and tucked it down into his saddlebag.

145

Ransom shot the sheriff a confident smile. "I always get my man, Sheriff."

"That's why I sent fer ya," Sheriff Mobley said. "You're jist about the best bounty hunter in this area."

"I am the best," Ransom bragged without hesitation. He turned and sauntered across the room, then stopped before the many Most Wanted posters nailed to the wall.

Slightly annoyed by his overly confident tone, Sheriff Mobely decided to needle the big man's ego a mite—just for the fun of it. As much as he respected Riley, he figured nobody ought to be that goddamned confident, no matter how good he was at what he did. "Word has it you're still lookin' fer that fella from up North." He paused, pretending to think. "He was from Detroit, wasn't he?"

"Yeah," Ransom drawled, his expression growing grim, his ego taking an icy plunge. He pretended to study the posters on the wall with intense interest.

"What's his name again?" the sheriff probed, enjoying the moment immensely.

"Walker," Ransom snapped. "His name is Robert D. Walker."

"Oh, yeah!" The sheriff paused again. "Now I 'member. He was a slippery fella, weren't he?" The old sheriff cackled with glee. When he finally got control of himself, his voice held a tinge of admiration. "Had every bounty hunter in these United States scramblin' to git that big fat wad o' money that rich son of a bitch up in Detroit offered for his recapture. Didn't do no good, though. All them Wanted posters nailed up in 'most every town in the Union, and still no one ever saw hide nor hair of him once he slipped outta that prison."

Ransom shot him a sullen glance over his shoulder.

"Don't mean someone won't sooner or later."

"Ya know what I think?" Sheriff Mobely queried. He stood and came around his desk, his expression suddenly sober and shrewd. "I think there has to be an awful good reason that rich fella is offerin' the reward 'stead of the law. Seems to me he wants Walker a helluva lot more 'an anybody else does." The sheriff's expression grew thoughtful. "I always did wonder 'bout that. . . ." He left off, still pondering the notion.

"You got any more of them posters layin' around?" Ransom asked, his mind working over a small niggling suspicion.

"Well, I don't know," the sheriff said and went back to his desk. "I jist might." He sat down and pulled out a drawer stuffed with a mess of old posters and papers. "It's been all o' six years or more since he up and disappeared, ain't it?" Taking a pile of papers out of the drawer, he slapped them down on his desk and began to rummage through them.

Meanwhile, Ransom busied himself with reading the posters on the wall, his mind furiously working over an unlikely but all too compelling thought.

After several minutes the sheriff's head came up. "Well, what d'ya know 'bout that!" he exclaimed. Ransom's head snapped around to look at him. "Here's one!" He held the yellowed poster out to Ransom.

He crossed the jail floor and took the paper from the sheriff's hand.

WANTED, DEAD OR ALIVE, the poster read. ROBERT D. WALKER. ESCAPED CONVICT. REWARD: $10,000.00.

For several seconds Ransom stared down at the faded image before him. It was difficult to tell the color of the man's hair because the picture was so aged and dull, but Ransom tried to imagine it light, almost a silver blond. The man in the picture wore a mustache, and his hair was short and combed back from his face.

Ransom's head began to throb as he imagined the mustache gone. He imagined the face a little older, the hair a little longer at the nape and falling forward over one side of the man's brow.

The truth struck him with the force of a lightning bolt.

Whitaker!

He remembered that Elnora had said Whitaker had sold her the book! Whitaker had thought he'd enjoy it!

Humiliation and anger made Ransom's face turn a deep dark shade of red. All this time Walker had been right under his nose, laughing at him.

"Can I keep this?" he asked the sheriff brusquely, his green eyes snapping with ire.

"Sure. Ain't nobody lookin' fer him anymore but you."

Ransom hefted his bag up onto his shoulder and, without a backward glance, stalked out of the Kansas City jail.

Lottie McGee stood outside the doors of the First Resort.

From inside her establishment came the sound of the piano player banging out a bawdy tune, while raucous hoots of male laughter and sultry feminine voices made a melody all their own.

Across the street the Last Resort competed for attention with a generous share of its own noise. The sounds emitting through the saloon's open doorway, however, were more masculine—the soft clink of glasses, the slap of cards hitting the tables, the sociable hum of male conversation.

She pulled her shawl tight against the cool night air and turned to gaze down Main Street. She saw him coming. The moonlight glinted off his hair, and, as always, his companion, Arthur, was at his side.

She waited until he drew abreast of her saloon, admiring his easy saunter and the attractive width of his shoulders. He cut a fine figure, she thought, wishing, as she often did, that she was younger and could have another go at some of life's more important choices. "Evenin', Russ," she said quietly as he passed by her establishment.

He halted his steps and turned, searching for her through the deepening shadows. "Evening, Lottie," he said, finding her, his voice smooth and deep and pleasant.

"Out for your nightly stroll, are ya?" She walked to where he waited in the street. Reaching him, she bent and gave Arthur an affectionate pat on the head.

"Just catching some fresh air," he said with a slight smile.

"Want some company?" She tipped her head to the side coquettishly.

He gazed down at her, and his smile grew. "It would be a pleasure." He crooked his elbow out to her, and she took his arm.

In companionable silence they strolled down Main Street while all around them the evening shadows lengthened. Noise followed them from both saloons, and on down the street a dog barked and a cat howled.

"Won't be long and summer will be here," Lottie commented conversationally.

"It's been a long winter," Russell said. "It'll be nice to see it end."

They fell back into silence for a while, then from out of the blue Lottie said, "You been a little long in the jaw lately, Russ. You got somethin' on your mind?"

He shot her a glance, raised an eyebrow, but kept his silence.

"Wouldn't have somethin' to do with that little Miss Perry, would it?" Lottie raised a skeptical eyebrow of her own.

They stared at each other a long moment, then a grin stole across Russell's face. "Sometimes I think you see too much for your own good, Lottie."

She chuckled deep in her throat. "A woman in my profession has to keep her eyes open all the time. If she don't, well . . . you know how it can be." She sighed deeply, then said, "You're sweet on that woman, ain't ya?"

Russell stared straight ahead, pondering her question. He gave a small defeated huff of laughter. "Yeah. I guess I am."

"You guess!" Lottie sounded incredulous. She tugged him to an abrupt halt before Maisie and Minnie's boardinghouse. Turning to him, she propped her hands on her ample hips. "Ya either are or ya ain't. Now, which is it?"

He gave her a long thoughtful look. "Yes. I'm in love with her," he admitted quietly.

"That's better!" She nodded, satisfied with his admission. " 'Bout time you men start speakin' up and say what you're feelin'." She gave his arm a tug, and they continued their walk past the boardinghouse, on past the *Harmony Sentinel* office, making a half circle in front of the church so they could head back down the other side of Main Street.

When they reached the First Resort, Lottie turned to him again. "So why don't you tell her?"

Russell gave a small dry laugh. "I'm afraid it's not quite that easy."

Her eyes rounded with frustration. "And why not?"

Russell's expression grew solemn. "I have my reasons."

She stared at him a long minute. "We all got our secrets, Russ. But I know a good man when I meet one. I always said you were the finest gentleman this town ever saw." She reached down into her pocket and pulled out a folded yellowed piece of paper. "I still say that." She held the paper out to him. "Here. I been holdin' on to this for 'bout four years now."

He looked down at the paper and took it from her hands. He didn't unfold it. He didn't have to. He knew what it was. His eyes came back to hers, and their gazes locked for a long meaningful moment.

When at last she spoke, her voice was soft with wisdom and compassion. "Seems to me folks oughta let the past be the past. If I'd had the good sense to do that, I mighta been in another profession a long time ago, 'stead of stayin' stuck in this one all these years." She paused. "Talk to your lady, Russ. Miss Perry's made of real fine stuff, even if she did seem a little starchy at first. Little by little, she's gettin' that starch ironed outta her, and when she's done, she's gonna make someone a fine wife. That girl's got spunk." Lottie nodded. "Trust me, I know."

A smile caught at Russell's mouth. He leaned over and pressed a light kiss to Lottie's still beautiful lips. "Lottie McGee," he said, "you're one helluva woman."

She flashed him a million-dollar smile. "Hell, I know that." She blushed like a schoolgirl, then reached down and gave Arthur a pat. "By the way, Russ," she said as she turned back toward her place of business, "them two old gals over at the boardin'-house were peekin' out at us through their window a few minutes ago." She gave him a broad wink. "There's gonna be talk in Harmony tomorrow."

He chuckled, his eyes twinkling with amusement, and slipped the folded poster into his coat pocket. Then he walked on down Main Street with Arthur at his side.

The third Tuesday in April dawned bright and clear. The air was sweet, smelling of freshly turned earth and the beginnings of new plant life. The surrounding fields were green once again, the trees no longer naked and barren, but resplendent and verdant. Birds sang, insects buzzed, and down in the meadows horses and cattle grazed alongside their young.

Meanwhile, young children caught the fever and became unruly, yearning to be turned loose to play outdoors.

So it was that Elnora woke Sam and Andy early that morning. Faith Hutton had promised her students a spring picnic, and neither boy wanted to be late for school today.

Elnora packed the boys' lunches with extra care, adding a few extra cookies and some of yesterday's apple pie.

Then she chased them out into the crystal clearness of the warm sunshine, feeling their excitement as if it were her own. "Have fun, you two!" she called out.

"We will," Sam hollered without turning.

"Yeah, we will," Andy repeated, right on his brother's heels.

Elnora went back into the house to see to the other children. A few minutes later Vivian came down the stairs with Alice in her arms.

Elnora turned to her and said, "I think I'll make a picnic and take the children outside to play for a while. We'll have our lunch down in the meadow. That way they can get rid of some their fidgets. Mark Anthony needs to stretch those chubby legs of his, and George is so squirmy, I'm beginning to fear for Prissy again."

"Oh, that sounds wonderful, Nora. It's such a beautiful day."

"Why don't you come with us?"

Vivian smiled a bit sheepishly. "I think I'd rather just sit and listen to the quiet for a little while. Selfish of me, isn't it?"

"Not at all," Elnora answered.

Once she had the lunch packed, she picked up Mark Anthony and shooed the rest of the children out the door in front of her. They all waved at Vivian, who stood in the doorway, watching them march off into the sunshine.

They found a perfect spot down in the meadow near a large cottonwood, not so far away from the house. Elnora spread a blanket out on the ground, half in the sun, half in the shade, while the children ran circles around her.

After she laid out the picnic, she called them to the blanket. They ate with a hunger born of fresh air, youth, and activity.

When they were done, they skipped off to play once again, making a fetching sight while they looked for crawly things and beat the meadow for gophers.

Leaning back on her elbows, the sun warming her face, Elnora allowed her gaze to wander languidly over the blue, blue sky, then back down to the children who played a short distance away.

Her thoughts turned to Russell, and she felt a sweet stirring within her breast. She had not seen him since the day of Alice's birth, but he was supposed to come for her tomorrow so that they could resume their quest. There were so few leads left, and Elnora wondered if maybe they never would discover who the author of the story really was—if maybe his identity would always remain a mystery.

Like Russell, she thought. In all the time they had spent together, he had never talked about his past or his family. It was almost as though he were two men—the one who looked at her with those deep, dark eyes and made her feel young and winsome and beautiful; and the other man who held himself away from her, away from everyone. A man with no past.

She wondered if she would ever have the answers to her questions. Time was ticking away quickly, and soon, whether Ransom returned or not, whether she and Russell ever discovered the identity of their author, she would be leaving Harmony. Sally's wedding was fast approaching, and she still needed a dress. It saddened her to think she might leave without ever telling Russell that she loved him. Could she—should she—tell him? she wondered. He had yet to fully reveal his feelings for her.

Elnora's mind lingered on those thoughts for quite some time until suddenly she noticed that the sun had all but disappeared. She lifted her gaze to the sky. It had grown dark and murky. A sudden gust of wind rippled across the meadow, and she felt a chill in the air that had not been there a moment ago.

Not terribly concerned, she picked up the book Russell had given her the day Alice had been born. She read a few pages, then glanced back up at the sky and felt a prickle of uneasiness. The sky had taken on a yellowish cast, and the gentle breeze of the morning had all but vanished. All around them everything was still as death, and a disturbing quietness had settled over the land.

Quite suddenly a flock of blackbirds, squawking loudly, left the sanctity of the cottonwood beside her, as though to seek shelter elsewhere.

Her instincts alerted, Elnora rose without further hesitation and hurriedly began packing the leftover items back into the picnic basket. "Come, children!" she called out to the four. "A storm is coming!"

She folded the blanket into a haphazard square and turned to find the children at her side. "Here, George." She handed the boy the blanket and cast another apprehensive glance toward the sky.

It was then she saw it.

Way out in the distance she clearly recognized the huge black swirling cloud for what it was.

"Oh, my," she whispered, her heart almost stopping dead within her chest. She swept Mark Anthony up into her arms. "Come, children! Hurry!" She started for the house, leaving the basket behind, hurrying Emily and Sara in front of her.

"What is it, Aunt Nora?" George asked, his short legs pumping at her side, while he cast a fearful glance over his shoulder.

"It's a twister." She tried to keep the panic from her voice, but it slipped through just the same. She gave each girl a none-too-gentle shove. "Hurry, girls!"

By the time they reached the yard, a wild wind had

picked up, gaining force by the minute. It whipped around her, tugging at her hair, tearing it loose. Her clothing pressed against her. Around her the air hummed, and an awful roaring filled her ears. Then the rain came. The drops were huge and pelted her and the children like stones, quickly and thoroughly wetting their clothing.

Mark Anthony began to cry, and Sara and Emily whimpered with fear.

Elnora went directly to the fruit cellar. She put Mark Anthony down between her legs and fought to get the doors open. When she finally did, she herded the children down the ladder, leaving them no choice but to obey her. Then she handed Mark Anthony to George and firmly ordered, "Stay there till I come for you. I'm going to get your mother and Alice." She climbed back up the stairs and, fighting the wind, lifted the doors from the ground to close them.

"Vivian!" Elnora cried out, running for the house, clutching her skirts high so they wouldn't trip her. She threw the kitchen door open wide, and the wind sent it crashing against the wall, sending two of Vivian's favorite teacups toppling off a shelf to the floor, where they shattered instantly.

Vivian ran from the parlor into the kitchen, her face marked with fear, Alice clutched in her arms. "Where are the children?"

"They're in the cellar," Elnora, said, gasping, breathless from her run. "Come." She held out her hand. "Hurry!"

Just then Gordon burst through the door. He grabbed Alice from Vivian's arms. "Let's go!" he yelled, raising his voice to be heard over the thundering wind. "I've already turned the animals loose."

They ran back out into the wind. The rain had

turned to hail. It pounded them with fury. They
glanced fearfully at the spinning column that was racing toward them. The pressure of wind was so fierce,
so intense, it hurt their ears. It took all three adults to
pry open the doors to the cellar, while Gordon held
a squalling Alice in one arm. Vivian and Elnora
climbed down the ladder first, then Gordon handed
Elnora the baby. He had to use every ounce of
strength he possessed to pull the doors shut behind
him.

Below, the children were crying. The three adults
gathered them close, while the wind roared above
them like a giant locomotive.

Despite her resolve to the contrary, Vivian began to
cry softly. Elnora hugged her close. "Sshh, Viv, don't
cry," she soothed.

"Sam and Andy," Vivian whispered in Elnora's ear
so the other children couldn't hear her. "What about
my other babies . . . ?"

"They'll be all right," Elnora returned confidently,
though she'd wondered the very same thing herself.
"Faith Hutton is a smart young woman. I'm sure the
boys are safe."

Then an awful deafening sound roared above them,
and the children screamed and clutched at the three
adults.

Within seconds the storm was over, and an eerie,
unnatural silence settled around them.

For several long moments the family huddled together, safe among last season's apples and vegetables, wanting to be sure the great spinning demon had
left—afraid of what they would find when at last they
emerged from their sanctuary.

Finally Gordon took a deep shaky breath. "I guess

we better get on outta here and see what's left of the farm."

"Papa," Sara sobbed tearfully, clutching at him, "what about Prissy?"

Gordon hugged her close and kissed her forehead. "Prissy knows enough to get outta the bad weather, honey. She's an old scrapper. The only thing she can't seem to avoid is George." He reached out into the darkness and found his son's head, ruffling his hair affectionately. Then he released Sara and climbed up the ladder. Taking another shaky breath, he used both arms and threw the double doors upward, letting them fall open onto the ground.

Amazingly enough, the sun shone down on them, heating them with its innocent brightness.

Cautiously Gordon stuck his head up out of the hole, while below, everyone waited with baited breath.

"Praise God Almighty," he whispered emotionally. Then in a much stronger voice he said, "She missed us!" He shot out of the cellar. "She missed us! How 'bout that!"

Elnora and Vivian helped the children up the ladder. They followed behind, stepping up into warm sunshine.

Gordon was right. The house and barn were still standing. But the Perry farm had not gone completely unscathed. There was nothing left of the chicken coop except kindling and feathers. The chickens that had survived were flapping around in circles, clucking and complaining loudly. Debris and tree limbs littered the yard, and the entire west corner of the barn roof was gone.

Yet they felt most fortunate to have fared so well.

Once Gordon had everyone settled in the house, he

turned to his wife and hugged her close. "I'm goin' on into town to get Sam and Andy."

She nodded.

"Meeeow." All heads turned to see Prissy come wandering out from under the kitchen table, sensuously stretching each of her back legs, as though she'd just awakened from a long luxurious nap.

They all laughed, feeling relieved by her seeming unconcern for the catastrophe that had just occurred. Gordon released Vivian and then strode out into the sunshine.

Elnora ran behind him, catching his sleeve. "Gordon!"

He turned to her.

Her eyes were dark with worry. "See if Russell is all right, would you?"

He studied her face a brief second, then leaned forward and kissed her cheek. "I will, Nora," he promised quietly. "Don't worry." Then he hurried off to the barn to get his horse.

Gordon met Russell on the road into town.

He was riding his horse, coatless, his expression marked with concern. The twister hadn't even been out of sight when he'd saddled his horse and set out for the Perry farm, his heart in his throat. "Hello, Gordon!" he called out before he'd reached the other man. "Is everyone all right at your house?"

Gordon reined in his horse, and Russell stopped beside him. "Everyone's fine," Gordon said, then paused a moment. "Nora's fine. She'll be glad to know you're all right, too." He watched as relief lifted some of the worry from Russell's face. "What about Harmony?" he asked, fearing the worst.

"We suffered a little damage, but not much. The

twister grazed the west end of town, causing a little damage to a few houses and business establishments."

"Anyone hurt?"

"Not that we know of. . . ."

Relieved, Gordon let his breath out, his eyes sinking shut.

"It's the children we're concerned about," Russell went on quietly.

Gordon's eyes snapped open, and his head came up.

"They didn't make it back before the twister hit. We're organizing groups to set out and look for them now."

"Oh, God," Gordon whispered, brushing a hand across his brow.

"I was riding out to check on you and your family, then Arthur and I were going to set out on our own." He thought a minute, then said, "I suppose we should ride back into town just to be sure they haven't shown up yet."

Gordon nodded, and together they rode for Harmony.

When they reached the school, they found a sizable group gathering outside the doors. Even Lottie McGee and several of her girls were in attendance, their expressions tight with worry.

Seeing Gordon, Mary and Samantha ran to greet him, their faces marked with concern. "Is everyone all right at your house, Gordon?" Mary asked.

Gordon nodded. "Everyone's fine."

"How about the Baileys and the Winchesters?" Russell asked. "Has anyone checked on them?"

"They're all fine," Mary said. "The Baileys are over there." She pointed toward the crowd. "And Edward and Fred rode into town just before you did."

Russell nodded and looked toward the school-house.

Kincaid Hutton, his face showing strain, stood on the top step, trying to gain some semblance of control over the panic-stricken parents.

Sheriff Travis Miller joined Kincaid on the step. He tipped his hat back from his dark blond hair and held his palms up, hoping to quiet the mumbling crowd. At thirty-five years old, he was well respected as Harmony's sheriff and had a way with calming the townsfolk. "We all know there are plenty of places Faith could have taken the children to. I'm sure they're fine. They're probably on their way home right this minute, so let's not lose our heads 'bout this. Everyone pair up and grab a lantern, and we'll get started. If all goes well, we'll all be home by night-fall."

Still on horseback, Russell turned to Gordon. "Let's stop by the store and get a lantern and Arthur, then we'll head out."

Gordon nodded and turned his horse to follow Russell back down Main Street.

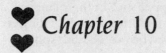 *Chapter* 10

THE TOWNSFOLK SPLIT up into small groups and fanned out in different directions, agreeing to meet back at the schoolhouse in two hours.

Russell and Gordon headed north, taking a rough, rarely traveled road that ran directly behind the schoolhouse.

Russell stole a look over at his companion. Gordon's face was stiff, his gaze constantly sweeping both sides of the road for any signs of Faith and the children. "We'll find them, Gordon," Russell assured him.

Gordon nodded but held his silence, hoping his friend was right.

Russell looked down at Arthur, who ran beside the horse, his nose lifted to the wind. "Go, Arthur. Find them," he ordered in a quiet but firm tone.

Arthur seemed to know what was expected of him. He shot down the road ahead of the men. After a short while he veered off the road into a field. The men followed, watching the dog sniff every pile of brush he passed.

"What do you think?" Gordon asked Russell after a few minutes. "You think he's on to something?"

Ahead of them Arthur sniffed a downed tree, then ran over to investigate a thick clump of brush. "Give him time," Russell said calmly.

Dusk came, and they stopped and lit their lanterns. Finally, growing weary and frustrated, Gordon looked over at Russell. "Maybe we should split up and set out in different directions."

Russell shook his head. "They're out here somewhere, or Arthur would be running beside us, not out there working the area the way he is. He smells them." He whistled sharply. Arthur was at the horse's side in a flash. "Come on, boy," Russell urged in a gentle but commanding tone, "find them!"

Arthur looked up at him, his golden eyes solemn. He whimpered and shot off once again, sniffing the ground furiously.

After a few minutes he lifted his head and went still as death. A low whimper escaped him, and his tail took to wagging. The whimper lengthened and became a series of sharp barks, and he raced off, disappearing behind a thick glade of trees.

Russell and Gordon kicked their horses and followed, each holding a lantern high to light the way.

Then they heard it.

"Help! We're trapped! Help us!"

The two men followed the voice and found Arthur barking with a frenzy in front of the mouth of a small cave. The opening to the cave was almost completely covered by a fallen oak tree.

Russell swung down off his horse and ran to the tree. "Faith! Is that you?"

"Oh, Russell," she cried out, "thank God, you've found us!"

Gordon was right behind him. He tried to peer through the branches to see the group hidden within the shallow mouth of the cave. "Everybody all right in there?" he asked, his heart thumping.

"We're all fine!" Faith called out. "But I'm missing Harry Taylor! He wandered off by himself, and I didn't have time to find him before the twister hit! So we hid in here, but the twister brought this tree down, trapping us."

"We'll find Harry," Russell said while he ineffectually pulled at the heavy trunk of the tree.

"Sam! Andy!" Gordon called out. He, too, pulled at the thick limbs, but the huge tree wouldn't budge.

"We're in here, Pa!" Sam hollered.

"Pa, I'm hungry!" Andy added.

Gordon's eyes slipped shut in relief, and he laughed a shaky laugh.

"We're going to need help," Russell said. "You stay here and keep everybody calm, and I'll ride back to town and get the others. We're going to have to cut this tree apart piece by piece to get it out of the way. Once I lead the others out to you, Arthur and I will set out and look for Harry."

"Hurry," Gordon said, slapping the other man on the shoulder.

Russell reached town in record time. He found several of the townsfolk back at the school, ready to set off on another search. "We've found them," he hollered, reining in his horse. "But they're trapped in a cave. A tree fell down in front of the opening. We need everyone to grab a saw and a lantern and follow me. I'll lead you to where they are."

James Taylor broke away from the crowd and rushed to his mercantile to get his tools.

Russell followed him. "James," he called out.

James turned.

Russell tugged on his horse's reins, his expression compassionate. "Harry isn't with them, James." Russell watched the color drain from the other man's face.

"That doesn't mean he's hurt or anything. It just means he's off somewhere on his own. We'll find him, though." He paused, then asked, "Can you get me something of his? Something that Arthur can smell his scent on?"

James was silent for a brief moment. "Of course," he said quietly and ran into his store. He came out a moment later with a scarf. Mary followed behind, her face drawn and tight. Lillie came out a moment later, holding her right palm pressed to her chest. She was unnaturally silent in her worry over her youngest son.

James handed him the scarf. "I'm gonna blacken that boy's hide when he gits home! It's just like him to do a crazy thing like this!" he whispered fiercely, finding strength in his anger. But both men knew he would do no such thing.

"Try not to worry, James." Russell lifted his gaze to the woman standing in the doorway and offered a reassuring smile. "Lillie, if anybody can sniff him out, Arthur can."

She nodded, and Russell turned his horse around and rode back to the schoolyard. Once there, he found all of the able-bodied males in town waiting for him.

"We're ready, Russ!" Travis called out. They mounted their horses, and Russell led the way.

The women waited behind, making preparations to tend any wounds that might exist when the group returned.

It didn't take Russell long to find the cave again. He'd left the lantern with Gordon, hoping that the children, seeing the light shining through the branches of the tree, would be comforted.

"Faith!" Kincaid called out, swinging down off his horse and running to the cave. "Are you all right?"

"I'm fine, Kincaid," she answered her husband. "Just get us out."

Some of the other fathers called out to their children and were greatly relieved when their children returned greetings.

Russell swung down off his horse. "You all right?" he asked Gordon.

"I'm fine," Gordon answered, although he felt exhausted. "Go find Harry."

"Arthur! Here!" Russell commanded. He took the scarf from his saddle and let the dog sniff it thoroughly. "Find him!" Russell ordered and swung back up onto his horse. He rode past James and said, "I'll be back as soon as I can."

The night had grown dark, lit only by a quarter moon and a few twinkling stars. Russell held his lantern high as Arthur ran ahead of him, zigging back and forth in an irregular pattern as he tried to pick up the boy's scent.

"Harry!" Russell called out, hoping the boy could hear him. "Harry Taylor!"

A hum of night sounds was his only answer. So he rode on, following Arthur, who led him off the road into a small clearing.

For a while he lost sight of the dog, but in time he was rewarded by the same low whimper he and Gordon had heard earlier when Arthur had found Faith and the other children.

A few seconds later Arthur began to bark furiously. His hopes rising, Russell guided his horse through the shadows toward the sound.

He came upon the remains of a cabin. The twister had reduced it to nothing more than a huge scrap pile of wood. Arthur ran frantically around the perimeters of the cabin, panting and whimpering.

Russell swung down off his horse, holding the lantern up. "What is it, boy?" he asked quietly. "Is someone under there?" He walked around to what had once been the front of the cabin, trying to assess the situation, while Arthur continued sniffing the pile of wood with a frenzy.

"Hello!" Russell called out. "Is anyone in there?"

Silence.

"Harry! Harry Taylor!"

"In here!" came the raspy reply.

Russell felt a rush of relief. "That you, Harry?"

Silence once again.

Arthur climbed up to the center of the pile and began to dig at something with vigor. Russell followed behind, trying to balance himself so he didn't fall through the shaky mess, while still holding the lantern high enough to light his way. When he reached the spot that Arthur was focused on, Russell found a place to prop the lantern so that it wouldn't topple over. Then he began to pick up pieces of wood, flinging them aside. "Hello!" Russell called out once again. "Can you hear me?"

"Yes." It was a hoarse whisper.

"Where are you?"

"Down here." The words were so muffled Russell could barely make them out.

"Hang on! We're going to get you out!" Russell threw aside another board, then another and another. Whimpering, Arthur backed out of his way. Russell worked on, his muscles straining. Sweat broke out on his forehead. Before long, his shirt was soaked clear through.

Finally he'd created a small opening, exposing the floor of the cabin. A little to the left he could see what appeared to be the trapdoor of the cellar. "Are you down in the cellar?'' he yelled.

"Yes," came the shaky reply.

Russell heaved aside a few more boards, fully exposing the door. He reached for his lantern and without hesitation pulled on the handle of the door, opening it. He shined the lantern down into the hole onto the face of the inhabitant.

His heart stopped dead.

Ransom Riley sat on the cellar floor, staring up at him, his right leg bent at an awkward angle.

But it was the expression on his face that unsettled Russell. It clearly mirrored his newfound discovery.

The two men studied each other in silence for a long moment, and Russell realized that the game was over.

"Hello, Walker," Ransom said at last.

Russell sat back on his haunches. After a few silent seconds he gave him a wry smile. "I wondered how long it would take you to figure it out, Riley."

"Long enough, I guess," Ransom said honestly, his expression growing sullen. "I suppose you've been chucklin' yourself sick over this."

"Not really," Russell answered truthfully, reaching his hand down to the other man. "Come on outta there."

Surprised at the other man's actions, Ransom held his hands at his sides and gave him a disgruntled look. "I can't," he said, his voice sulky. "I think my leg's broke."

Russell stared at him for a short while. "Well, how the hell did you do that?"

His voice full of self-disgust, Ransom explained, "I was in such a hurry to git away from the twister, I fell down this hole 'stead of climbin' down."

"How'd you get the door shut?"

Ransom shrugged. "Hell, I don't know. The wind blew it shut, I guess."

Incredulous, Russell retracted his hand. "You mean you can't get out of there on your own?"

"That's right," Ransom answered, peeved beyond words at his condition and also becoming more than a little worried.

Russell lifted an eyebrow. "I suppose you want me to come down there and help you."

His expression stubborn, Ransom didn't answer.

They stared at each other a long, long time, realizing the ramifications of their situation. They both knew Russell could very easily shut the door and once again bury the opening to the cellar. He could walk away as though he'd never found the other man, and Ransom could and probably would die before anyone else came along.

Russell rose to his full height, and Ransom knew fear. He watched the man disappear, his panic rising. But a moment later, Russell returned, propping his lantern into a hole near the cellar opening.

With a great sigh Russell turned and climbed down the ladder to the hard, dirt-packed ground below. "Come on." He stooped down, taking Ransom's arm and placing it around his neck, while he wrapped his arm around Ransom's waist. With a loud groan he hoisted the heavier man to his feet. "Anybody ever tell you you're heavier than a bull?" he asked, disgruntled.

Greatly offended, Ransom's brows dropped, but he kept his silence in lieu of loosing his rescuer.

Holding tight to Ransom's arm, Russell turned his back to the man. "Grab tight around my neck, and wrap your good leg around me. Hang on the best you can."

"Shit, I'll choke ya."

"Yeah, you probably will," Russell agreed dryly. "But I don't know how else to get you out of this hole."

Ransom did as he was told, and though their progress was slow, and Russell was gasping for breath and seeing stars for lack of air, he climbed the ladder rung by rung. When they reached the top of the opening, Russell clenched his teeth and said, "Let go of me and grab on to the door there." When Ransom did, Russell used one hand to push, as Ransom dragged himself up and out of the cellar. Once Ransom was out, Russell followed behind.

Together they collapsed onto the woodpile, panting. After a few minutes Arthur joined them and sat down between them, glancing curiously from one to the other.

"Arthur," Russell said quietly, "how the hell did you come up with him when we were looking for Harry?"

Arthur laid his ears back, whimpered, and wagged his tail.

"That who you were lookin' for?" Ransom asked, his tone surly. His leg was hurting him like the devil.

"Yep." Russell sighed. "I was."

They fell silent for some time, each lost in his own thoughts.

"I lost my goddamn horse," Ransom said more to himself than to Russell. "And my goddamn money. Hell, it's probably layin' all over some farmer's field by now."

"At least you're alive." Russell rose to his feet and picked up the lantern.

Narrowing his eyes, Ransom angled him a skeptical stare. "Why is that, Walker? Why am I alive?" When

Russell didn't answer him, he got mad. "Answer me, goddamn it! We both know you could have left me down there to rot!"

A half smile tugged at Russell's mouth. "That wouldn't've been playing fair, Riley." He offered his hand, and after staring at it a second, Ransom took it. Russell hauled the heavier man to his feet and wrapped an arm around his waist, steadying him.

"This ain't a game, Walker. They say you're a murderer."

"Do you believe everything you hear?" Russell asked evenly.

"Hell, no! To tell you the truth, I don't give a goddamn whether you killed anybody or not. I still plan to take you back to Detroit and claim my money!" He looked over at his rescuer. "Soon as we get to town, I'm tellin' Travis Miller who the hell you are, and I'm havin' you locked up. Once my leg is healed, you're goin' back where you belong—"

"You talk too damn much," Russell interrupted, not bothering to look at him. "Let's go. I'm tired. Besides, I have to get back and tell James I didn't find his boy."

With Russell's weight supporting him, Ransom awkwardly limped over the woodpile. He slid Russell a belligerent glance, his chin stubborn. "Just 'cause you saved my hide doesn't mean I owe you a thing," he went on defensively. "Not a goddamn thing, you hear me?"

"Never said you did." Russell stopped before his horse. Ransom held on to Russell's shoulder while Russell bent over. Locking his fingers together, he made a cup out of his hands. "Here. You ride. I'll walk. Both of us would be too heavy, and I'm not about to kill my horse."

Agitated by an odd jumble of conflicting emotions,

Ransom grumbled something unintelligible and placed his foot in Russell's hands. He grabbed the horn on the saddle, and allowed Russell to help him up onto the horse.

Grimacing, Russell straightened and placed a hand on his lower back. "Jesus, Riley, you're killing me." He went to get his lantern. "Arthur!" he called, then whistled sharply. Arthur came running, and, lantern in hand, Russell took the horse's reins and led the way through the murky darkness.

After some time Ransom's voice broke the silence. "Walker?"

"Yeah?"

"You sold Elnora that book. Why did you do it? You had to know I'd figure it out 'ventually. You might as well have turned yourself in."

Russell was silent a long minute. He'd often asked himself the same question and had yet to come up with an answer that made any sense. "I don't know why I did it," he said truthfully. "Maybe I was tired of running and hiding." He threw a glance over his shoulder. The light from the lantern revealed Russell's smile. "Maybe it was just a game. I don't know. It just seemed like the thing to do at the time."

"But how'd you know who I was?"

Russell gave a soft, short laugh. "Riley, I've been watching you for almost as long as you've been hunting me. I know more about you than you probably know about yourself." He paused a moment, then said, "I made it my business to know about the men who were most likely to hunt me. I wasn't a Detroit newspaperman for nothing."

Bewildered, Ransom thought about that all the way into town.

* * *

When they reached town, it was well past midnight. Russell went straight to the mercantile, even though he dreaded having to tell James and Lillie he hadn't found Harry. James was waiting up for him, and so was Harry, who had returned on his own, safe and sound.

He'd wandered off by himself, all right, but seeing the twister approaching, he had had enough sense to find a ditch and press himself into it. He'd found his way back into town while the men were still cutting away the tree that had trapped his teacher and classmates.

Russell was relieved to know the boy was safe.

He said his goodbyes to the Taylors, then his mind returning to more pressing matters, he went back out to join Ransom. "I'll take you on over to see Doc Tanner," he said and took the horse's reins once again, leading him toward the doc's office.

As they passed the Last Resort, Travis Miller came out of the saloon with Cord Spencer at his side. Seeing Russell and Ransom, the two men walked toward them.

Realizing the full impact of his predicament, Russell felt a heavy sadness overtake him. He thought of Elnora—he'd never told her he loved her. Well, maybe that was best. If he had told her, and if she had returned the sentiment, it would be all the more difficult to lose her, to see the condemnation in her eyes when she learned the truth about him.

His chest hurt as he thought of the future, stretching on empty and barren without her. Still, he reminded himself, when Riley handed him over to Marcus Powell, he would be lucky to live long enough to have a future of any kind.

"Hey, Russell!" Travis called out cordially. "Who ya got there?"

"Riley," Russell called back.

Cord laughed. "That sure as hell don't look like Harry Taylor on your horse." He smiled up at Ransom. "How ya doin', Riley?"

Ransom didn't answer him. His thoughts were in turmoil. Robert Walker had saved his life, knowing he would give up his own, or at the very least, he would give up his freedom.

Hell, what does it matter to you? Ransom asked himself. *Turn him in and you'll have all the money you need to start your life with Nora.*

"You hurt?" Travis asked, peering up at him. He shook a lock of his blond hair out of his eyes.

"My leg," Ransom found himself saying. "I think it's broke. I got buried under a cabin when the twister passed over. Walk—Whitaker found me."

Russell looked up sharply.

"I think I need to see the doc," Ransom went on.

"Well," Travis said, "hope you're feelin' better tomorrow."

"Me, too," Ransom said truthfully.

"Well, good night, fellas," Cord said and turned back to his establishment.

Puzzled, Russell took the horse's reins and led the way to Doc Tanner's office.

"We ain't done yet, you and me, Walker," Ransom promised, his voice not nearly as determined as it had been earlier.

"You're right about that," Russell replied.

"I still mean to take you in, so don't you think you can take off runnin'!"

Russell smiled into the night. "I wouldn't think of it, Riley."

* * *

Ransom's leg wasn't broken, however, it was badly sprained, and he had a pulled muscle so severe that Doc Tanner said he'd shoot him if he were a horse.

It took all of ten minutes, with Russell holding Ransom down as he moaned and groaned loud enough to wake the dead in three counties, for Doc Tanner to wrap his leg so that the pain wouldn't be so intense.

When the doctor was finished, Russell went over to the livery and got his rig, then returned and helped Ransom up into the seat. "I'm taking you out to Gordon's," Russell told him. "I figure your family will want to see you."

His leg throbbing, Ransom sulked all the way to the Perry farm, rankled by his predicament. The last thing he wanted was to be beholden to a murderer; worse yet, the murderer whose bounty he'd been dreaming about collecting for all of five years. It galled him so badly he almost feared he'd choke to death before he ever got home.

When they reached the farm, all was quiet, the house dark and still.

Russell jumped down from the rig and strode to the front door, wishing he didn't have to wake Gordon at this late hour.

Still, he was as anxious to be rid of his burden as his burden was to be rid of him—at least for the time being.

He knocked loudly on the door and waited. Within seconds a light showed in an upstairs window. A few minutes later Gordon opened the door.

"Russ," he said, surprised.

"Gordon," Russell greeted. "Sorry to wake you, but I've got Riley out in my rig." He thumbed in the direction of his buggy. "I found him buried beneath a cabin while I was out looking for Harry. He hurt his leg and pulled a muscle pretty badly, but other than that he's fine."

Gordon helped Russell get the big man out of the rig and into the house. They sat him down in a chair at the kitchen table, then turned when they heard someone coming down the steps behind them.

"My goodness! What's going on down here?" Elnora asked, tightening the belt of her robe around her narrow waist. Behind her Vivian followed, her expression one of confusion. Seeing the three men, Elnora stopped at the bottom of the staircase. Her eyes fixed on Ransom, then lifted to Russell.

She felt a sweet rush of relief and joy at seeing him safe, and as they stared at each other, their eyes spoke what their lips had not. Elnora wondered if Ransom could know, just by looking at them, the truth of their feelings for each other.

Ransom watched the silent exchange between the two, and jealousy pricked him sharply. Inwardly he seethed, for his instincts told him that much had occurred between them during his absence.

"Ransom!" Vivian cried and rushed to her brother's side. "What happened?"

"I hurt my goddamned leg and pulled a muscle. But I'm fine," he grumbled, not in the mood to relay once again how Whitaker had come to his rescue.

Vivian turned to Russell. "Thank you for bringing him home." Without hesitation she took his hand in her own and gave it a gentle squeeze, then said to her husband, "Let's put him in the back bedroom. That way he won't have to fight the stairs."

Gordon and Russell raised Ransom to his feet, and with Gordon on one side and Vivian on the other, they helped him down the hall, leaving Elnora and Russell alone.

Elnora crossed the floor to stand before him. "I'm so glad to see you." Her voice was soft but shaky with emotion. "I was so worried when the storm . . ." She left off as he gently laid his palm against her cheek.

"Sweet Nora," he whispered, a wry smile touching his mouth. She was mussed from sleeping, her hair hanging down her back loose and free. He thought her lovely.

She tipped her head, laying her cheek into his hand, her eyes closing.

He swallowed, feeling his life and his freedom ebbing away, even as he touched her. Soon he'd only be able to hold her in his dreams. "I was worried about you, too," he said and bent to place a kiss on her temple.

She opened her mouth as if to say something, but he stayed her, placing his finger against her lips.

Then he turned and left, leaving her to stare after him, her heart aching to share the newfound discovery of her love for him.

Exhausted, Russell lay awake in his bed, thinking, brooding.

If he had any sense, he knew he'd be packing his bags right now. By daybreak, Harmony could be far behind him.

Riley had given him a fair chance—a head start, an opportunity to continue his life of anonymity somewhere else.

But another life in another town held little appeal for him now. The years stretched before him, empty and long, leaving him feeling bereft and lonely.

A lifetime without Elnora would be no life at all.

So instead of running, he lay in his bed, staring up at the ceiling and fighting an intense wave of envy.

At this very minute Riley was sleeping under the same roof as Nora. When he woke tomorrow morning, he would eat the food that Nora's hands prepared; he would share the table where she ate. Her hands would tend him, her mouth would smile at him, and his eyes—her beautiful eyes—would look at him.

Russell groaned and rolled onto his side. *It's all your fault*, said a small voice from within. *You could have left him to die.*

No, Russell told himself, he couldn't have. No, Russell told himself, even though he knew Riley would take him back if he stayed.

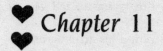 *Chapter* 11

"YOU'VE BEEN SEEING him!" Ransom accused the next morning when Elnora brought a breakfast tray to his room.

Blushing profusely, she placed the tray over his lap and asked, "What are you talking about, Ransom?"

His expression thunderous, he adjusted himself more comfortably in his bed. "You know damn well what I'm talkin' about. Whitaker!"

Her eyes widened as she feigned innocence, even while guilt pricked her sharply. "Russell?"

"Oh, so he's Russell now!" Ransom's green eyes flashed with jealousy. "What happened to 'Mr. Whitaker'?" He coated the title in a thick layer of sarcasm.

Irritation replaced her guilt, and Elnora shot him a disgusted look. "Will you please lower your voice? Does everyone in this family have to know the entire context of our personal discussion?" She dropped her gaze and gave special attention to straightening the coverlet on the bed. "Russell and I have been spending a good deal of time together, so it's silly for us to be calling each other by our formal names. In the beginn—"

"What the hell do you mean, 'spending time together'?" Ransom roared, his voice still loud enough to rouse a bear out of his winter's nap.

181

Refusing to be cowed by his anger, Elnora huffed and said, "Ransom, please. I'm trying to tell you, if you'll just let me finish."

His expression bullish, he folded his arms across his chest and waited.

"As I was saying," she went on calmly, returning to her task of straightening the bedclothes, "in the beginning we were spending time together mainly to pacify Maisie and Minnie. They wanted us to discover the identity of the author who writes the weekly series featured in the *Sentinel*."

"In the beginning?"

"Yes, in the beginning."

"And now?"

"Now . . ." Elnora raised her eyes to his, paused a moment, then quite honestly said, "There have been no proclamations of love between us, if that is what you mean."

They stared at each other in silence for several heated seconds, while Ransom's face purpled with fury. "I don't want you seeing him," he stated flatly.

Elnora straightened her back, and a fire lit within the depths of her eyes. She raised her eyebrows, and her determined, dimpled chin jutted forward ever so slightly. "I beg your pardon?" She blinked at him, once, twice.

"I said I don't want you seeing him! Not ever again!"

Her eyebrows lowered, and she propped her hands on her hips. "Since when, Ransom Riley, do you have the right to dictate who I can spend time with and who I can't? Need I remind you that I'm a fully grown woman and that we are not promised to each other?"

He jabbed an accusing finger at her, his face beet

red. "You said you'd wait for me!"

"I did wait for you." Her tone was even, but her gaze was not nearly so steady.

He studied her a long moment. "I was gonna ask you to marry me when I came home."

His words caught her off guard, taking the starch out of her stance. She stared at him openmouthed for a long moment. "I—I don't know what to say...."

Smitten by her sudden look of surprise, his affection for her overrode his anger, and he softened his next words. "There are things about Whitaker you don't know, Nora."

"Yes," she agreed, some of her spunk returning. She lifted her chin a notch. "I imagine there are." She raised one eyebrow. "And I'm quite sure there are things about you I don't know either, Ransom." With that said, she turned on her heel and left him to eat his breakfast alone.

Maisie and Minnie came to visit that afternoon.

"Is everyone all right here?" Maisie asked, glancing around the kitchen as though she expected the twister to have blown it away.

"We're fine," Elnora answered. "Gordon has some work to do around the farm, though. He lost part of the barn roof, and the chicken coop is in a shambles. But for the most part, we fared well."

"Praise the Lord!" Minnie exclaimed and sighed, seating herself at the table.

"How is everyone in town?" Vivian asked, joining the three women with Baby Alice in her arms.

"Fine. Fine." Maisie bobbed her head and smiled down on the baby.

The four women chattered for a while, comparing notes about this person and that, until finally Maisie turned to Elnora and pointedly asked, "So . . . when are you and Russell going to continue the search?"

The question took Elnora by surprise, especially after the discussion she'd had with Ransom just hours ago. "I'm afraid we've only a few more people to talk to," she answered quietly. "I'm not sure we'll ever discover your author for you. I'm sorry, ladies."

"But you must!" Minnie cried.

"Yes, you must!" Maisie repeated.

Elnora smiled, and Vivian laughed.

Maisie pouted. "Lady Elvia and Sir Ruggard have yet to find the blue diamond. They haven't given up. How can you?"

"It's not the same thing, and you both know it," Elnora chided with a gentle smile. "Sir Ruggard and Lady Elvia are fictional characters, created out of the mind of your author."

A knock sounded on the door, and Elnora rose to answer it.

She opened the door to find Russell standing on the porch, looking every bit as gallant and handsome as the silver knight who still haunted her dreams. "Russell . . ." Her voice was soft with surprise, warm with pleasure at seeing him.

"Nora . . ." He paused a second, knowing he was a fool to seek out a chance to see her again. But he simply couldn't help himself. He'd vowed to leave town by the end of the week, and he wanted to see her while he could. He wanted to be the one to tell her that he was going away. "We had plans today, I believe," he said at length.

Elnora stared up at him, her heart lifting. She had not expected him to keep their engagement, especially after the terrible day they'd all experienced yesterday. She thought a moment. "Why, yes, we do. But after yesterday I wasn't sure . . ."

"Are you up to it?"

Suddenly she felt up to almost anything. She turned and glanced over her shoulder at Vivian.

"Oh, go on, Nora. We'll be fine," Vivian said with a smile. "Have a good time."

Elnora turned back to Russell. "Of course I'm up to it. Just let me get my shawl."

From his bedroom window Ransom watched Russell hand Elnora up into the buggy. Furious, his pride wounded, he stepped back from the window and let the curtain fall back into place.

All right, Walker. You had your chance, goddamn it!

He limped back to the bed and struggled to get his trousers on. His good foot got caught, and he almost fell over onto the floor, but he caught himself on the edge of the bed, righting himself. Finally, with the aid of the makeshift crutch Gordon had brought him, he stood.

He limped down the hall, bumping into the wall every few feet, cursing a colorful stream of obscenities. When he reached the kitchen, the three women stared at him in bald surprise and shock.

"Ransom!" Vivian exclaimed. "Well, for heaven's sake! What are you doing out of bed?"

"I'm goin' to town," he grumbled bad-naturedly and thumped off toward the door.

Vivian rose from the table and handed Maisie the baby. "You'll do no such thing!" she said as she followed him.

He turned and fixed her with a stubborn gaze. "I'm goin' to town, Viv," he told her in a voice that said he would not be dissuaded. "I'll be home later." He ground his teeth together in pain and hobbled out onto the porch, grumbling new vulgarities every few steps.

She stuck her head out the door. "How are you going to get up on a horse?"

"I'll manage," he said without turning. "Just leave me be."

Heaving a disgusted sigh, Vivian stepped back into the house, her hands on her hips.

"Well, I never," Maisie said, exasperated. "Body hunters. Humph! A bad lot!"

Minnie shook her head in disgust. "He's a bull-headed one, isn't he?"

Vivian stared after him, a frown marring her pretty face. "As bullheaded as they come," she said quietly, knowing he was up to something and wishing she knew what it was.

The sun warm on their faces, Elnora and Russell headed out to visit Tom and Inga Lind—Faith Hutton's parents—on their farm.

When Russell and Elnora had talked to Faith about their quest, she'd jokingly told them that her father had sat at the kitchen table many a cold wintry night, telling his children stories about knights and fair ladies, about sorcerers and dragons.

Since Russell and Elnora were fresh out of leads, they figured the Lind farm was the only place left to go.

The truth was he wanted to spend one more day with her.

The truth was she wanted one more day with him, too.

After they'd ridden along for a while, she turned to him. She looked up at him, glad no helmet hid the beauty of his silvery blond hair.

He looked down at her, his smile warm. "I'm glad you came for me today."

His smile held strong, but his usually smiling eyes clouded. "I am, too."

Her gaze dropped to her folded hands. "I suppose our search will soon be over...." Oh, how she wished it wouldn't. Oh, how she wanted to confess all she felt for him, but she held her silence, uncertain of his feelings for her.

"I suppose so..." he returned in an unusually husky voice, wishing he had the right to share his life with her, wishing for all the world that things could be different.

Saddened by their thoughts, they rode on in silence, each savoring the moments they still had, wishing they could say all that was in their hearts, wishing their quest would never end.

By the time Ransom made it into town, he was furious. He'd taken Trudy, Gordon's oldest mare, hoping her gait would be smoother than the young gelding's. But the old mare's back was so swayed, her hips so bony, Ransom's backside literally ached from the bumpy ride, and his bad leg hurt him so much he almost felt like bawling.

And it was all Walker's fault, by damn.

Embarrassed, his ego stung by his predicament, he slipped off the old mare as gracefully as possible, glancing covertly around him, hoping no one had witnessed his humiliating ride into town. Using his crutch, he hobbled up the steps to the mercantile and banged his way through the door.

Seeing him, James came out from behind a counter that was littered with jars of peppermints and other sweet treats. "Ransom! How are you?"

"I've been better," he grumbled.

James rushed to his side. "Here, let me help you."

Ransom waved him off with a frown. "I don't need your help. What I need is to send a message by telegraph. Can you do that?"

"Of course. Come on over here," James said pleasantly and motioned to a desk in the corner of his large store. He led the way past a table stacked with linens and other fine materials. "Sit down and make yourself comfortable." He gestured to a side chair, while he settled himself in the one in front of the desk. He waited while Ransom awkwardly lowered himself into the chair, then asked, "Now, who is it you want to send the telegram to?"

Ransom's face was grim. "Marcus Powell in Detroit, Michigan."

James clicked out the message with patience. "And what do you want it to say?"

Ransom paused a second, feeling an uncomfortable bolt of shame course through him. He squelched it quickly, thinking of the reward that would soon be his, thinking of Nora and their future. "Just say, 'The search is over. Meet me in Harmony, Kansas, as soon as possible. Bring the money. Riley.' "

"That's all?" James lifted a curious eyebrow.

Ransom nodded brusquely. "That's all. He'll know what it means."

Nora and Russell's trip out to the Lind farm yielded them nothing more than sunburnt noses.

Tom and Inga Lind were as pleasant a couple as any two people could be. They were openly affectionate with each other and, like Gordon and Vivian, were the parents of seven children. But when Elnora asked Tom Lind if he was the author of the series, he just chuckled, while Inga teased, "He'd better not be! Whoever that man is, he's sweet on you, Elnora!"

On the way home Russell and Elnora were as silent as they'd been on the ride out to the Lind farm. They felt their time together slipping away, like sand through their fingers, yet each felt unable to stop the flow.

They rode on, and the sun slipped slowly into the western sky, casting a peachy glow across the horizon. The wind whispered gently through the treetops, teasing Nora's and Russell's hair, kissing their cheeks.

Unable to stand another silent moment, Elnora abandoned prudence and was determined to express her feelings. She turned in the seat to face Russell and placed her hand over his. He pulled lightly on the reins to stop the horse, and turned to her, his eyes questioning.

As she looked up at him, her expression was soft and vulnerable, but her voice was steady. "There is something I must ask you. Something I must know. I am not a young schoolgirl with my entire life stretching out ahead of me. I don't have time to play co-quettish games, nor do I have the heart for it. I never did. I'm a grown woman with a grown woman's heart." She swallowed, suddenly afraid, her heart thumping, knowing she needed to know the truth for herself, for him. "If I never know anything else, Russell, I would like to know this one thing."

Russell sensed danger. His eyes slipped shut, and he brought her tiny hand to his mouth. "Nora," he said softly, wishing he had the strength to stop her, knowing he didn't.

She took a deep, almost painful breath. "Do you care for me, Russ?"

He opened his eyes, and his hand found her cheek

in a gentle caress. "Oh, Nora," he whispered, "you know I do."

Her eyes became suspiciously damp, but her gaze remained direct and determined. "Do you love me?"

He stared at her a long moment, while her heart thudded and the wind lifted a chestnut curl away from her face. When he finally spoke, his voice was thick with emotion. "I love you more than I can ever tell you, more than I have ever loved anyone in my entire life. I believe I would gladly lay down my life for you."

A soft sob escaped her. "Why have you never told me?" she asked, her voice a fierce whisper, her honey-gold eyes anguished.

His expression became as pained as her own. "Because I thought it best that I didn't. I thought it best for you."

"But why?"

He shook his head, and she knew the depths of her frustration. Confused by his refusal to explain, she spoke the first thought that came into her head. "Is it because you have a wife?"

"No," he answered quietly, a shadow of a smile pulling at his lips. "I have no wife, Nora. If I did I would want her to be you."

The words touched her, igniting a latent fire, shooting warm darts throughout her body. "Then what? What is it?"

Russell heaved a heavy sigh, his expression sober, his dark eyes solemn. "I'll be leaving Harmony very soon, Elnora. I wish I could tell you why, but I can't. It was selfish of me to spend this time with you, to kiss you, to hold you, to fall in love with you. But I couldn't help it. I wanted a chance to know you. And I had that chance." He gave her a sad smile. "It was the best time of my life, Nora. You're like sunshine, only better. Your warmth and beauty never fades."

"Oh, Russ . . ." She dropped her gaze, her emotions in turmoil. She took his hand and pressed her lips into his palm. "Don't you see? There is nothing you could tell me that would change the way I feel for you."

But he didn't believe her. So he held his silence and placed a tender kiss on her lovely mouth. It wasn't until he was on his way home that he realized she had never said exactly what she did feel for him.

But he knew. He knew.

That night Ransom made a point to seek Elnora out.

He waited until the children were tucked into bed and Vivian and Gordon were seated in the parlor; then, before she could slip off to her room, he came up behind her and touched her arm. "We have to talk," he told her firmly.

Disturbed by his tone, she finished straightening the kitchen, then grabbed a shawl and followed him outside.

The moon was a thin crescent above them. Out in the yard fireflies had begun their twinkling dance in earnest.

Ransom took her arm and led her toward the barn, to the very spot they had shared that wintry Christmas Eve many months ago. He hooked his foot on the bottom rung of the fence and rested his arms on the top rung while he stared off into the distance. "Nora . . . I'm sorry about this morning."

She pulled her shawl tighter, feeling a sudden chill in the late April air. "You needn't be. I think I understand."

He turned his head to look down at her. "I don't think you do."

She gazed up into his face and, once again, realized the truth of her affection for him. She loved him. But she loved him as she loved Gordon, the way she loved all her brothers. Time would not change that. Neither would marriage. She read in his eyes what few people ever did—vulnerability and integrity—and she felt the need to tell him the truth. She was sorry to hurt him, but she knew she would be sorrier still to marry him and regret it for the rest of her life. Even if she and Russell could never be together, even if she were to go to her grave a lonely old maid, she could not take advantage of Ransom. She knew she could never be the wife he needed, the wife he deserved. He deserved a woman who would love him with her whole heart.

"Ransom . . ." Her voice was gentle. "I have to tell you something."

"No, Nora, listen—"

"Please—"

"Nora—"

"I'm in love with Russell Whitaker," she blurted.

He looked as though he'd been kicked in the stomach. He stared at her for a full twenty seconds, then dropped his boot to the ground with a heavy thud. He turned to face her fully. "You don't know what you're sayin'!" he boomed, taking her roughly by the shoulders.

"Yes, I do," Elnora returned evenly, her chin set with determination. "I know you think I've played you false, and maybe I have. I know you don't like him for some reason. But I love him, and he loves me." Her eyes begged for his understanding. "I didn't plan to fall in love with him, Ransom. I just did. I don't even know if we can be together, I—"

"Stop it, Nora. Stop it right now! You don't know

what you're sayin'!" His brow tight with frustration, Ransom gave her shoulders a rough shake.

"Ransom, please—"

"He's a murderer, Nora!" he yelled, unable to stop himself. "He's the man I've been huntin' all these years! He's not who you think he is!"

The blood drained from her face, and she went deathly still. Slowly her gaze lowered to his chest.

The seconds ticked by; the stars twinkled; the fireflies danced. . . .

"Do you hear me, Nora?" His face was close to hers, so close he could see the slight trembling of her bottom lip as she digested his statement. Her pain was so evident, so tangible, he was suddenly very sorry to have told her, suddenly very sorry he had ever discovered the truth about Russell Whitaker. "Aw, Nora . . ." he said in a pained voice and tried to pull her into his embrace.

But she stayed him, placing her palms flat against his chest. "I hear you," she whispered tonelessly, refusing to look at him. "I hear you." She took a step back, and his arms fell from her shoulders.

Then very slowly she turned and stiffly walked back to the house.

In the opulent study of an impressive house in the richest section of Detroit, Marcus Powell sat in a leather chair and reread the telegram he held in his hand.

"At last," he said to the man who stood before him. "At last we have him."

He stood and paced a determined path over the elegant expanse of the imported Oriental rug that graced the floor while he smiled to himself and felt a rush of elation and relief.

"When do you want to leave, sir?" asked a tall, thin, balding man who stood in the doorway.

"At dawn." Powell turned and smiled over his shoulder. "I won't give him another chance to get away."

"And when we get to Harmony?"

"We pay Riley his money and we take Walker into custody."

"And then?"

"Then," Powell said quietly, his mind clicking over his plan, "Robert Walker will mysteriously disappear, just like he did those many years ago, and no one will ever know we ever found him."

"What about Riley? He'll know."

Marcus strode to his desk and poured himself a generous measure of his best bourbon, not bothering to offer any to the other man. He raised the glass to his nose, sniffed, then savored the rich taste on his lips. "Riley will be too busy counting his money to waste a second thought on Mr. Walker."

"I hope you're right, Mr. Powell."

"Collins," Powell said with a harsh glint in his eye, "I've only been wrong once in my life. That was when I tried to buy Walker's silence. I should have killed him then and been done with it."

It was well past midnight when Elnora eased from her bed. She gave no thought to prudence or propriety. She forgot there was a time, not so very long ago, when she would not have thought of leaving her bed at such an hour, let alone leaving her bed to seek out a man.

But that was another time and another woman. That was before she'd met Russell Whitaker and before she'd fallen in love with him.

Her hair hanging loose and free down her back, she dressed in only the briefest of undergarments and a simple skirt and blouse. Then, holding her shoes in her hands, she slipped down the staircase, silent as a shadow.

She took her shawl from the peg near the door and made only the softest click as she opened and closed the door behind her.

Once on the porch she put her shoes on, then ran as swift and light as the wind across the yard to the barn.

Saddling a horse was a difficult task for such a small woman, but she persevered, her determination giving her a strength a much larger woman would not have been able to muster.

When she was finally sure she had everything in place and firmly buckled, she swung up into the saddle. Then she pulled her skirts up in the middle for comfort and rode for Harmony.

♥ Chapter 12

ELNORA RODE DOWN Main Street, her mind focused on only one thought: She had to see Russell.

She'd lain awake for hours, waiting for the household to quiet, her heart aching, her mind replaying Ransom's angry words over and over again.

Was he telling the truth? She had to know. She couldn't let Russell leave Harmony until she did.

She rode past Harmony's two saloons, where lights still glowed in their windows. A soft hum of voices came from the buildings and mingled with the dulcet twitter of the crickets.

From somewhere far out in the distance a wolf howled, and from somewhere much closer an owl hooted softly.

When she reached the bookstore, she reined in the horse and slipped from the saddle, then led the horse around to the rear of the building and tied him to a post near the back door.

Without hesitation she climbed the porch steps and knocked at the door.

Her heart pounding, she waited, hearing muffled sounds of movement coming from within. Then he opened the door and was standing before her.

They stared at each other in silence for a moment, their eyes speaking volumes. There was no pretense of surprise. They both knew why she had come.

His silvery hair was tousled, and he was clad in only his trousers and a white shirt that he'd not taken the time to button. His expression solemn, he stepped aside, holding the door open for her. "Come in, Nora," he said softly and allowed Arthur to slip past her out onto the porch.

Without a thought to convention, she entered his private room for the first time, noting with a quick sweep of her gaze how masculine yet how tidy everything seemed. The room was lit by the soft glow of a lamp that sat on a dark polished desk. The desk stood against the wall, facing a window to the east. In the middle of the room a large four-poster bed held court. On the far wall, directly in front of her, was a fireplace and a leather wing chair. Beside the chair stood a small square table, on which sat a short stack of books.

The fire in the grate had burned down to nothing more than a glowing heap of embers. Silently Russell closed the door behind her. Noting her sudden shiver, he went to the fireplace and added a log, sending a burst of smoke shooting up the chimney. He took a poker and settled the log into place. Within seconds, hungry flames ignited, adding warmth to the chilly room.

Slowly he straightened and turned to face her. Their gazes locked. His dark eyes were sad, bereft of amusement. Hers were rife with questions and doubt.

They stared at each other in silence for what seemed like an eternity, until Elnora could stand it no longer. "Who are you?" Her question was an intense whisper.

He looked to the floor and sighed deeply while he pocketed his hands and searched his mind for the

right words. There were no right words, he realized
with a heavy heart. There was only the truth, and
though he could offer her little else, he could offer her
that.

"My name is Robert Walker," he said quietly.

Her eyes slipped shut.

He crossed the room to stand before her. Gently he
took her by the shoulders. "I'm sorry, Nora. I never
meant to hurt you."

She opened her eyes and searched his face. "Who
is Robert Walker?" She paused a moment, and when
he didn't answer, she said, "I have to know."

A sad smile caught at his lips, and he nodded, understanding her need. He allowed his hands to slip
from her shoulders down to her hands. "Come. Sit
down, Nora. It's a long story." He led her to the chair
near the fireplace and waited until she was seated.
Then he pushed his hands down into his pockets once
again and began to pace the room.

"My name is Robert David Walker," he repeated
quietly. "I'm from Detroit, Michigan. I'm the oldest
of three children. I have a younger brother, Patrick,
and a younger sister, Laura. They're both married and
have children of their own. My parents are dead.
They died within a few years of each other." He
turned to her and gave her a wry smile. "I'm a reporter—a newspaperman by profession. At one time
it was said that I was one of Detroit's finest."

At her soft gasp his smile grew sad once again.
"Does that surprise you?"

She thought a moment, her eyes fixed on his face,
then honestly said, "No. I should have known all
along. It suits you somehow."

"Well," he said and gave a short humorless laugh,
"I loved it at the time. It was exciting and sometimes

dangerous work." He resumed his pacing. "Unfortunately not everyone loved me. I had a way of irritating people—of upsetting the cart, so to speak. There were certain influential men in our city who were involved in some rather questionable activities. I didn't hesitate to investigate their dealings and write about them—once I was sure of the truth. If I believed something was unjust, I said so. If I discovered some source of corruption, I exposed it, regardless of the consequences to the guilty individual. . . ."

His steps halted, and he took a deep breath, his dark gaze returning to her once more. "I guess I was an idealist of sorts. I paid a price for my idealism, though." He grew silent a few moments and looked down at his bare feet. "There is a man named Marcus Powell. . . ." His tone grew bitter. "He's very rich and very powerful. He's involved in politics, and his aspirations to political office are lofty. I know things about him that could ruin his chances of ever serving high office in this country. I know things about him that could put him behind bars for the rest of his life."

He lifted his gaze and stared unseeing at the wall before him. "It all started as a small thing actually. I was investigating some of Powell's financial dealings in the city, and before I knew it I was caught up in something much bigger than I had anticipated. I discovered how he'd made his money, which led to my discovery of the role he played during the war." Russell looked at Elnora. "He's a traitor to his own country. He made a fortune by playing both sides of the government during the war, with little regard for the lives of the men on either side. If that truth is ever known, he'll be ruined." He gave a brief derisive laugh. "I made the stupid mistake of letting him know what I knew. . . ."

He took a deep breath and pulled his hands from his pockets. "He knew of my investigations, and one night he and one of his henchman, a man named Bradley Collins, came to my apartment. Powell offered to buy my silence, then he offered me a job. I turned him down on both offers. Although I didn't say so, I planned to write the story that night and give it to my editor in the morning. Anyway, Powell left in a fury, and I wrote the story that night. I didn't fall asleep till almost dawn.

"I was awakened by the police banging on my door. When I went to see what they wanted, there was a man lying in front of my door. He was dead. I knew him. His name was Jack Sloan. He was one of my connections. He used to work for Powell. He was the one who'd helped me gather the information on Powell.

"The police hardly gave me time to finish dressing, let alone a chance to defend myself. They hauled me downtown and locked me up. I figured Powell had bought them off. But I wasn't really worried. I knew I was innocent, and I figured my lawyer would prove it sooner or later."

He gave a dry laugh, and his smile grew bitter. "But I had no idea the extent his power could reach. Not only had he bought the police off, but also he'd bought off my lawyer, who I thought was my friend. I soon found out no one could help me, not even the *Detroit Times*, the paper I worked for.

"They couldn't actually prove I had killed Sloan in cold blood, but they had enough trumped-up evidence to put me away for a very long time. Before I knew what was happening, I was on my way to prison."

Elnora listened, her heart aching for him. "What

happened to the story you'd written about Powell?"

"It disappeared." Russell cocked his head to the side, his brows lifting in a gesture of self-mockery. "Most conveniently."

"Oh, Russ . . ." she said in an anguished whisper.

He went on as though he hadn't heard her. "I knew he would have me killed at the first opportunity. He would never rest until he knew I was silenced forever. He would have killed me the night he came to see me, but he knew it would be too obvious that way, especially since my editor knew I was working on a story about him. So he set me up instead for a murder I didn't commit, planning to have me killed later.

"I knew he wouldn't wait too long. He couldn't take a chance that my friends or family might be willing to help me prove my story even though I was behind bars. So I planned my escape and bided my time." Russell offered Elnora a shadow of a grin. "Powell would have been furious to know he was the one who gave me my chance. Apparently he'd hired someone within the prison walls to kill me. To that man's credit, he tried by knifing me in the back.

"I was hurt pretty badly, but obviously not fatally. The prison guard sent a doctor to my cell to clean and bind the wound. I saw my chance and took it." Despite himself, Russell grinned again. "I'm afraid I scared the doctor to death, but I didn't harm him. I merely relieved him of his clothing and money, gagged him, tied him up in my cell, and walked on out as though I were him. It was easier than I'd ever anticipated. When I was sure I was a safe distance away, I wired my sister a message, and she sent me the money I'd been smart enough to place in an account in her name.

"I found Harmony by accident really. I'd planned

to head farther west, maybe even take a ship out of a San Francisco port and settle in some remote part of the world. I hoped to return someday, prove my innocence, and expose Powell for the traitor and murderer he is.

"But when I stopped here I knew this was where I could fit in, where I could live peaceably and still keep an eye on what was happening with Powell." He shrugged a shoulder. "So Russell Whitaker was born, along with Whitaker's Bookstore."

"What about Ransom?" Elnora asked. "What role does he play in all this?"

"When I first made my escape, Powell must have been frantic. It wasn't long before I saw sketches of myself popping up in every town I passed through. He must have sent them out all over the country. He was offering the reward himself, in an amount far exceeding anything the government would have offered."

He gave her another wry smile. "The government did not put near as much value on my hide as he did, you see. Anyway, every bounty hunter in this country would have loved to collect that money. So I shaved off my mustache, grew my hair a little longer, and kept an eye on the papers while I did my own share of investigating to find out the names of the best bounty hunters in the country. Ransom Riley was one of the best. So I learned everything I could about him.

"Most of the others gave up the hunt after the first two years, but somehow I knew Riley never would. It was a coincidence that Vivian was his sister and that he came to town to visit on occasion. I hadn't planned on that."

His voice grew soft and wistful. "It was a coinci-

dence that I met you. . . ." He paused. "I did not plan
on you either, Nora."

Their gazes met and held, and time seemed to stop.
With a rush of relief, she realized she had not been
wrong about him. He was a good man, the finest. He
was the man she loved.

She rose from her chair and crossed the floor to
stand before him. While she gazed up into his handsome, beloved face, she forgot that she had once been
proper and concise, that she had once been predictable and conventional. She simply remembered that
life was a tenuous chain of events, often full of sur-
prises—some wonderful, like Alice's birth, some dev-
astating, like the twister that had ripped through
Kansas two days ago.

She knew she would be a foolish woman indeed
not to take a chance at tasting love, even it meant she
would never taste it again.

Her heart pounding with determination, she said,
"I love you, Robert Walker, Russell Whitaker—whoever you are." She went up against him, and a moment later she heard his deep groan and felt the
reassuring weight of his arms embrace her, pulling
her close.

They stood that way a long time, hardly breathing,
letting their emotions soar freely for the very first
time.

Emboldened by her love for him, Nora placed her
palms on his chest, then slowly slipped them inside
the open wedge of his shirt, pressing it back, feeling
his warm, hard flesh beneath her hands. "Oh, my,"
she whispered, her eyes on his chest, "look at you."
He was beautiful indeed, and look at him she did. His
chest was wide and firm and covered with a light
dusting of silvery-blond hair. She closed her eyes and

slid her hands up to his nape and touched his sun-kissed hair, threading it gently between her fingers, reveling in its softness.

Trembling beneath her touch, his heart thudding wildly, he took her hands from his neck and held them clasped to his chest, stilling any further exploration. She opened her eyes and stared up at him in confusion. Her face was lovely and stark, her eyes wide and questioning. Her hair hung down past her shoulders in thick chestnut waves, and he felt an intense desire to touch it, to wrap his fingers in its length.

His eyes dropped to the hollow of her throat, where a light pulse beat visibly and every bit as rapidly as his own. He was suddenly conscious that each second that passed threatened to shatter his control.

"You should go, Nora," he told her in a hoarse voice, struggling with himself to do the noble thing.

Hurt by his suggestion, she shook her head. "I don't want to go. I—"

He pressed his fingers to her mouth, stopping the words before she could utter them and strip him of any chivalry he might still possess.

He saw her swallow, watched her bottom lip quiver with a sudden uncertainty, and the need to hold her one last time overrode any other thought. He reached for her, pulling her into his embrace almost roughly. "I love you, Nora," he whispered hoarsely. "I love you. I love you . . ." The words became an intonation on his lips, a music sweeter than any she had ever heard.

"Who would have thought . . ." she murmured, leaving the rest unsaid, feeling a river break loose within her heart and wash over her with a miraculous, healing sweetness.

Her arms, so long denied, curled around his neck, and she pressed her mouth into his hard shoulder, kissing him, tasting him, wishing the moment could last forever.

They stayed that way, clinging, their hearts thrumming, holding tight to what little time they had.

When she lifted her head and looked up at him, he lowered his head to kiss her, finding open lips, soft and waiting, wanting and willing. He touched them with his tongue, and she responded in kind. Passion took flight and bore them up on a journey beyond reason. With a painful sound deep in his throat, Russell deepened the kiss, and it turned hungry. Their tongues danced and stroked, searching, learning, leaving them both breathless and aching for more. His mouth moved over hers restlessly, as though he couldn't get enough of her.

His hands slipped from around her back to her waist, then down to her hips, bringing her flush against him; and despite her soft gasp of surprise, his hands slipped around to cup her buttocks gently.

He lifted his head and gazed down at her. Her eyes were closed, and her dark lashes trembled upon her pale cheeks.

Sighing, he rested his cheek on the soft crown of her head. "Oh, God, Nora. You're fine and pure and special, the kind of woman a man courts and woos and, if he's lucky, eventually wins for his wife. I don't want to hurt you. I don't want to leave you with nothing but my memory."

She pulled away slightly and looked up into his face. "All of my life I've wondered about love, while I've spent most of my life giving to others, loving others. And I'm not sorry. I was glad to do it. But for all that I loved them and they loved me, I've never had

anyone of my very own. Someone who loved me—
not for what I could do for them or for what I could
be for them, but simply loved me for who and what
I am. I've never had this—what I have with you, at
this moment, right now. . . ." She left off, offering him
a tremulous smile. "It's worth everything to me to
have this time with you. Even if after we are done all
I'll have left is your memory. Don't you see, your
memory is so much more than I've ever had before."

Her eloquent words moved him, and he swallowed
the knot in his throat. "I could leave you with a baby,
Nora. Don't you understand that?" The thought
frightened him. How would she ever manage alone if
there was a child? And what about her reputation?
Taking a chance wouldn't be fair. It wouldn't be right.

He mentally weighed his choices, as he'd futilely
done so many times in the past twenty-four hours: He
could not take her with him. She would be in danger
with him. If he stayed, Riley would take him in eventually. Riley had only given him a head start out of
some sense of fair play.

"Nora," he said, "if I left you with a baby . . ."

Her eyes misted, and she gave him a tender, wistful
smile. "Then you would leave me with much more
than a memory, wouldn't you?"

His throat burning, he tried to muster a disapproving frown. "I would leave you as fodder for the gos-
sips, Miss Perry."

"Imagine that," she said softly, lifting an eyebrow.
"What an interesting notion."

He stared at her a long moment, his need to protect
her warring with his need to love her. "I love you,
Elnora Perry."

"I love you, too. . . ."

His expression solemn, his deep brown eyes earnest, he asked her one last time, "Are you sure?"

She smiled up into his face. "I've never been more sure about anything in my entire life."

So he took her hand and led her to the bed.

When he turned to face her, she read the hesitation in his eyes, even while she felt the heat of passion in his touch. "Please," she said, placing a palm to his bare chest, "don't make me wonder any longer, Russ."

His eyes full of love, he stooped before her, taking her hands and placing them on his shoulders for balance. Gently he took her shoes off, placing each one beneath his bed, noting with a sudden flash of amusement that she wore no stockings. Elnora Perry, riding about in the dead of night without her stockings. Who would believe it?

He stood, and very slowly his hands found the buttons on the front of her blouse. His gaze holding hers, he undid each one. Then, with silent reverence, he peeled the blouse away from her shoulders and bent and kissed each shoulder.

She sighed and slid his shirt off his shoulders, down his arms, to the floor below.

He pulled back and let his eyes drift over the thin cotton shift that covered her, his gaze fastening on the vague impression of her tiny nipples pressing against the soft fabric. His throat suddenly tight, his breathing labored, he reached for her waist and unfastened the button on her skirt, then sent it sailing down her hips to join his shirt on the floor.

She stood before him, clad only in her shift and bloomers, without the protection of a corset or a bustle or even her staunch Presbyterian propriety. She wasn't afraid. Her hands found the waist of his trousers and unbuttoned them. He helped her and soon he was standing before her, tall and naked and lean and far more beautiful than she had ever imagined him to be.

His control weakening, he untied the ribbons on her shift, then parted it and slipped it down over her shoulders, baring her breasts to his view. His gaze lingered there for several seconds.

"God, Nora," he said as his hands came up and gently cupped the small perfect globes, "you're so lovely." Wanting to see the rest of her, he rolled the garment down over her hips, catching her bloomers with it, letting them float down to lie around her tiny bare feet.

She stepped free of her clothing and, for the first time in her life, stood unclothed before a man. She was not ashamed; she was only glad that the man who stared down at her was the man she loved.

Unable to wait any longer, he took her hand, and they stretched out on the bed.

His hand found hers, and she felt only the slightest hesitation, but it soon faded into infinity. He whispered soft words of love and touched her, oh, how he touched her, kissing, skimming, exploring breasts, belly, and lower . . . his hands working a magic all their own, drawing from her a series of soft gasps and surprised sighs.

"It's so much nicer than I ever imagined it to be," she whispered, her voice holding a note of awe and wonder.

"How did you imagine it to be?"

"I don't know. Not like this."

They kissed once more, hearts drumming, hands searching, and after a while he took her hand and placed it on the most intimate part of his body. Her eyes raised and locked with his. He was firm and smooth and hot, wondrously different from herself, and she didn't know what to do next.

But her confusion lasted only the sparest of moments, as his lips found hers again and they came alive together. While the lamplight glowed and the night sounds floated in through the partially open window, he rolled over and hovered above her, pressing his body to hers with promise.

"Nora . . ."

"Yes . . ."

"I love you. . . ."

She smiled up at him and knew her quest was about to end. Anticipating the discovery, she opened to him, inviting him to ease himself into her virgin body, while tears of joy leaked from her eyes and down the sides of her face.

"Oh, my," she said softly, unable to express all she felt.

He went still within her, letting her adjust. "Hurt?" he asked, pressing his lips to her shoulder, willing himself to wait for her acceptance of him.

"Oh, no . . . no . . . it's . . . it's wonderful. . . ."

A ghost of a grin caught at his mouth. "Why, Miss Perry," he whispered, "whatever would the ladies think?"

She shut her eyes and chuckled softly. "They'd think I'm quite wicked, I suppose. . . ."

He lifted his head and began to move with care. "You're not wicked, Nora. You're just a healthy, wonderful, woman. You're . . ." He left off, unable to continue speaking as desire overtook him. His strokes became silken and smooth, harder and deeper. Overcome by the depths of her newfound passion, she arched and gasped and drew him deep, her arms clasping his wide shoulders as together they moved as one. Their joining was tender and lush, sweet yet somber. It was music, a unique melody, much more beautiful than she had ever hoped it would be.

In time she was surprised anew by a sudden liquid swell of sensation, followed by his powerful shudder and his deep groan of release.

Then came the beautiful stillness that followed, broken only by their labored breathing and the solemn ticking of the clock on his fireplace mantel.

He lay upon her, sated, his eyes shut, his arms lax, his lips pressed to her shoulder. Her heart full, she threaded her fingers through his hair, down to his nape, imprinting in her mind the feel of him in her, on her. She hugged his neck and felt a deep sense of serenity replace the hunger that had so long burned within her heart.

After several still moments he withdrew from her and rolled to his side, pulling her close, stroking her back, holding her as the night hours passed, until the inevitable pink rays of dawn pressed ruthlessly against his window.

"Nora," he said. "I'm sorry—"

"Shhh . . ." She pressed a soft kiss to his mouth. "I'm not." She gazed into his beloved eyes. "I'm not at all sorry."

"Oh, Nora," he whispered, aggrieved.

They lay close, belly to belly, hugging tight, wishing time would cease.

"When will you go?" she asked at length.

He shook his head. "Without you there's no place to go. . . ."

"You have to," she said fiercely. "You must. I would rather know you're safe and alive someplace away from me than have you stay and risk being captured once Powell learns where you are."

His chest hurting, he touched her cheek, her hair, her eyelids. He knew she was right. He had no choice. "Tomorrow." He paused a minute, then said, "I'll go tomorrow."

They found Arthur waiting for them out on the porch. The sun had crested the horizon and had turned the sky into swirls of pink and gold satin.

Elnora looked up into Russell's face, forever imprinting his features into her memory.

He looked down at her, heartsore, thinking love was a painful thing.

"Nora . . ." he said quietly.

"Yes?"

"Would you do something for me?"

"You know I will."

"Take care of Arthur."

She nodded. "I will." She paused a moment, feeling as though her heart would break. But she gathered herself and gave him a brave smile. "Goodbye, Sir Knight."

A ghost of a grin caught at his mouth, and he inclined his head slightly. "Goodbye, my lady."

Then she turned and ran down the steps to her horse.

Within seconds he heard the muffled sound of hoofbeats as she rode away.

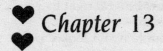

Chapter 13

BY THE TIME Elnora reached the farm, the sun had fully risen. She rode the horse into the barn, unsaddled him, then turned to find Gordon standing in the open doorway.

"Where have you been, Nora?" he asked, his tone and expression revealing his concern. "I was just about ready to ride into town to look for you."

Her gaze unwavering, she looked him straight in the face and told him the truth. "I've been with Russell."

His face registered surprise, and his breath whooshed out, but all he said was, "I see." He passed a hand over his face and sighed wearily. "Are you all right?"

"Yes, Gordon, I'm fine." She stood her ground, her chin lifted slightly.

He crossed the hay-dusted floor to stand before her. His hand came up and touched her cheek in a tender, affectionate gesture. "You're in love with him, aren't you?"

"Yes, I am."

"Does he return the affection?"

"Yes." Her eyes misted, and she dropped her gaze to the floor.

Stricken by her tears, Gordon pulled her into his

embrace and hugged her. "Then what is it, Nora? Russell is a good man. I know he'll do right by you."

"He would if he could."

He set her back away from him and looked down into her face. "What is that supposed to mean?"

Elnora kept her gaze lowered and shook her head. "I can't tell you. I wish I could, but I can't." Gently she pulled away from him. Her eyes found his. "Don't worry about me, Gordon. I'm fine. Really." She gave him a shaky smile, then turned and ran for the house before he could question her further.

When she entered the kitchen, Vivian was at the stove, preparing breakfast. Hearing the door open and close, she turned, her eyes worried. Seeing Elnora, she gave a sigh of relief. "Oh, thank God it's you, Nora. Where—"

"Don't ask me anything right now," Elnora pleaded quietly. "Please, Viv."

Vivian paused a moment, then acknowledged her request with a slight inclination of her head. "Would you like some breakfast?" She gestured to the table where the six children sat staring up at their aunt with open curiosity.

"No, thank you. Not right now. Actually I'd like to speak with Ransom. Is he up?"

"I haven't heard him moving about yet, but I'm sure he's in his room."

"Good," Elnora said, relieved. She went over to the table and kissed each child. "Good morning, darlings," she said, ruffling their hair and giving them hugs. When she was done, she crossed the kitchen floor and halted near the hallway, one hand on the door molding. "Vivian . . ."

"Yes?" Vivian looked up from the pan of frying bacon.

"Thanks for not asking."

Vivian smiled, her kind blue eyes filled with understanding. "I really didn't have to, dear."

Elnora nodded, then disappeared through the doorway that led down the hall to Ransom's room.

Ransom had spent a restless night, tossing and turning, trying desperately to fall asleep.

But his conscience was not about to give him rest.

It had smote him with a vengeance, keeping him awake long into the early-morning hours.

He'd no sooner drifted off than he was awake again. Once during the night he was certain he'd heard hoofbeats. But by the time he'd managed to get out of his bed and hobble over to the window to look outside, all was still and silent once more. All he could see through the meager light afforded by the thin slice of moon were swaying shadows.

When at last he'd fallen asleep once again, he'd had a horrible nightmare. He dreamed he was Walker, and Walker was him. Everything was switched around. Instead of Walker turning him in for the bounty money, he had let him go.

Ransom had woken then, feeling guilty and ashamed. So he had an argument with his conscience: He wasn't Walker, goddamn it! And Walker wasn't him! He'd given him a fair chance to get away. What the hell more could he want, for Christ's sake! He'd be damned if he'd just forget about the whole thing, forget about the bounty money and let him continue to live in Harmony, free as he pleased, and court and maybe even end up marrying his Nora!

Nosiree! There was no way he'd let Nora marry a dirty convict!

Still, for all his convictions, for all his justifications,

his conscience was not salved, and he felt no better for having sent the message off to Powell.

Finally, in the wee hours of the morning, he'd managed to drift back off to sleep again only to be rudely awakened by his bedroom door slamming into the bedroom wall.

"Ransom! I have to talk to you!"

It was Nora's voice. His eyesight still bleary, he rubbed the sleep from his eyes and tried to focus on her.

"It's about Russell," she said, her voice shaky with emotion.

That woke him.

He shot up into a sitting position, causing himself a considerable amount of pain from his damaged leg. "Nora," he bellowed, pulling a sheet up to cover his nakedness. "What the hell are ya doin' in here? I ain't even dressed."

She paced back and forth, not the least bit concerned with his naked body. "I have to tell you something, and I want you to listen to me very carefully." She turned and pinned him with her determined golden gaze. "Russell is an innocent man."

"His name is Robert Walker," Ransom corrected firmly, his eyes flashing with ire.

"Fine. You call him by whichever name you want, but it doesn't change the truth." Then she went on to tell him the whole story exactly as Russell had told it to her.

When she was done she fell into silence a moment, and he gave her skeptical stare. "Nora . . . a man like him would tell you anything to save his hide," he said, but his voice lacked conviction.

She came around to the side of the bed and sat down. "He told me the truth, Ransom. I know he did.

Please. I love him. Please don't take him away from me."

As he looked in her eyes, he realized the depth of her feelings. She did love the man. She loved him with all of her heart and soul. Ransom now knew she would never love him the way she loved Walker.

He clutched the sheet to his wide hairy chest and looked up into her sweet face, feeling a fierce rush of affection for her. Her story about Walker's innocence did little to ease his already stinging conscience. He wished things could be different. If ever there was a woman he could have loved, Nora would have been the one.

He also wished, as he had last night when he'd told her about Walker, that he'd waited to send the message off to Powell. In doing so, he'd not only struck a blow to Walker, but he'd hurt Nora, too. He cared far too much for her to see her hurt in any way.

He had wired the message on an angry impulse, born out of jealousy and frustration. He had to admit that he, like Sheriff Mobely, had long questioned Powell's motives at offering such a large bounty at his own expense. It had never made any sense. But he hadn't wanted to face that suspicion. He hadn't wanted to give up his dream of gaining the bounty he'd lusted after for so long. But when Walker had saved his life, deep in his heart Ransom had known the truth.

The man was innocent.

A cold-blooded murderer would never save the life of the bounty hunter who had been chasing him all these years.

Robert D. Walker was a decent, innocent man.

Ashamed, Ransom dropped his gaze. "It's too late, Nora." His voice was heavy with regret. "Marcus

Powell is already on his way. I expect he'll be here by tomorrow sometime."

A coldness came over her, and her face paled as she rose from the bed slowly. "My God . . .What have you done?"

His sad, green eyes lifted to hers. "I wired him a message. I'm sorry."

Slowly her hand came up and covered her mouth while her mind worked furiously. After several seconds she whispered, "I have to warn him. He has no idea. He didn't plan to leave until tomorrow."

Ransom's head snapped up. "He planned to leave tomorrow?"

"Yes."

Another wave of remorse rushed in to choke him.

"I have to do something," she mumbled, casting her gaze around the room fervidly, as though the answer to the dilemma were somewhere there before her. Without another word she turned and ran for the door.

"Nora, wait!" But it was too late, she was already through the door and running down the hall.

Mumbling something especially vulgar, he swung his legs over the bed, grimacing with pain. With a superhuman effort he managed to get into his trousers, took his crutch from where it was propped against the wall, and hobbled after her as fast as he could.

When Nora burst through Russell's door that morning, he was surprised to see her. He had just returned from having breakfast over at the boardinghouse, and although he had unlocked the front door, he had not yet opened the shop for business.

"Russell!" she said, her eyes frantic with fear. "You

have to pack, now, today.''

He came around the counter and took her by her shoulders to steady her. ''What are you talking about?''

''Marcus Powell,'' she said as she gasped for breath, ''he's on his way here this very minute. Ransom wired him a message yesterday.''

He studied her face for several long moments, then sighed. ''It's too late, then.'' He pulled her into his arms, embracing her tightly. He cupped the back of her head with one hand and inhaled deep of her sweet, clean scent.

''No!'' She shook her head vigorously against his chest. ''It's not too late. It can't be!''

''Nora, I can't keep running. He'll talk to people here. He'll soon know what I look like. Now that he knows for sure that I'm still alive, he won't rest until he finds me. There's no place for me to run anymore, no place for me to hide.''

Aggrieved, Elnora lifted her head from his chest and looked up into his face. ''But—''

''Yes, there is,'' said a deep voice from the door.

Elnora spun and moved to stand protectively in front of Russell.

She held Ransom's gaze solidly, but Russell took her firmly by the shoulders and moved her aside.

''Riley,'' Russell said, his eyes wary.

The two men stared at each other a long moment, assessing, studying, until at last Russell broke the silence. ''What do you want, Riley? If it's your bounty, you'll have to wait till Powell shows up.'' There was no bitterness in his voice, only a resigned acceptance. ''You've waited this long—another day won't make that much difference.''

Chagrined, Ransom adjusted his stance, but his

gaze never wavered. "It's not the bounty I'm after. I came to help." He paused. "I know where you can hide. At least for now."

Russell's keen gaze grew wary once again. "Why would you want to help me?"

Feeling extremely uncomfortable, Ransom shrugged a meaty shoulder. "Hell, I don't know." In a stronger voice he amended his statement with "You saved my life. I figure I owe you somethin' for that." His gaze found Elnora, and his voice grew softer. "And for Nora. I'd do it for Nora. I'd do anything for her."

Russell watched Ransom's face intently. He was telling the truth. His affection for Elnora was plainly etched into his earnest expression.

Ransom looked Russell in the eye again. "I have a plan. I don't know if it'll work, but we got nothin' to lose by givin' it a go. I figure I'll need to convince Powell you lit out this morning. I doubt he'll believe me outright, but sooner or later he'll leave town to search for you. Once he does we'll figure out where to go from there. You'll need supplies while you're in hidin', but we'll bring 'em out to ya—"

"What makes you think I'd trust you?" Russell interrupted, cocking one eyebrow.

Aggravated, his pride still stinging, Ransom narrowed his eyes. "The way I see it, Walker, you don't have a helluva lot of choice, now, do ya?"

Russell realized the truth of that statement and gave the other man a long deliberate stare, while a slow smile caught at his mouth. "I suppose I don't." Then, his voice all business, he said, "I'll need a couple of hours. There's something I have to do first."

Ransom nodded. "Get it done, whatever it is."

"Take Nora and Arthur with you."

Elnora opened her mouth to protest, but Russell stayed her with a gentle, "Go with him. I'll see you later."

Caught in a web of uncertainty, she glanced from Russell to Ransom. Could she trust Ransom to help them? And if they didn't trust him, what would they do? Where could they go?

Russell read her mind. "Go, Nora." He shoved her gently toward the big man. "He'll help us. It'll be all right."

The cabin was exactly as Russell and Ransom had left it—a shambles, nothing more than a huge pile of wood and debris.

Russell raised his eyebrows and turned to give Ransom a disbelieving stare. He pointed to the cellar opening. "You want me to go down in there?"

Feeling better than he had all day, Ransom nodded and grinned. "Yep."

Elnora bent over the gaping hole and looked down into the cellar. "It's pretty dark down there."

"It sure as hell is," Ransom agreed.

Early the next morning a knock sounded at the Perry door.

Elnora almost jumped out of her skin. She shot a worried glance at Vivian, who knew nothing about the danger Russell was in, and went to answer it.

She found Maisie and Minnie standing on the porch, nearly dancing with their impatience.

"The quest is over!" Maisie shouted, holding up that morning's edition of the *Sentinel*.

"How wonderful!" Elnora tried to sound excited, but her enthusiasm was dampened by her worry over Russell. She'd had very little sleep the past two nights,

and her nerves were stretched taut. Ransom had told
her to act as if nothing were out of the ordinary. She
was trying, but it was far more difficult than she had
ever imagined it would be.

"Please, come in and sit down, ladies." Elnora ush-
ered them in.

Once they were seated, Minnie turned to Elnora
and Vivian. "I know you probably want to read the
story for yourselves, but we simply can't stand it. We
must tell you what happened."

Vivian laughed at their girlish excitement. "So tell
us."

"Well," Maisie began, "you know the Black Knight
has been searching all over the kingdom for Sir Gawain."

"Yes." Elnora affected interest while she told herself, *Be calm, act normal. . . .*

"Well, he never did find him, so he returned to
King Nefan's court. He did not return empty-handed,
however. Although he did not find Sir Gawain, he
discovered something of vast importance—"

Minnie clapped her hands with glee. "He brought
back evidence proving Sir Gawain's innocence! King
Nefan was right!"

"And," Maisie added, "since Sir Ruggard had yet
to return with Lady Elvia, the king sent the Black
Knight off to aid them in their quest so that both his
best knights could return to his service as soon as possible."

Vivian set the teacups on the table. "Did the Black
Knight find them?"

Maisie nodded. "Well, yes, he did. But not until
after Sir Ruggard had already found the blue diamond for Lady Elvia."

Her interest perking, Elnora looked up from her teacup. "He found it?"

"Yes," Minnie cut in. "He found it. But he had to fight for it. The band of insurgents was fierce and the odds were against him, but the Black Knight arrived in the nick of time and helped him to win the battle. Together they were able to return the blue diamond to Lady Elvia."

"However"—Maisie sat forward in her seat—"Sir Ruggard took a terrible wound to his chest."

"No!" Vivian cried, completely caught up in the fantasy.

"Yes," the twins said and nodded.

Minnie pressed forward, too excited to hold back the ending. "So the Black Knight put Sir Ruggard on his steed and led him all the way back to Lady Elvia. When he saw the stricken look on her face, he realized how much Lady Elvia loved Sir Ruggard. Because the Black Knight loved her, too, he vowed to do everything he could to save Sir Ruggard's life."

"Oh, thank goodness!" Vivian cried, pressing her palm to her chest and returning to the stove for the teapot.

"Yes!" Maisie exclaimed. "Thank goodness, indeed!"

It was Minnie's turn to break in. "Sir Ruggard remained awake until he saw Lady Elvia and handed her the diamond. Then he slipped into unconsciousness. The Black Knight knew they would have to nurse his wound at once or risk losing him. So while Sir Ruggard was unconscious, the Black Knight started to undress him. He began with removing Sir Ruggard's helmet, and . . ." She paused, letting the tension build. "You'll never guess what he and Lady Elvia discovered."

Smug in their newfound knowledge, the twins sat back in their chairs.

Vivian pressed forward expectantly, while Elnora's brain began to click. Her eyes took on a tender sparkle, and she softly said, "Sir Ruggard is Sir Gawain."

"Elnora!" Disgusted, both woman huffed and deflated back down into their chairs. "How did you know?"

A smile caught at her mouth. "I just knew somehow." She paused a moment. "It seems to fit."

"So will Sir Ruggard live?" Vivian asked.

"But, of course," Maisie assured her. "There will have to be a wedding."

Minnie looked doubtful. "Unless our author decides not to write us a wedding."

Appalled at the thought, Maisie's mouth fell open. "He wouldn't dare! After all he's put us through, he'd better give us a wedding. Why, my nerves are stretched thinner than thread!"

Vivian chuckled and poured them all another cup of tea. "Well, if he doesn't he'll have himself a royal fight on his hands, that's for sure."

Maisie pinned Elnora with her sharp gaze. "Have you and Russell discovered who the author is yet?"

Elnora's smile was sad and wistful. "Not for certain. But I have a notion."

"Tell us!" Minnie exclaimed.

"Yes, do tell, Elnora!" Maisie insisted.

"I'll be happy to tell you when I know for sure." She clamped her mouth shut tight, refusing to budge an inch, while she thought about a certain score she would have to settle should her notion prove correct.

"Funny thing," Minnie said, pursing her mouth thoughtfully. "Russell never showed up for breakfast this morning."

* * *

When the Kansas Pacific pulled into the Harmony depot later that same afternoon, Marcus Powell and his companion, Bradley Collins, descended the steps of the train.

Powell's cool gaze swept over the multicolored town with a chilly detachment, while his upper lip curled in distaste at what he saw.

Finally his eyes came to rest on the pink hotel that sat beside the train depot. He turned to his servant. "We'll check into the hotel, then we'll find out where Riley is staying." His steps determined, Powell headed straight for the hotel.

Collins nodded and followed behind, carrying both their traveling bags.

Meanwhile, having finished their lunch at the hotel, which also served as a restaurant and a meeting place for the locals, Sheriff Travis Miller, Cord Spencer, Frederick and Edward Winchester, and Zeke Gallagher were gathered outside the open doors, passing the time of day.

When Powell strode by, Frederick tipped his hat and called out a courteous, "Hello, gentlemen!"

Travis followed with "Welcome."

Powell ignored their greetings and turned his disdainful gaze on all of them. "Do any of you know a man named Riley? Ransom Riley?"

The five men looked at one another, then back at Powell.

"Who's askin'?" Travis's voice was low and cautious, instantly alert to trouble.

Powell's smile was thin and perceptive. "Ah, I see that you do. Well, tell him that Marcus Powell is in town. Tell him I'll be at the hotel waiting for him." Without waiting for an answer, he turned and brushed past the group with an air of preeminence, followed faithfully by Collins.

The five men stared after them silently for several moments, then looked at each other once again.

Greatly offended, Frederick huffed and said, "My word. Stuffy old cock, isn't he?"

Disgusted, Cord shook his head. "Takes all kinds. I hope they don't visit my place. My regulars don't take to rudeness. Those two are liable to get their heads busted."

Zeke said, "I don't like the looks of them. What do you think he wants with Riley?"

Travis rubbed his chin thoughtfully.

Edward turned to Travis. "You'll be watching them, I presume."

Travis smiled humorlessly. "You can bet on it."

Within the hour Travis was on his way out to the Perry farm. The folks of Harmony had a way of looking out for their own, and since Ransom was Vivian's brother and had spent some time in their midst, Travis figured he belonged to Harmony as much as anybody else did.

When Travis reached the farm, he saw Ransom outside the barn, struggling to hitch up the rig. Noting his struggle, Travis reined in his horse beside him. "How ya doin', Riley?" He swung down off his horse, then took the bridle from Ransom's hands and placed the bit in the horse's mouth.

"I've been better," Ransom answered truthfully. "This leg hurts like hell. It slows me down more than I care to admit."

"I don't suppose you should be up on it," Travis commented conversationally. He cast his gaze around the perimeters of the farm. "Everything all right out here?"

Ransom immediately sensed Travis's tension. "Everybody's fine." He fixed his gaze on the sheriff's face. He knew he hadn't come clear out to the farm for the sole purpose of sharing small talk. "What is it, Travis? What brings ya out this way?"

Travis halted his movements and turned to face Ransom. "Two strangers came into town on the train 'bout an hour ago. They were askin' for ya."

Ransom's face was impassive. "They give their names?"

"One did. He left a name and a message for you." Travis paused. "Said to tell you Marcus Powell is in town and staying at the hotel."

Unblinking, Ransom nodded. "Thanks for the message."

The two men stared at each other a long moment. Finally Travis asked, "You in some kind of trouble, Riley?"

Ransom gave a soft laugh and shot him a lopsided grin. "Hell, no, Travis."

Travis's gaze held steady. "You need help of some kind?"

"If I do, I'll let ya know."

"I don't like the looks of them two. I got a bad feelin'—"

"Ain't nothin' I can't handle, Sheriff."

Travis stared at him a few more seconds, then nodded. "If you say so." He finished hitching up the rig for the other man. When he was done, he swung back up onto his horse and pinned Ransom with his steady gaze once again. "Funny thing 'bout my feelin's. They're seldom wrong." He paused. "If you need me, all you gotta do is let me know.''

Ransom nodded. ''I'll remember that, Travis.''

Elnora handed Russell down the sack of food she and Ransom had brought him. ''Hello,'' she said softly, warmed by the sight of him. Their fingers brushed briefly, leaving them starved for more of each other.

''My lady.'' Russell gave her a cocky bow and winked, hoping to lighten her heart. Worry was etched around her eyes, and he felt a twinge of guilt for having been the one to put it there.

Ransom and Arthur stood guard near the rig, keeping a lookout for danger, while giving Russell and Elnora a few minutes alone. ''You all right down there, Walker?'' Ransom called out.

''Fine!'' Russell called back, suddenly glad of the other man's reassuring presence. Riley would see Nora through if anything happened to him. The thought was hard to face, but he found comfort in it nevertheless.

From where he stood waiting, Ransom looked down at the dog, then reached out and petted his head. Arthur wagged his tail so hard his rear section jerked back and forth erratically. ''You're all right, fella,'' Ransom said quietly. ''When all of this is over and done, maybe I'll just get me a dog. They're easier to figure out than women.'' He gave a snort and asked the dog, ''Who'da thought she'd pick him over me?''

Arthur responded with an answering whimper, while back at the cellar door, Elnora asked Russell, ''Are you cold?'' She reached her hand down for his.

He took her hand and gripped it tight in his much larger one. ''No.''

''Does the lamp give you enough light?''

"I'm fine, Nora. Quit worrying."

Valiantly she struggled to clear her expression of tension and tried to smile. "It's so hard." Her voice was an anguished whisper.

"I know."

"I love you."

"I love you, too."

Growing impatient, Ransom clumped over to Elnora's side. Behind him, Arthur followed. Leaning on his crutch, Ransom peered down into the hole. "You got enough food to hold ya for a while?"

"Plenty."

"We might not make it back for a day or two."

"I'll be all right." Russell slid Ransom a questioning look. "He show yet?"

Ransom glanced over at Elnora, then back at Russell. His nod was slight. But not so slight that Russell didn't catch it.

♥ Chapter 14

RANSOM RODE INTO Harmony at dawn the next morning.

He headed straight for the hotel, knowing Powell would be up and waiting for him.

Although they'd never met face-to-face, Ransom felt as though he knew the man. They'd corresponded regularly in the past several years, comparing notes as their search for Walker had continued.

When he reached the hotel, Ransom stopped the rig out front. Holding his injured leg in front of him, he awkwardly slipped to the ground, gritting his teeth in pain. His leg was aching something terrible. Doc Tanner had told him to stay off the damn thing, and he would like to, but he had to put things right for Nora first.

He took his crutch from the seat and placed it under his arm, then limped around to the hitch rail. Once he secured the horse's reins, he thumped his way up to the door of the hotel and let himself in.

Kincaid Hutton was already at the front desk.

He looked up without surprise. Word got around fast in Harmony, and everyone knew the two strangers had come to town looking for Ransom.

"He's in Room Ten, Ransom." Kincaid jabbed a thumb over his shoulder at the stairs. "Can you make it up all right or you want me to go get him?"

"I'll make it," Ransom said and limped off toward the staircase. "Thanks, Kincaid."

"You need anything you let me know," Kincaid called from behind.

"I'll do that." Ransom took the steps slowly, his mind working over the details of his story. He knew Powell wasn't gonna believe him, but it didn't matter. Powell could ask the townsfolk all the questions he wanted, but no one other than himself, Nora, and Arthur knew where Russell was, so Ransom figured Powell would not get the answers he sought.

He and Elnora had been careful to take enough of Russell's personal belongings from the bookstore so that it looked as if he had, in fact, left town. Not seeing him around, the townsfolk had already begun to question his disappearance. Ransom and Elnora figured that was just as well. Their questions would give some credence to Ransom's story.

When he reached the top step, he heaved a sigh of relief, then headed on down to door ten. He knocked twice and waited.

He didn't have to wait long. A tall, thin man answered the door, opening it wide. "Are you Riley?"

Ransom nodded.

"Come in." The man stepped aside.

A shorter, much stockier man stood with his back to the door. Slowly he turned and smiled. But the smile was cold and never quite reached his eyes.

Ransom knew him immediately. He was dressed much finer than the man who'd answered the door. His gray suit and polished black shoes looked expensive.

"Ah, Mr. Riley." Marcus Powell crossed the room, extending his hand. "We meet at last."

Ransom took Powell's hand and gave it a brief shake, and as he did, the story Elnora had told him about Powell and Walker replayed over again in his head.

If he'd had any doubts about Walker's story, they dissipated completely. There was a calculated coldness about the man who stood before him. His eyes were flat and mean. This man, Ransom knew, could and would kill without guilt, without empathy. He'd met other men like him through the years. They were the most dangerous animal in existence.

"Where is he?" Powell asked immediately, his impatience growing with every passing moment. His quest for Walker had far surpassed the simple desire to see the man dead. Oh, he wanted to see him dead, all right. But it was much more than that. He wanted to kill Walker himself. Walker had challenged his power, his authority, had dared to throw his offer back in his face. He was the only man living who had ever risked such a thing. Walker's open contempt of his power ate at Powell's dark soul every hour of every day.

Ransom shifted his weight to accommodate his throbbing leg. "I'm afraid we have a problem."

Powell's eyes narrowed slightly. "What do you mean, we have a problem?" His posture went suddenly rigid.

Ransom met his gaze evenly. "Walker is gone. He left town yesterday."

Powell stared up at the bigger man for all of half a minute. A black rage rushed over him, but his voice was ominously quiet when he asked, "How could you let him get away?"

Ransom looked down at his leg, then back up at Powell. "I didn't have much choice about it. I didn't know who he was till a few days ago. I hurt my leg the same day I found out. That's why I wired you to come to Harmony 'stead of tryin' to bring him in myself."

"Why wasn't he locked up in the jail?"

Ransom raised a skeptical eyebrow, and a half smile touched one side of his mouth. "I had a feelin' you wouldn't want the law in on this."

Temporarily appeased by Ransom's insight, Powell smiled and gave a soft humorless chuckle. "You're smarter than I thought you were, Riley." He paused. "Where do you think he'd go?"

"I have a feelin' he'd head west."

"What was he doing in Harmony in the first place?"

Ransom saw no reason to lie. Powell could get the answer to that question from anyone in town if he showed them Russell's Wanted poster. "He's been livin' here for about six years. He was using the name of Russell Whitaker and owned Whitaker's Bookstore."

Powell gave a harsh laugh and turned to look out the window at Harmony. "Imagine that. All this time he was right here, in this little town." He fell into silence while Ransom waited, his nerves beginning to bunch.

"What now, Mr. Powell?" Collins asked from behind.

Powell's rage returned in a quiet rush. "What now, indeed?" He turned and faced Ransom. "I suppose you know you've forfeited the bounty money."

Ransom knew it would not be wise to appear to give up so easily. He lifted his chin a notch. "He can't be far. Soon as my leg heals some, I plan on lightin' out after him."

Unblinking, Powell stared up at Ransom a long time. Then Powell took a step toward him and very softly said, "Why is it, Mr. Riley, that I'm getting the distinct impression that you're not telling me everything?"

His face carefully blank, Ransom stared down at the other man. "I don't know, Mr. Powell. You tell me."

Slowly Powell walked a circle around Ransom, his gaze never wavering, then he stopped before him again. "I would hate to find out that you're lying to me. It would be"— he looked over at Collins—"shall we say it would be unhealthy for Mr. Riley if we should make that discovery, Collins?"

"Yes, sir," the other man said without hesitation.

Rankled by the threat, Ransom stared down at Powell for several moments. "I don't take kindly to threats, Mr. Powell," Ransom warned quietly. He turned and slowly limped toward the door.

"We had an agreement, Mr. Riley!"

Ransom looked over his shoulder, his green eyes as icy as Powell's blue ones. "Sometimes agreements change. Sometimes things just don't work out like ya planned."

Powell lifted an eyebrow and inclined his head. "They do for me. I'm a very powerful man. You'd do well to remember that."

They stared at each other a long moment, while tension crackled between them.

"This ain't Detroit, Powell. You'd do well to remember that." Ransom walked out into the hall, leaving the door open behind him.

For three days Powell watched and waited for some sign of Walker.

His watching and waiting was in vain, however.

He knew Riley was lying. He felt it in his soul. Walker was close—so close Powell could almost sense his presence.

He considered wiring a message to Detroit, ordering more of his men to join him, but he realized their presence would benefit him nothing.

They could not bring Walker out from wherever he was hiding, and even if they could, they would only prove a detriment to him in the end. The more witnesses he had when finally he was able to dispose of Walker, the harder it would be to keep them all silent.

Collins was the only man alive who knew as much as Walker did, and once Walker was dead, Powell planned to see that Collins suffered an unfortunate accident while cleaning his gun one day.

On his fourth day in town, his frustration mounting, Powell went to see Sheriff Miller.

He found him at the Harmony jail, seated at his desk.

Powell approached him with an air of authority, and Travis looked up from his desk.

"I'm looking for someone." Powell tossed the poster of Russell on the desk and waited, watching the sheriff's expression carefully.

Unimpressed by Powell's arrogant manner, Travis took his time reaching for the poster. When he did pick it up, he studied it in silence for a long time, carefully masking his surprise.

"Have you seen him?" Powell's question was an insolent bark.

Slowly Travis lifted his gaze, his face impassive. "What has he done?"

"I'm asking the questions here, Sheriff!" Powell snapped indignantly.

His brows lowering, Travis stood and hooked his

hands on his hips. "This is my town, and I'm the sheriff here. Now, let me ask you again . . . why are you lookin' for him?"

Infuriated, Powell nearly shook with anger. He was fast losing control. To be so close and not be able to find Walker was playing havoc with his nerves. "He's wanted for murder, you fool! Surely you can read the poster! Now!" he boomed. "Let me ask *you* again—have you seen this man?"

His jaw tightening, Travis met the other man's gaze squarely. He knew Russell Whitaker. He also believed he could no more be a murderer than he, Travis, was a fool. Something was very wrong with all of this. He didn't understand how Russ had managed to get his face on a Wanted poster, but he meant to find out.

Travis stepped out from behind his desk and approached the other man. "First of all," he said, his tone soft and deadly, "I am no fool. Second, I haven't seen this man since the day before you arrived. He left town, and no one seems to know why. I'd like to know the answer to that question myself." Coldly dismissing Powell, Travis turned back to his desk and sat down, returning to his work. "Sorry, I can't help you."

Incensed, Powell spun toward the door, nearly running over Collins, who'd been standing behind him.

"Mister," Travis said from behind, lifting his gaze from his records, "I think your visit in Harmony is about over."

Powell turned and gave him a cold glare, then without uttering another word, he left the jail with Collins following.

Throughout the rest of the day, Powell questioned the townsfolk about Russell's whereabouts. But the locals just looked at him blankly and told him the same thing Riley and Sheriff Miller had.

Powell suspected they were telling the truth—they didn't know where Walker was—but he'd also begun to suspect that if they knew where to find him, they would not have told him anyway.

The next day Powell and Collins boarded the Kansas Pacific and left town.

Travis watched them go, glad to be rid of them.

Although he didn't understand what was going on with Russell, he knew it had something to do with Ransom, and he planned to get some answers to his questions and fast.

His jaw set, he swung up onto his horse and headed out to the Perry farm.

Russell was growing restless. The minutes and hours seemed to drag by. Three days had passed since Ransom and Elnora had visited. His food and water supply was diminishing fast, and still they had not returned.

That meant Powell was still in town, hanging on, hoping for a clue to his whereabouts.

Weary, Russell passed a hand over his face, noting the growth of his beard. He needed a shave and a bath. He was so damned tired of hiding, of waiting, that he'd begun to consider leaving the cellar, walking into town, and facing Powell head-on.

But he knew the odds were stacked against him. Who would believe him? Besides, Riley had made him promise he would let him handle Powell—for Elnora's sake.

So Russell waited, his nerves wearing thin, his heart heavy. He worried about Elnora. His arms ached to hold her, and his body ached to love her one last time.

But there would be no time for that. Once Powell

was gone, he would have to gather what little he could carry and leave Harmony.

The thought did little to comfort him.

He should have known his past would catch up with him eventually.

Lonely and bereft, he laid his head back against the cellar wall and waited.

It was well past midnight when Ransom and Elnora stopped the rig next to the cabin. The moon was a full creamy disk, lighting the night with an iridescent glow.

May had brought milder winds and warmer temperatures, and the night was filled with the sounds of the coming summer.

Arthur jumped from the rig and, whining, shot off for the cabin in search of his master.

Ransom helped Elnora down, then grabbed the basket of food and followed Arthur. "You all right?" he asked, keeping his voice low.

She nodded. "I'm fine." Her voice was a trifle too high, her back a little too stiff.

"You shouldn't have come."

"I had to."

Ransom shot her a disgusted look. "Who would have thought a little thing like you could be such a pigheaded woman?"

Annoyed, she cast him a sidelong glance. "Size has nothing to do with this."

"I should have tied you up."

"It wouldn't have done any good. I would have found a way to get loose. You forget, I have an ally in young Sam."

"Humph!"

When they reached the cellar door, Ransom reached

down and knocked twice. "It's us, Walker," he whispered. "Open up."

Russell pushed the door up and open, then held the lantern up to their faces. His gaze found Elnora, and he smiled. He looked over at Ransom. "It's good to see you. Both of you."

Ransom nodded. "Powell left town today."

"Are you sure?" Russell asked, his smile fading, his expression becoming cautious.

"No. But they both got on the train. Travis saw them."

"That doesn't mean a whole lot."

"Yeah, that's what we figured." Ransom rubbed the back of his neck wearily.

Russell started to climb out of the hole, but Ransom put a hand out to stay him. "You just stay down there," he ordered, his voice firm and quiet. "At least for now."

Russell cocked his head, his gaze narrowing. "What's going on, Riley?"

"Just do as I say."

"Trust him, Russell," Elnora said softly. "He knows—"

"Yes, he knows. So why don't you let him come up?" interrupted a chillingly familiar voice. "It's been a long time, hasn't it, Mr. Walker?"

Elnora gasped, and Ransom went deathly still.

An icy coldness pervaded Russell's body. His first thought was for Elnora's safety, then he thought of Ransom and felt a twinge of regret and sadness. Powell would kill them both. He would leave no witnesses. He had to distract Powell long enough for them to get away. Somehow he had to save them. He climbed the ladder to the top and agilely lifted himself out of the cellar and up onto his feet. "Hello, Powell,"

Russell said with a humorless smile. He crossed the short distance between them, his saunter almost arrogant, and stood face-to-face with the man who had lusted for so long after his death.

"Ah, Mr. Walker." Powell's voice was silky smooth. He smiled up at him. "You're looking quite fit for a convict."

"I take care of myself," Russell retorted coolly. Beside him, Arthur emitted a low, threatening growl. Russell quieted him with a gentle hand to his head.

Powell nodded. "I see that you do." He took a deep satisfying breath. "You've led me on quite a chase these many years, you know that, don't you?"

"It's been my pleasure." Russell's smile was grim.

The smile dropped from Powell's face. "You won't have that pleasure any longer, I'm afraid."

Seemingly unconcerned, Russell shrugged and pocketed his hands. "What good will it do to kill me, Powell?" he asked, stalling for time. "Sooner or later someone else is going to learn the truth about you. It'll eventually come out that you're nothing more than a murderer, a traitor. Someone else will write my story one day."

"Yes, you're probably right. But I'll worry about that when the time comes." He glanced over at Elnora and Ransom. "It's a pity you involved these good people. Now it seems they'll have to join you in your death."

"Let them go, Powell," Russell said quietly, his smile fading, his cool facade disintegrating. "They haven't done anything to deserve this."

"Ah, but you see that doesn't matter to me one way or the other. They are here with you, and that's offense enough." Powell's narrow gaze fixed itself on Ransom, and he lifted one thick brow. "Mr. Riley, I can't tell you how disappointed I am in you."

Ransom gave a short snort. "I'm sorry as hell 'bout that, Mr. Powell." His tone was openly sarcastic.

"Yes, I'll bet you are." Powell paused. "I have to say it was awfully noble of you to give up the generous reward you would have earned had you turned Mr. Walker over to me like we'd planned."

"Yeah, I'm one helluva nice guy," Ransom admitted, realizing with a start that it was true.

Powell gave a soft, bitter chuckle. "I'm surprised you really believed I would leave Harmony so easily."

"I'm also dumb as dirt," Ransom agreed, his mind working frantically.

"Collins," Powell said quietly, "you have the guns loaded, I presume?"

"Yes, Mr. Powell." Collins stepped out of the darkness and handed Powell a pistol, keeping one for himself.

Her fear temporarily suspended, Elnora stared at the man in outrage. "How can you do this?" she whispered fiercely.

His eyes on Elnora, Powell leveled his gun on Russell's chest. "Quite easily. It's going to be such a pleasure, I assure y—"

But he never completed his sentence.

Russell lunged and pandemonium broke loose.

Elnora felt herself knocked to the ground by Ransom, while Russell grabbed a long piece of wood and brought it crashing against Powell's shoulder, causing the gun to discharge into the night with a resounding crack.

Russell felt the bullet graze his arm, but he ignored the pain as he struggled for possession of Powell's gun. Disabled by his leg, Ransom crawled toward

Collins, but Arthur was there before him. The big dog leaped forward and caught the man in the chest with all fours, sending him to the ground with a heavy thud. The gun bounced out of Collins's hand, and Ransom scrambled for it.

Without a thought for herself, Elnora rushed in, pummeling Powell's shoulder and back, trying to aid Russell, but Powell slapped her hard across the mouth, sending her flying backward into the debris.

Distracted, Russell turned to her and yelled, "Nora!"

Seeing his chance, Powell raised his arms and brought the butt of the gun down sharply on Russell's head.

Dazed, Russell stumbled and dropped to his knees, and Powell lowered the gun, pointed it at his head, and said, "Goodbye, Mr. Walk—"

A second shot exploded into the night, followed by a loud, "Now, hold on there!"

Everyone went still.

The silence was broken only by the twitter of crickets, mixed with a host of heavy breathing.

"I'd put that gun down if I were you, Mr. Powell!" From out of the darkness came Travis Miller, his pistol aimed dead straight at Powell's chest.

Behind him followed a small group of men: Cord Spencer, Frederick and Edward Winchester, Zeke Gallagher . . .Their expressions grim, the five circled the cabin, their gun barrels leveled on Powell and Collins.

For a moment Elnora's heart stopped beating as she watched Powell consider Travis's order.

Powell's gaze challenged Travis. "I could pull this trigger and kill him before you could stop me."

Travis nodded. "Maybe. But if you try it, you'll die, too. That I can promise you."

Powell stared at the sheriff for a long second, weighing the threat in his words. Then he looked down at Walker, and the obsession to see him dead quickened. He pulled back the hammer on his gun, the ominous click sounding incredibly loud.

"No," Elnora whispered, "please."

"You can't kill us all, Powell," Cord said quietly. "You may silence him, but there's all of us, and we all know the truth about you. Like the sheriff said, you pull that trigger, we'll kill you."

A long, long moment passed while everyone waited, holding his breath. Slowly Powell lowered the gun to his side. He wanted Walker dead more than anything in the world. But he was a coward and could not risk his own life to fulfill his desire.

"That's better. Now throw the gun over there, nice and easy like," Travis ordered.

Powell obeyed, then slowly raised his palms.

His head clearing, Russell lurched to his feet and rushed to Elnora. He bent over her. "Oh, God, Nora . . ."

She went up against his chest, wrapping her arms tight around his waist. "I'm all right. I'm all right." Their emotions raw, they held each other close for a long moment with no thought for the others around them.

Then she felt it, something warm and sticky beneath her cheek. She pulled back and searched through the shadows to see what it was. "My, God! You're wounded!"

"Shhh," Russell said. "The bullet just grazed me."

"Your shoulder?" She looked up into his face.

"My arm."

"Oh, Russ . . ."

"Shhh . . ." He pulled her close once more.

Winded and sweating profusely, Ransom rolled onto his back, his leg causing him considerable pain. "Well, it sure as hell took ya long enough!" he said, disgusted.

"Hell, Riley, you said to wait till he'd said enough to hang himself," Travis answered with a grin.

"Yeah, but I didn't want him to hang for my death!"

Travis chuckled good-naturedly. Ransom had told him the entire story the day he'd ridden out to tell him that Powell had left town. Together they reasoned that Powell hadn't left Harmony for good, and they'd agreed to set a trap, enlisting the aid of their friends, who were all too willing to go along on the adventure.

"Get on over here, Powell," Travis said. "Seems you got a lot of explainin' to do to the marshal. Then you're gonna be takin' a long ride back to Detroit in a prison wagon."

Powell walked out of the debris and stood before the sheriff's horse. He brushed some of the dust from his expensive coat. "You can't prove a thing, Sheriff," he said with a sneer. "I'm a powerful man. No one will believe you."

"But they'll believe all of us," Edward Winchester cut in. "We all heard what you said. We all know what Russ was going to write in his story about you. And I don't need to remind you that we are all witnesses to what you just tried to do. Whitaker isn't a murderer. He never was. But you are."

Travis nodded and repeated the words Ransom had spoken to him days ago. "This ain't Detroit, Powell."

"If we have to, we'll all come to Detroit to testify against you," Zeke added.

Frederick nodded. "It would be a pleasure."

"I doubt we'll have to." Cord cast a glance over at Collins, who was being guarded by Arthur. "I have a feeling your friend over there might be willing to fess up to everything he knows, now that his silence will no longer benefit him."

Russell stood and helped Elnora to her feet. Arms linked around each other, they walked over to Ransom. They helped him to his feet and supported him. Together the three walked out of the rubble.

When they reached their friends, Russell and Elnora looked at each of the men, their hearts filled with gratitude. "I don't know what to say," Russell said. " 'Thank you' hardly seems—"

"Oh, hell," Travis said, "we needed a night out anyway, Russ."

"Yes, indeed." Frederick nodded. "It was an exciting evening, to say the least. I've been living like a recluse for months."

Edward looked over at Russell, cocked an eyebrow, and repeated the words he'd said to him that long-ago day in the bookstore. "We all have our reasons for living our lives the way we do, don't you agree, Russ?"

Russell nodded, and a slow grin stole across his mouth. He realized that Edward, like Lottie, had suspected who he was long ago. And like Lottie, he had chosen to judge him by his character, not by what a poster had said about him. "Indeed I do," Russell said quietly. He looked down into Elnora's beautiful eyes. "Indeed I do."

♥ Chapter 15

IT WAS ALMOST dawn when Elnora and Ransom returned to the Perry farm.

Travis had taken Powell and Collins into custody, and Russell, Ransom, and Elnora had ridden into town with the group so that Doc Tanner could tend Russell's wound.

Russell was right. The bullet had only grazed his bicep. Doc Tanner cleaned the wound, added a few stitches, and said to Russell and Ransom, "You two keep my night business booming." Then he asked Ransom, "How's the leg?"

Ransom frowned and grumbled, "You might as well shoot me, Doc, and get it over with. I ain't never gonna get enough rest to heal it."

Ransom and Elnora saw Russell home, and Ransom waited in the rig while Russell took Elnora aside, placed a light kiss to her forehead, and said, "I'll see you soon."

The sun was high when Elnora finally rose from her bed that day. A breeze sifted in through her bedroom window, ruffling her curtains. The air was warm and sweet and ripe with promise.

Her heart light, she took extra care with her toilet, arranging her hair up into a shiny, puffy nest. Her hands shaking with excitement, she dressed carefully in a light blue bustled skirt and a high-necked white blouse.

Something wonderful was going to happen today. She could feel it.

She found Vivian in the kitchen, waiting for her.

Vivian tipped her head to the side. "Now will you tell me what's going on?"

Elnora smiled. "Yes. Now I will." And for the next hour she did.

When she was done, Vivian collapsed into a chair and slapped a palm to her chest. "My goodness! Who would imagine such goings-on!" She sat stunned and silent for several seconds, then her eyes rounded. "Oh, my goodness! I almost forgot!" She reached down into her apron pocket and pulled out a sealed envelope. "This came for you earlier this morning."

"For me?" Elnora raised her brows and took the envelope with her other hand. She hesitated a moment, anticipation tingling through her, while Vivian pressed forward expectantly.

"Oh, open it, for heaven's sake!" Vivian said.

"Who delivered it?" Elnora asked, easing the seal open.

"Harry Taylor. And, no, he wouldn't tell me who asked him to deliver it." Vivian looked disgusted. "Apparently the sender had paid him well to keep his identity a secret."

"Imagine that." Elnora smiled, then looked down at the note. Quite suddenly her cheeks took on a warm glow. Her voice soft, she read the fancy script.

"My Lady,

If you would discover the identity of your author,

meet me at the town livery this evening at 7:00.

> With deepest affection,
> Your Knight"

Slowly Elnora's head came up, and her gaze met Vivian's. She lifted one eyebrow, and her eyes took on a sparkle. "So we'll meet at last."

Vivian clapped her hands together. "Finally! Oh, I can't wait to tell Minnie and Maisie!"

The sun had just begun its descent when Elnora stopped the rig before Jake Sutherland's livery that evening.

She'd come to the livery alone, although she was sure, thanks to Vivian, almost everyone in town knew she was supposed to meet the mystery author tonight.

She climbed down from the rig and, with painful slowness, brushed the wrinkles from her skirt, prolonging the moment she would enter the building. Her heart was thudding with anticipation; her palms were damp.

What if her notion was wrong? But what if her notion was correct?

Straightening her shoulders, she took off for the building, her small steps determined.

Taking the double doors in hand, she swung them open wide, then stepped into the cool, shadowy interior.

A medley of smells reached her: leather, oil, horses. From somewhere within the barn a horse whinnied a greeting and stomped his foot.

She crept into the interior a few feet. "Hello!" Waiting for a response, she turned and closed the doors behind her.

Another whinny from the horse was her only answer.

She took a few more steps into the barn. Then her mouth dropped open, and her eyes widened. Awed, she stared at the scene spread out before her.

The interior of the barn was draped in lengths of colored materials, decorated in preparation for a magnificent event. Over in the far corner of the barn a table held the beginnings of a bountiful feast.

"Hello?" she said again, the simple word a dubious question.

A sudden clink of metal caught her attention, and she took a few more steps forward, very curious now.

Then she saw him.

He stood tall and erect, dressed in a suit of silver armor. His face was concealed beneath his helmet, and in his hand he held a tall lance, propped up on the hay-dusted floor.

One eyebrow lifting, she straightened. "So, we meet at last, Sir Knight." Her voice was soft and silky.

Holding his silence, the knight bowed slightly and, with effort and a fair amount of clanging and clinking, closed the space between them.

She lifted the other eyebrow and peered up into his visor, trying to see his eyes. "You've gone to an awful lot of trouble to keep your identity hidden from all of us."

He nodded but didn't answer.

"I would know who you are," she told him at length.

Slowly the knight reached up and took hold of his visor. "My lady," he said quietly and went down on one knee, slowly lifting his visor to reveal his face.

Her heart quickening, Elnora's mouth fell open as their eyes met and held. She felt a sweet rush of gladness that it was him and no other, followed by a slow burn of aggravation at his deceit.

Within two seconds her aggravation won out. She clamped her mouth shut and shoved at the knight's shoulders, sending him crashing and clanking to the floor, his visor slamming back down to cover his face.

"Russell Whitaker! How dare you!"

Stunned, Russell lay on his back, flailing his arms like an upside-down turtle. "How dare I what?" he croaked from within his helmet.

"How dare you lie to me all this time!" Furious, she stomped her foot. "You've allowed me to chase all over this town like a fool, questioning all these people, looking for a . . . a . . . oooh!" She was so angry she couldn't even get the words straight. "A secret author!" she finally managed. "And all this time it was you!"

"I thought you'd be glad it was me!" he muttered, sounding injured.

"I am glad!" she hollered.

"Well, you've got one hell of a way of showing it, Nora." He rolled onto his side with effort, then sat up, lifting his visor once again. He stared up at her, and his dark eyes took on an amused twinkle. "I never lied to you, Nora."

"Ohoooo, yes, you did." Her brows met crossly, and she plunked her hands on her hips. She bent over and went nose to nose with him. "I asked you directly the day we went to visit Samantha who you thought the author was—"

"And I said that Samantha was right. Whoever he was, he had lost his heart to you."

"That's lying!"

"It isn't!"

"I feel like an idiot!"

"Why should you? I didn't lie to you. I love you!" he yelled up at her. "I did lose my heart to you!"

She was silent a moment, her injured pride warring with her soaring heart—she still hadn't become used to hearing him say those beautiful words. "That doesn't excuse the fact that you deceived me."

"I wanted to spend time with you."

"Then you should have come courting."

"I would have if it hadn't been for my past. I didn't think I had anything to offer you, Nora." His voice grew soft and husky. "But I wanted to be near you. I think I started to fall in love with you from the very first time I saw you sitting on the wagon seat beside your brother."

With both hands he struggled to pull his helmet off his head. Finally he managed to uncork himself and flung the helmet aside.

Eyeing his suit of armor, she gave a small huff of disgust and rolled her eyes. "For heaven's sake, where did you get that thing?"

Russell grinned. "Fred loaned it to me. He had it up in his attic. Said it belonged to one of his ancestors. Said it'd get to you. What do you think?" He held his hands out at his sides, his dark eyes glittering with mischief.

Despite herself, Elnora almost laughed. He looked so ridiculous sitting there in a suit of armor, his legs sprawled out before him, his silvery hair mussed. But she refused to let him off so easily. She straightened her spine and folded her arms over her chest. "You'll have to do better than that, Mr. Whitaker."

"Then how about this?" Before she realized what he was doing, he reached for her and pulled her down into his lap. The metal was cold beneath her skirts, but he held her fast, his arms tight around her waist. "Now, Miss Perry," he said, "I have something I would like to ask you."

Stubbornly avoiding his gaze, she sighed and lifted her nose into the air, while her stomach turned flip-flops and her heart skittered and spun.

He took her dimpled chin in hand and turned her face to his. His deep brown eyes earnest, he quietly said, "I love you, Elnora. If you'll marry me, I will love you every second of every day for the rest of my life."

Abashed, her jaw slackened, and she stared up at him. Her emotions billowed and took flight, and her anger died. All of the lonely, sterile years of her life faded away as the promise of a new and joyous life unfolded before her like the blooming of the fairest rose of summer. Her throat tight, she touched his handsome face with a brush of her fingertips, as tears of joy stung her eyes. "That's not playing fair," she told him, trying to muster a disapproving frown.

"No, I suppose not. Neither is this." He lowered his head and kissed her mouth softly, letting his lips linger over hers for a long tender moment.

When finally he lifted his head, she sighed and, with her eyes still closed, whispered, "I was supposed to go to my cousin Sally's and help her with her wedding dress. . . ."

He kissed her again. "I suppose you'll have to send her a message saying you won't be available."

"But I promised—"

"She'll forgive you."

"I suppose. . . ."

"Well, then," he prodded, dropping a series of light kisses on her nose, chin, neck . . .

"Oh, yes . . ." she murmured and hugged his neck.

"Yes, what?" he teased, wanting to hear her say the words aloud.

"Yes, I'll marry you." She opened her eyes and stared up into his face.

A slow grin caught at his mouth. "I'm not sure I heard you correctly. What did you say?" He cocked a hand at his ear.

She gave him a disgruntled glance and shouted, "I said yes, I'll marry you!"

"Well, it's about time!" Zeke boomed, throwing open the livery doors. "We're all 'bout starved to death, waiting for you two to get things settled."

Behind him marched most of the town, arms laden with food and goodies. Even Lottie and her girls were in attendance. Russell had sent them an invitation himself and dared anyone in town to challenge it.

Mary and Samantha sauntered past, their smiles revealing their happiness, their eyes twinkling with mischief. Samantha winked, and Mary said, "I told you we'd see."

Her cheeks blazing with embarrassment, Elnora covered her face with her hands. "Oh, good heavens!" she moaned. "What have you done?"

Russell hugged her close, not in the least bit affected by the presence of his neighbors and friends. "I invited them over to celebrate our engagement."

Amazed at his audacity, she dropped her hands from her face and widened her eyes. "Before you even asked me?"

Russell chuckled. "I was hoping you wouldn't say no and embarrass me."

She thought a moment, then her eyes narrowed with suspicion. She stabbed a finger at his armored chest. "Did they know you were the author all along?"

"They didn't know till about four hours ago."

Appeased, Elnora smiled and laughed. "I bet the ladies almost fainted with surprise."

"They almost did."

"Come on, everybody!" Maisie called out. "Let's eat!"

Two weeks later Elnora helped Ransom haul his belongings out to where Vivian and Gordon waited with the children in front of the house.

Everyone wanted to say goodbye.

"I wish you would stay for the wedding," Elnora said, glancing up at him.

"Aw, you know me, Nora," Ransom said without looking at her. "I ain't much for weddin's and such. I don't imagine I ever will be."

"We'll miss you."

" 'Course ya will." He winked and shot her a light-hearted grin that reminded her of the Ransom she'd first come to know.

She smiled and shook her head. "You're an incorrigible flirt."

"Ain't I, though?" he said, his eyes laughing.

When they reached the others, Vivian hugged her brother tightly. "Don't you dare wait so long to come back, you hear me?"

He chuckled and gave her a squeeze. "I hear ya, Viv." When he released her, he turned to Gordon and gave his hand a firm shake. "You take good care of my sister."

Gordon nodded. "I always give it my best."

Ransom went down on his good knee and opened

his arms wide, and the children rushed in to hug him.

"When will you come back?" Sam asked.

"Yeah, when?" Andy wanted to know.

"Next summer," Ransom said.

"You promise?" George asked.

Ransom ruffled his hair. "You bet." Then he frowned and shook a finger under the boy's nose. "You stay out of Miss Lottie's house, ya hear?"

His expression sober, George nodded, then suddenly he grinned, revealing a wide empty gap where his front teeth had recently been.

Ransom rose and turned to Elnora, who felt her chest growing tighter by the minute. She stared down at the ground, blinking, blinking, trying to keep the tears at bay.

Noticing her effort, Ransom shifted his weight, suddenly uncertain about what to do with his hands. "Aw, jeez, Nora, don't ya go cryin' on me."

She lifted her head and stared up into his dear face. "Oh, Ransom . . ." She paused, her throat burning. "You take good care of yourself."

On impulse he swept her into his arms and gave her a big hug. "You be happy, honey."

She nodded against his chest, and he released her.

"Well, I'll be seein' ya next summer." He swung up into his saddle and gave his horse a slight nudge. He looked back once, waved, then rode away, feeling more than a little sorry for himself.

On his way through Harmony, Ransom stopped in front of Whitaker's Bookstore. He swung down off his horse and tied him to the hitch rail. He limped up the steps and into the store, the bell above the door announcing him. Although his leg still ached, he was getting around much better these days.

Russell looked up from the counter, and Arthur walked over to greet his friend.

"Hello, Riley." Russell came out from behind the counter, crossed the floor, and stood in front of the other man.

Ransom gave the dog a few good pats, then looked up at Russell. "I just stopped by to say I was leavin'." He tried to affect a stern expression. "I'll be back from time to time, so you better treat Nora right, or I just might persuade her to run off with me." He flashed Russell a lopsided grin. "Women have a helluva time resisting me."

A grin caught at Russell's mouth, also. "I don't doubt it for a minute." He extended his hand, his expression sobering. "Riley, you're a good man. Thank you for giving me my life back."

They stared at each a long moment, feeling their respect for each other take hold and grow.

"Oh, hell," Ransom said, embarrassed, "next thing you know, we'll be actin' like we like each other." He shook Russell's hand, giving it a hearty squeeze, then he turned and thumped off toward the door. When he reached it, he looked over his shoulder. "You know that book Nora bought me, *Les Misérables?*"

"Yes." Russell pocketed his hands, still smiling.

"Does Javert ever catch that man Valjean?"

Russell lifted one eyebrow, and his smile grew mysterious. "Finish reading the book, Riley. We'll talk about it next time you come through town."

Ransom gave a small huff of disgust, then shrugged. "I'll be seein' ya, Walker." He turned and hobbled out the door and on down the steps to his horse.

He unbuckled his saddlebag and peered inside. The book was there. He buckled his saddlebag again and swung up onto his horse and headed down Main Street.

He was almost past the First Resort, when Grace Bloomfield came strutting through the doors, carpetbag in hand. "Hey, Grace," he greeted, tipping his Stetson and flashing her a wide smile.

"Hey, Ransom, honey." Grace returned his smile.

He reined in his horse. "Where you off to in such a hurry?"

She sighed heavily and hung one hand on her ample hip. "I'm not sure yet." She squinted up into the sun, giving his question some thought. "I'm leavin' town, though. Kinda tired of this one." She tossed her long blond hair over her shoulder and angled him a sultry glance from beneath her lashes. "Which way you headin'?"

Ransom grinned, his mood lifting by leaps and bounds. Grace Bloomfield had always been one of his favorites. Grace had a grace all her own, and she was bloomin' in all the right places. "Darlin'," he drawled, "I'm headin' any way you wanna go." He held out his hand, his self-pity all but forgotten. "Come on up."

The headlines on the front page of the *Harmony Sentinel* on the morning of May 15, 1875, read: LADY ELVIA AND SIR GAWAIN WED AT LAST. Below in smaller print, "Story Inside."

Maisie and Minnie wasted no time sitting down and opening the paper to the appropriate page.

They smiled as they read how Sir Gawain and Lady Elvia were wed at King Nefan's castle. By order of the king, everyone in the kingdom attended the ceremony.

Flags and banners flew; trumpets sounded. Entertainers danced and tumbled, and a trio of jousts took place. There were gorgeously garbed ladies and gentlemen everywhere, and the galleries were decorated and canopied in various flamboyant colors. Food was abundant, as was merriment and gaiety.

Lady Elvia was uniquely lovely in her ivory gown and her steeple-shaped cap, with its veil that floated down to the floor around her tiny slippered feet. Her hair hung down her back in a cascade of chestnut waves, and her golden eyes were alight with love and happiness.

Her chosen knight, Sir Gawain, was handsome indeed. He was dressed in a red and white tunic that bore his coat of arms. He wore knee-high leather boots with golden spurs that signified his knighthood, and his sun-struck silvery hair was bared for all to view its glory.

When at last the final vows were spoken, and they shared their first matrimonial kiss, all of the kingdom rejoiced and celebrated, even the Black Knight who gave his blessing, then rode off on another exciting adventure.

It was a beautiful story indeed, eliciting a good measure of sighs, and more than a few misty eyes among the townsfolk—though none of the men would admit to such sentimental dribblings.

But their joy did not end with Sir Gawain and Lady Elvia's wedding.

Beneath the headlines of the day was another large caption of even greater interest to the folks of Harmony:

Mr. Robert D. Walker of Detroit, Michigan, (our own Russell Whitaker of Whitaker's Bookstore) to marry Miss Elnora Perry of Wichita, Kansas, at 3:00 this afternoon. Everyone is invited to attend.

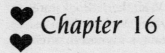 *Chapter 16*

IT WAS A splendid day for a wedding.

The sky was blue, the air balmy.

Horses attached to the hitch rails lazily swished flies from their rumps, while bees hummed and songbirds sang.

Children raced across the grassy churchyard in wild abandon, wrinkling their freshly laundered clothing and earning them tart scoldings from their mothers, who were still sighing and tittering over the details of Lady Elvia and Sir Gawain's wedding.

In time, the Reverend Johnson and his wife, Rachel, came out of the church doors to usher everyone in for the ceremony. Talk of the fairy-tale wedding faded away as the townsfolk looked forward to the joining of two of their very own.

With quiet dignity Arthur waited at the door while the townsfolk filed into the church, one by one, two by two, their conversation humming with their excitement and joy.

Once everyone was seated in the polished pews, the chattering ceased, and Lillie Taylor, seated at the organ, solemnly lowered her gaze to the keyboard and began to play a soft tune to announce the bride.

Shoulders swiveled, and heads turned.

Within seconds Elnora's two little nieces appeared.

Both girls were dressed in frilly confections, complete with lace and bows and ruffles, their hair caught up in curls and adorned with ribbons.

Sara came down the aisle first, followed by Emily, who as usual had her thumb in her mouth.

But no one seemed to mind today. The ladies giggled with delight, and the gentlemen chuckled with amusement.

When at last the organ music droned to an anticipated halt, a hush fell over the crowd, and Elnora appeared at the back of the church.

She was dressed in a simple gown of ivory satin that boasted a small bustle in the back and a train that trailed a long way behind her. The neck was high and demure, and the sleeves of her gown, though puffy at the top, narrowed down the length of her arms to pointed, lace-trimmed cuffs at her wrists. On her head was a delicate crown of daisies, woven with ivory lace and pearls.

Her cheeks were rosy and bright, her hair resplendent, piled on her head in a stylish, modern arrangement.

But it was her eyes that made her friends and neighbors blink back tears. Her honey-gold eyes were striking, sparkling as they were with love and happiness.

She was, indeed, a lovely bride.

Vivian, her arms clutching Baby Alice, began to cry, and Gordon, his own eyes damp and weepy, hugged her close.

Young Sam smiled, not at all distressed by his aunt's decision to marry Mr. Whitaker. He'd begun to notice that Rebecca Talbot, the little redheaded girl who sat behind him in school, wasn't really so yucky-looking after all.

Andy, George, and Mark Anthony looked on, trying not to fidget overmuch.

On Gordon's left was his and Elnora's father and mother, and the four other Perry brothers and their wives. Beside them was their cousin Sally. They'd all come, hearts aglow, to see their dear, lovely Elnora, the one who had cared for them all so often, now moving on to a new life—a richer, sweeter life. The life she'd always deserved.

Her groom stood in the front of the church, waiting for her, his heart hammering, his eyes warm with appreciation.

When finally she reached him, she smiled up into his face and thought him the most handsome groom she'd ever seen. He was indeed her knight in shining armor, the silver knight of her dreams.

He stood before her, tall and lean and broad-shouldered, every inch the gentleman, dressed in a sparkling white shirt and his best dark suit and tie. His silvery-blond hair fell forward onto one side of his forehead, and his deep, brown eyes, those dancing, laughing eyes that she loved so much, smiled down on her, promising her a lifetime of faithfulness.

A slow familiar grin caught at his attractive mouth, and he held out his hand to her. She took his hand with a secret smile of her own, and another host of sighs and sniffles rippled around them.

Smiling, his eyes damp, the Reverend Johnson held up his hand to quiet the assemblage. This was an especially bittersweet moment for him and his wife. They had decided to leave Harmony, and this would be the last ceremony he would perform here among his dear friends. Clearing his throat, he solemnly began the ceremony. "Dearly beloved . . ." he began quietly.

Elnora and Russell stood gazing at each other, their emotions billowing, thinking they were luckier than most.

Somehow God had seen fit to guide them to a town called Harmony. Somehow he had seen fit to have them meet, to let them fall in love with each other.

How wonderfully blessed they were.

The Reverend Johnson's voice broke into their thoughts. "Do you, Russell Whitaker—" He smiled a bit sheepishly. "Do you, Robert David Walker, take this woman to be your wife?"

His chest suddenly tight, Russell gave Elnora's hand a gentle squeeze. "I do." His deep voice was soft but sure, bringing a rush of tears to Elnora's eyes.

"Do you, Elnora Perry, take this man . . ."

Steeped in emotion, her heart swelled. "Oh, yes . . . I do."

The reverend continued with more of the lovely, age-old words, and Russell gently slipped a thin, gold band onto her dainty finger.

Time ceased, and hearts hovered. Slowly Elnora lifted her gaze to that of the man before her. Seeing her tears, his hand touched her cheek. "My sweet lady," he whispered.

While their hearts reached out and entwined, the Reverend Johnson spoke the most beautiful words of all. "I now pronounce you man and wife. You may kiss the bride."

Everyone waited while the tall, handsome gentleman took the lovely little lady by the shoulders. Everyone watched while he dipped his head and placed a gentle kiss upon her lips. When they parted, moved by the awesome beauty of the moment, everyone sighed, sniffled, and honked with irreverent noisiness into their handkerchiefs.

Lottie McGee and her girls could have won a ribbon for having the pew with the loudest sniffles, but the pew where Maisie and Minnie and Zeke sat would have placed a close second. Faith Hutton, Samantha Spencer, and Mary Hubbard embarrassed their husbands by openly weeping in their joy over Elnora's happiness.

"Well," Maisie said, vaulting from her seat, "it's about time you two got hitched." She turned to her sister and smiled. "We did it!"

Minnie nodded. "We did, indeed!"

"Pa," George announced, his voice echoing throughout the auditorium, "I gotta go!"

Later that evening, when the festivities were over and twilight fell around them, Russell and Elnora stood at the back door of Whitaker's Bookstore.

As though she wasn't quite sure she could believe it, she looked up at him and said, "We're married."

He smiled down on her. "Yes, we are."

Amazed by the reality, she shook her head. "It's so hard to believe."

"Is it?" He lifted one brow. "Why is that?"

Suddenly self-conscious, she dropped her gaze. "I just never thought it would happen to me."

He took her chin in hand and raised her face. "Nora, you were meant to be loved."

Staring up into his eyes, she believed him and she asked the questions she'd wondered about so often since she'd discovered his true identity. "Do you ever want to return to Detroit, Russ? Did you leave anyone behind?"

"I missed it at first. And there was someone a long time ago. But she wasn't like you. I never loved her like I do you," he told her honestly. His expression grew earnest, his eyes tender. "Harmony is my home now. This is where I belong. Here with you." He paused a moment as he thought of home and what it should mean for a woman. "There's a small piece of ground I've had my eye on for some time. It's a little ways outside of town. I thought you might like a house of our own. Someplace where we can raise our children."

Her mouth dropped open slightly. "Ohhh," she whispered at last, pleased, moved beyond words. A house . . . Children, too . . .

He stepped in front of her and opened the door. "Well, for now, welcome home, Mrs. Walker."

She smiled up at him, and a sudden thought came to mind. "What about Whitaker's Bookstore? Will we call it Walker's Bookstore now?"

"No." He shook his head and laughed. "Somehow it just doesn't sound right. Whitaker's Bookstore it is, and so it shall remain."

He swept her off her feet and into his arms, carrying her over the threshold, while she hugged his neck and laughed.

She raised one eyebrow. "And who am I, pray tell? Mrs. Whitaker or Mrs. Walker?"

"You, my dear, are both." Holding her in his arms, he kicked the door shut behind him and lowered his head to kiss her. His lips whispered across hers, once, twice, then he playfully nibbled at her bottom lip.

"Imagine that." She sighed softly. "Married to two men. And they're both you. I think I like that." She closed her eyes as her head lolled back onto his arm, and her smile grew tender. Slowly her eyes opened. "You'll always be Russ to me."

"And you'll always be Lady Elvia to me," he said and kissed her again, this time running his tongue over her lips to each corner of her mouth, tasting her, fitting his mouth to hers with a mastery of perfection.

When at last he lifted his head, he let her feet slip down to the floor and steadied her by holding his hands at her waist.

"Russ . . ." She felt a moment of shyness, a moment of uncertainty. For so very long she'd dreamed of having someone of her own, of having someone who not only needed her, but loved her, too. Truly and completely. For one breath of a moment she worried that everything—him, the wedding, even the one night they'd shared together—had been nothing more than a beautiful fantasy, a wondrous dream.

"Hmmm . . ." His voice was deep and rich.

She touched his face with her fingertips, as though to make sure he was real. "I do love you."

His gaze caressed her warmly. "I love you, too, Nora."

Her doubts fled, and a mischievous twinkle entered her eyes. "Was Lady Elvia really me?"

His eyes took on that familiar amused glitter. "Of course she was."

She cocked her head to the side. "But how could you know from the very beginning that you were going to love me?"

His smile grew secretive, and he kissed her dimpled chin. "Trust me, I knew," was all he would tell her.

With a maddening slowness, his hands moved up from her waist to her breasts and touched her there, molding, lifting, holding, lingering over her hardening nipples.

Arousal drugged her, and her breathing grew heavy. Her arms went around his neck, her fingers lacing through the silvery hair at the nape of his neck.

His lips found her throat, her face, her hair. Gently

he reached up and undid the crown of flowers, loosening it, sending it sailing onto a nearby chair. Then, one by one, he plucked out her hairpins, casting them to the floor with heedless abandon.

Her eyes opened and rounded as her hands caught at his, trying to still him. "I'll have to find them all tomorrow. . . ."

"I'll help you," he said and continued his task until, at last, all her hairpins were lying on the floor. He combed her hair loose with his fingers, lifting it away from her head and letting it fall in silken waves around her shoulders.

His breath teasing her cheeks, he worked at her clothing next. Unbuttoning buttons, untying ties, taking his time—they had all the time in the world now—until he could skim it all down, leaving her standing in only her shoes, stockings, chemise, and pantaloons.

Her face glowing, she watched him while he stepped away from her and bent and removed his shoes. When he straightened, she closed the space between them and helped him unbutton his jacket, his shirt, his trousers, gently pushing the garments away until he stood before her as beautifully unclothed as he had the night he had taught her the secrets of love.

His eyes dark with passion, he dropped to one knee and eased her shoes from her feet, then slowly, ever so slowly, he slipped her stockings down her shapely legs, pressing a kiss to each knee before rising to stand before her.

"I . . ." she began but never finished, as he worked at the tiny buttons on her chemise. When they were free, he brushed the garment aside and slipped his hands inside, laying his palms against the firm mounds of her naked breasts.

"Oh . . ." she whispered, her eyelids drooping, desire rippling through her trembling limbs to the very center of her belly. She covered his hands with her own, feeling his warmth infuse her, even as she shivered beneath his touch.

"Nora . . ." he said softly and gentled her with his caresses. He touched his lips to hers once more. When arousal grew rife, he urged her lips apart, and the kiss became wanton and greedy, tongues touching, twirling, dancing.

In time, his breathing labored, he drew back and slipped away her chemise and pantaloons, leaving her standing naked before him. He drew her close, letting his hot flesh press into her belly while his hands roved over her satiny skin.

"Russ."

"Yes?"

"I am wicked." Unencumbered by false modesty, she drew away from him and let her hands discover his body anew, exploring, stroking, while his breath caught in his throat, and a fire lit in his eyes.

His groin aching, he became impatient and swept her up and carried her to the bed, dropping down beside her, pressing kisses to her face, eyelids, chin, neck. He flattened his palm over her smooth abdomen, then his hand drifted lower, touching her gently, finding her warm and wanting.

He rolled above her and propped himself up on his elbows. He took her face in his hands and said what was in his heart. "How did I ever find you?"

Her heart brimming, she smiled up at him. "I guess you were just lucky." Then her smile sobered. "We were both lucky." She lifted her arms and drew him down and, with her small hands, guided him home.

His entrance was an enchanted thing. They moved

together as one, learning a rhythm all their own, savoring each stroke in a joining that was golden.

Their first time had been bittersweet, beautiful, but tinged with sorrow at their impending separation. Ah, but this time they had all of the sweetness and none of the sadness, only the sublime promise of their lifetime together.

When he shuddered with his release, she watched his face, thinking it lovely, reveling in his beauty and masculinity, then she closed her eyes and went the same way he had gone just seconds before her, to a mystical land full of wonder that belonged to them alone.

In the minutes that followed, they lay, limbs entwined, hearts beating out their love. A sudden thought occurred to her, and she tipped her head up to stare at him. "Our children. How many did you want? We've never talked about it."

He smiled down at her, while he lovingly kneaded the small of her back. "We'll have as many as you like."

"Oh," she said, never having considered the thought of numbers. She'd had no reason to until this day, this perfect moment. She hugged his waist. "Three would be nice." She thought of Gordon and his brood and cast her husband a narrow glance from beneath her lashes. "Not seven."

His lifted his eyebrows. "No?"

"No," she said, her voice firm, her pointy chin determined.

He chuckled, and in time they fell silent once again, wondering about the faces of those three children, thinking about each other, planning their future.

After a few moments she looked up at him again,

her expression sober. "Do you think Ransom will ever come back to visit us?"

He brushed her hair back from her face, kissed her forehead, and thought about that a minute. "Yes," he finally said and smiled into the darkness. "We have an appointment to discuss the ending of a certain book a certain lady gave him."

"Ahh," she said, understanding. She sighed, heartened by his answer. She turned onto her side, and they snuggled, back to front, spooned to each other in a perfect fit. She pulled his arms around her and hugged them close. "Will Lady Elvia and Sir Gawain be happy?"

Russell brushed her hair aside and kissed the back of her neck. "Very."

"Will you write about them anymore?"

"No. The rest of their story belongs to them alone."

Elnora smiled to herself. "That's as it should be." She paused. "And what of the Black Knight? Will he ever find a lady of his own?"

Russell thought a second. "I don't know," he answered honestly. "I guess that'll have to be up to him."

She paused. "That day . . . the day Ransom came to help us. You stayed behind to write the story, didn't you?"

"Yes."

"Why? When everything else was happening, why was it so important?"

"It needed to be done," he said quietly. "For me. For all of us."

Silence, then, "I should have known it was you." She chuckled. "A dog named Arthur . . . Humph."

He hugged her close.

"I love you, Sir Knight," she whispered sleepily,

her search for love over at long last.

"I love you, too, my lady," he whispered into her hair, silently vowing to love and protect her till the day he died.

When at last she drifted off to sleep, there was no longer a need for her to dream of a chivalrous knight in shining armor. He was there beside her, holding her in his arms as the night shadows deepened and the silvery moonbeams filtered in through the window and glinted off his hair.

He laid his cheek against her soft neck, and he knew he no longer had to hide from his past. He could take off his armor.

His quest was over. He had gained his freedom. He had won his lady.

Together, they would live out their days in their own little kingdom, in the quiet little town of Harmony, Kansas.

*Come take a walk down Harmony's Main
Street in 1874, and meet a different resident of
this colorful Kansas town each month.*

A TOWN CALLED
❧ HARMONY ❧

__**KEEPING FAITH**   0-7865-0016-6/$4.99
      by Kathleen Kane
__**TAKING CHANCES**   0-7865-0022-2/$4.99
      by Rebecca Hagan Lee
__**CHASING RAINBOWS** 0-7865-0041-7/$4.99
      by Linda Shertzer
__**PASSING FANCY**   0-7865-0046-8/$4.99
      by Lydia Browne
__**PLAYING CUPID**   0-7865-0056-5/$4.99
      by Donna Fletcher
__**COMING HOME**   0-7865-0060-3/$4.99
      by Kathleen Kane
__**GETTING HITCHED** 0-7865-0067-0/$4.99
      by Ann Justice
__**HOLDING HANDS**   0-7865-0075-1/$4.99
      by Jo Anne Cassity
__**AMAZING GRACE**   0-7865-0080-8/$4.99
      by Deborah James (March)

FREE
Romance
(a $4.50 value)

Send in the Coupon Below

To get your FREE historical romance and start saving, fill out the coupon below and mail it today. As soon as we receive it we'll send you your FREE Book along with your first month's selections.

Mail To: **True Value Home Subscription Services, Inc. P.O. Box 5235 120 Brighton Road, Clifton, New Jersey 07015-5235**

YES! I want to start previewing the very best historical romances being published today. Send me my FREE book along with the first month's selections. I understand that I may look them over FREE for 10 days. If I'm not absolutely delighted I may return them and owe nothing. Otherwise I will pay the low price of just $4.00 each: a total $16.00 (at *least* an $18.00 value) and save at least $2.00. Then each month I will receive four brand new novels to preview as soon as they are published for the same low price. I can always return a shipment and I may cancel this subscription at any time with no obligation to buy even a single book. In any event the FREE book is mine to keep regardless.

Name _____

Street Address _____ Apt. No _____

City _____ State _____ Zip Code _____

Telephone _____

Signature _____
(if under 18 parent or guardian must sign)

Terms and prices subject to change. Orders subject
to acceptance by True Value Home Subscription
Services. Inc.

0075-1